Copyright © 2020 by Dave Blackwell

All rights reserved.

Cover and Book design by Dave Blackwell

No part of this book may be reproduced in any form or by any electronic or mechanical means including information storage and retrieval systems, without permission in writing from the author. The only exception is by a reviewer, who may quote short excerpts in a review.

This book is a work of fiction. Names, characters, places, and incidents either are products of the author's imagination or are used fictitiously. Any resemblance to actual persons, living or dead, events, or locales is entirely coincidental.

Dave Blackwell

Visit my website at https://www.facebook.com/DBlackwellNovels

Printed Globally.

First Printing: December 2020

Deaf Like Me

Monday

Debbie walked up to the door, putting her ear against it, and knocking it gently.

"George?" She said. "Are you awake?"

She knocked again, louder.

"Georgie!" She said louder. "Are you awake?

Tall and slim, wearing jean shorts and a small white t-shirt, Debbie's hair is long, blonde, and messy. Down her right leg is a badly done tattoo of a snake and on the other leg, a ladder. Both tattoos start on the side of her thighs and run down to her foot.

Pushing open the door, trying not to make too much noise, she popped her head in, looking at the bed. The bed is under a large window, thick black curtains drawn, slightly open at the centre and letting in light that illuminated the room just about for Debbie to see. The king-sized bed is made of solid pine, the wardrobe and chest of draws either side matched. Against the wall opposite the bed, a long shelving unit in black that spanned the wall, filled with hundreds of books. The room is tidy and everything straight and clean.

"Georgie!" Debbie said. "Wake up!"

George did not respond.

Debbie opened the door fully and made her way towards the bed, not noticing the dumbbells in the middle of the floor on a red yoga mat.

Yelling out in pain when she kicked one of them, she fell forward, crashing into the floor so hard a couple of books fell from the shelving.

George stirred and rolled over, flipping the duvet cover off him.

"Weird dream, he said and looked towards the door, looking at it curiously. "I closed that," He said to himself.

Debbie stood up suddenly and George yelled out in fright, sitting up and cracking his head on the wooden headboard.

"Jesus!" He grabbed his head and moaned. "What are you doing in here?!" He growled.

"I called for you to wake up," Debbie said sitting on the corner of the bed and rubbing her foot.

George looked at them, the soles black.

"Get your bloody feet off my bed," He moaned. "They are disgusting!"

George pulled the duvet over himself, covering his legs. Wearing nothing but shorts, he reached up for his glasses, putting them on and rubbing his head, the hair cut very short. George is five foot nine and average build. On the top of his chest, he has a long thick scar on the right side.

"Are you awake?" Debbie asked, putting her foot down on the floor.

"Shut up a minute," George said. "Let me get my implant before you natter on about nothing."

She shook her head in frustration.

George reached up for a small black box on the headboard, taking a cochlear implant processor from it and a battery, he installed the battery, watching as the four green lights flashed followed by a red. He fitted it over his ear, and attached the magnet to his head, flinching at the crackling that went through his head when it activated.

"I said..." Debbie is cut short by George.

"Wait," George snapped. "It needs a few seconds."

Debbie sighed heavily, crossing her arms, and waiting.

"Now you can talk," He said. "What do you want?"

"Aren't you supposed to be at work?" She asked.

"No," George said. "I told you last night I am off for two and a half weeks."

"Oh yeah," She giggled. "I forgot, I did knock your door a few times, but you didn't answer."

"What did you expect?" George said.

"Thought you might answer me?" She said.

"You do know I am deaf huh?" George said. "Probably told you a million times!"

"Don't you wear that in your sleep?" She pointed to his implant.

George looked at her, no expression on his face.

"What do you think?" George said tutting. "Are you going to leave now?" he pulled the duvet up to his abdomen. "I'd like to go back to sleep."

"I hurt my foot on that," she pointed to the metal dumbbell. "Why did you leave it in the middle of the floor?"

"For you to trip over when you sneak into my room," George said. "Worked didn't it?"

"Couldn't you have put it somewhere else?" Debbie asked.

"No," George said bluntly.

"Why?" Debbie said, hurt from his reaction.

"Well it is my room," He said. "Your eyes work, don't they?"

She giggled.

"What do you want?" He asked bluntly.

"Someone is here to see you," Debbie said. "They are waiting downstairs."

"Well, why didn't you start with that?!" He groaned. "Jesus Christ!" He huffed. "Who is it?"

"Some woman," Debbie said. "I don't know."

"Didn't you ask?" George shook his head. "Normal practice when you let someone into the house."

"She said she was your bosses, boss or something like that," Debbie said. "Apparently a work emergency."

"Short podgy woman, short black hair?" George said. "Wearing a suit?"

"That sounds about right," Debbie said. "She said she wouldn't have come unless it was important."

"You really need to try and learn to prioritise!" George flicked the duvet off him and got up.

Debbie looked him up and down.

"Do you mind?" George said.

"Never seen you topless before," She smiled.

"Last time you will too," He said. "So, bugger off so I can get dressed."

"I am going out now," She got up.

"Going to work?" George asked.

"No," Debbie said. "We are still closed with this pandemic thing going on, when will it finish?" She asked.

"How do I know?" George scoffed. "Probably when people stop being idiots."

"I do wash my hands," Debbie said.

George looked at her.

"What do you want?" He said. "A fucking medal?"

Debbie giggled.

"Always makes me laugh when you say it like that," She sighed. "I'll let her know you will be down soon."

"Thank you," George grunted. "Try not to fall over on your way out."

Barbara sat at the kitchen table, her hands around a black mug. Her black hair is wet and messy. She is wearing a grey suit, underneath a light grey shirt. He shoes, black and heavily polished, the light glinting off them. She is wearing a surgical mask, covering her mouth and nose.

She looked around the small kitchen, the four-seater pine table at the middle, the L shaped worktop that ran under the window and to the side, a door next to it leading to the garden. The white tiled floor is clean, one tile in the middle with several cracks in it. The yellow walls made the room brighter but did not go well with the grey worktops and the silver cooker, washing machine, dryer, and refrigerator.

George walked into the kitchen, covering his mouth when he yawned. Wearing black jogging bottoms, grey slippers, and a white t-shirt.

"Hey Barbara," He said smiling. "Got a drink?" He noticed the mug. "Good."

Barbara started to talk, and George pointed to the mask.

"Do you mind?" He said. "Cannot understand you otherwise."

"Sorry," She pulled it off. "I forget."

"No problems," George smiled. "I got a negative result, so I am clean."

"I know," She said. "I did try and call you earlier," Barbara said. "But no one would pick up."

"I don't take calls," George said. "Cannot hear on the phone too well to follow a conversation, so I prefer texts or emails."

"I know," Barbara nodded slowly.

"So why did you call?" George said, looking at her screaming in his mind.

"I forgot that is all," Barbara smiled. "No offence intended."

George shrugged his shoulders.

"That young lady," Barbara indicated towards the door. "Is that your partner?"

"Oh, hell no!" George scoffed. "She is a housemate, a friend of a friend I am helping out."

"Oh," Barbara nodded. "Those tattoos," She hesitated. "They do stand out."

"She got them done a couple of years ago in Las Vegas," George said. "Some back-street amateur, they look terrible!"

"What do they mean?" Barbara asked.

"What snakes and ladders?" George said yawning. "It's weird."

"Okay," Barbara said. "I'm just curious that is all."

George stopped at the sink and turned around.

"Her first time," George said. "She went on a date with a guy, he didn't make the move so when they got the game out, she jumped him."

Barbara coughed, her hand in front of her mouth as she smiled.

"Well," She said embarrassed. "Serves me right for asking."

"Yeah," George said and turned around.

"George," She said. "I am very sorry to visit you at home, and please understand it is an emergency."

George picked up a glass from the draining board and filled it with water, sitting down at the table opposite Barbara.

"Did someone die?" He asked.

"What?" Barbara is shocked at his response. "God no!"

"You do know I am on leave for a month?" He said. "I have not had any leave in a while, and I need it."

"I understand," Barbara said. "I didn't know what else to do."

"So?" He said sipping from the glass. "Why are you visiting me at home?"

"Well," She said breathing out heavily.

"Sacking me?" George chuckled. "Wouldn't surprise me after the issue with the agency twat."

"Sacking you?" Barbara said, confusion on her face.

"Yeah," George replied. "Not too bothered either way."

"No," Barbara said. "Nothing like that, if anything I need your help," She hesitated. "What happened with the agency employee?"

"I told him to pack his stuff and go," George said. "Was a bloody danger and embarrassment to everyone!"

"You can update me on that later," She said. "I need you to come in."

"No way," George said groaning. "Four weeks I in a year, that is all I have asked for!"

"Harold had an accident," Barbara said abruptly. "A bad one and he has been admitted onto level three."

"Orthopaedics," George said. "What's the old sod done now?"

"Shouldn't call him that!" Barbara said in shock. "Human resources would have a field day!"

"Harold and I go way back," George said. "Don't worry about it."

George got up and switched on the kettle, removing a mug from a hook under the counter.

"Do you want a fresh one?" He said, pointing to the mug.

"No thanks," Barbara said. "I got your information from Marvin."

"Why?" George said. "He can manage things, he used to be a manager at another trust."

"He can't," Barbara said. "He was off last year with a condition."

"I know," George nodded. "Lazy bastard had a heart attack doing nothing."

Barbara laughed nervously.

"Marvin contacted me when Harold didn't show up," Barbara said. "He called Harold's wife who wasn't home, he went around and spoke to the neighbour and they filled him in that he was in Lavender ward recovering."

"What happened to him?" George said. "Did he fall off his arse or something?"

"He has two broken legs, cracked ribs and concussion," Barbara said. "He won't be coming back any time soon."

"Jesus Chris!" George snapped. "How did he manage that?"

"Oh, it is terrible," Barbara said.

"It's Harold," George said. "Anything is possible with him!"

"He was mauled," Barbara put her hand to her mouth, shock in her eyes.

"Mauled?" George said, not sure if he heard her properly. "By what?" He thought about it. "Not that little rat of his surely?"

"A cow," Barbara said.

George burst out into hysterical laughter, removing his glasses, and placing them onto the table.

"A cow?!" He shouted. "Did you say a cow?"

Barbara nodded.

"That is the stupidest thing I have ever heard," He scoffed. "Cows don't maul people!"

"This one did," Barbara said. "Apparently, his dog, Little Tyson wanted to play with the cow."

"That little shit doesn't play anything unless he has killed it," George said, putting his glasses back on. "He attacks or humps anything he can, nasty little rat!"

"What was he?" Barbara asked. "What kind of a dog?"

"Jack Russell," George said. "They used to have two and all they did was bark and snap," George clicked his tongue. "And bang each other."

"What happened to the other one?" Barbara asked curiously.

"Well," He sighed. "Harold always used to tell us that he was intelligent, and never needed to be on the lead," George said. "Well someone walking on the other side of the road dropped food, and Bugs ran for it."

"Oh no," Barbara said.

"Yeah," He raised his eyebrows. "Wasn't too intelligent then, died instantly, like a bug on a windscreen." He sniggered.

"You are mean!" Barbara said, forcing herself not to smile.

"So did Little Tyson learn his lesson?" George said.

"He died," Barbara said. "Harold was so upset."

"Died?" George said, biting his lip. "Oh dear, how?"

"The cow freaked and fell over, and Little Tyson was in the wrong place at the wrong time."

George covered his mouth, trying to stifle the giggles.

"It isn't funny!" Barbara said.

"At least both dogs had something in common when they died," George said. "They both met their ends with something beginning with C."

"Stop it!" Barbara scoffed. "It's not funny!"

"No, it's hysterical!" George said. "So how did Harold get hurt?"

"He tried to push the cow off Little Tyson, and when it got to its feet, it kicked out and caught Harold on the knee," Barbara explained. "When Harold went down, it trampled him."

"That must have hurt," George said. "Where was Mavis during all this?"

9

"She was sitting by the fence, watching it," Barbara said. "She thought they were playing!"

"Mavis has some memory issues," George said. "Has anyone contacted their kids?"

"I think so," Barbara said. "They have a son and daughter, don't they?"

"The son lives in the states, doubt he will be much use and the daughter lives in London," George explained. "I can probably track her down."

"Marvin said he would call her on my behalf," Barbara said. "Or try to, I don't know," She laughed nervously. "He drones sometimes."

"Yeah he does that," George said. "I just switch off," He pointed to his implant.

"I came in earlier today and it was bedlam," Barbara sighed. "The new admin started, and I don't know anything about your department."

"Hence why we kept inviting you down," George said. "You have cancelled every meeting in a row for the last three months."

"It has been busy," Barbara said. "I have had so much to deal with."

"Us too," George sat down, placing the white mug on a mat. "We have had nothing but new stock arriving every day, he held up a finger, I asked for overtime but it was refused, and last week alone I did an additional thirty-five hours, just to get things out."

"If you can come back, and manage the team, I will assure you that you will get the help you need," Barbara said. "I promise."

"You can also take care of my villa cancellation in Cornwall," He said bluntly. "If I don't show up, I have to pay a week's money."

"I will take care of that," Barbara sighed.

"I'll claim it back as expenses then," George said and looked at the clock on the wall. "I can get to work in an hour or so."

"Could you check that the new lady is okay?" Barbara said. "I cannot remember her name."

"Kirsty is it?" George said. "I need to check my emails."
Barbara finished her coffee.

"I do appreciate it," She said. "I'll try and pop in later."

"You won't," George replied.

"I will try," She said again, firmly.

"Okay," George nodded. "I'll email you with details of an agency I want to use."

"I am going back now," Barbara stood up. "So, I will let Marvin know you will be coming in shortly."
George nodded.

"I am very sorry," Barbara said. "I didn't know who else to ask."

"This is why Trevor should have stayed," George said. "He could do anything in the department."

"I know," Barbara sighed awkwardly. "But we had to make three people redundant."

"How did that work out?" George said. "Seems you took on new people and paid them more!"

"I know," Barbara nodded. "Mistakes were made."

"Well If you want things to go smoothly," George sipped at his coffee, blowing it. "I am going to ask if he can come in on the agency."

"Might be a little complicated," Barbara's face said she did not want to do it.

"Your choice," George said. "But if it hits the fan, it is on your head."

"I'll see what I can do," Barbara said. "I cannot make any promises," She held out her hand and then quickly retracted it. "Sorry," She chuckled. "Force of habit, I will let myself out and will probably see you later, give me a call if you need anything."

"Sure," George said. "Will do that."

George sat down, watching as Barbara walked out of the front door, slamming it behind her. George flinched and shook his head.

"Why do people keep slamming doors?" He groaned. "Looks like Cornwall will have to wait, again."

11:25

George sat parked in front of the barrier to the car park, the small screen flashing red and stating to press the help button.

"Bloody thing," He muttered. "Never bloody works!" He leaned out the window and pressed the button, listening against the traffic and background noise. The panel beeped several times until there was a click.

"Hello, how can I help you?" The female voice came over.

"Hi, I am deaf so be patient, I may struggle," George said. "My name is George Shades and I work in Medical Tech Services," he screwed up his eyes, trying to listen. "For some reason, my number plate won't read."

"What is your name please?" The woman said.

"Just told you," George said. "George Shades."

"And where do you work?" She said.

"Jesus," George mumbled. "Thought I was the deaf one."

"Repeat that please," The woman said.

"I am sorry I cannot hear you," George said, struggling with the traffic going by. "I need to get into the car park."

"What is your profession here?" The woman shouted.

George still could not understand her over the noise.

"I am deaf, and this is now really stressing me out," He growled.

"I will do my best to help you," The woman said. "What department do you work in?"

"George Shades from Medical Tech services," George said bluntly. "I am in a rush, so could you please raise the barrier, it's like the fifth time this week!"

"Oh, I have spoken to you before," The girl said. "You are the deaf guy from tech services!"

"Oh, for fucks sake!" George groaned quietly.

"I'll open the barrier, have a nice one!" She said.

There was a beep as the barrier opened, George drove through aggressively, frustration on his face as the wheels squealed around the corner.

11:49

George stepped up to the screen in the coffee shop, looking up at the choices on the board. He removed his mask and put it into his pocket, looking around at the empty café that was only doing takeaway service. The long worktop separating the kitchen area, a refrigerated display cabinet with fruit, cakes, sandwiches, and various confectionary.

The two teen girls stood behind the plastic screen, watching something on a mobile phone. One short and overweight with long black messy, wearing a green tunic that barely fit her, her black trousers dirty and creased. The other, slim build with short brown hair, wearing a short grey skirt and a similar tunic.

"Hi," George said forcing a smile. "Could I get a coffee please?"

"Sure one moment," One of the girls said. "Just need to finish this."

"Okay," George nodded, breathing out heavily. "Good job I am not a customer."

One of the girls looked at him, shaking her head in annoyance.

"What do you want?" The slimmer girl said, banging her phone down on the counter.

"Some customer service would be great," George smiled. "Don't strain yourself though."

"Someone got out of bed on the wrong side," The other girl said and giggled. "Grumpy."

"Sorry, what was that?" George said, not hearing her correctly.

"Nothing," She said. "Just asked what you wanted."

"Could I have a large black coffee," George said. "And a chicken baguette please."

"To have in or go?" The girl asked, leaning against the counter.

George looked around at the empty café, the tables and chairs no longer where they used to be, the main seating area now blocked off with caution tape.

"I think I will take it to go," George said. "Unless you have some deckchairs?" He looked over the counter.

"Good morning George!" The voice caused him to jump. "Thought you were off for a month, you lazy git?"

George turned round to see a tall slim man in a navy-blue suit, shaved head, thin glasses, and a well-groomed beard.

"I am Steve," George said. "Harold had an accident, and no one has any sense, so here I am," He scoffed.

"What happened to him?" Steve asked in concern.

"Got mauled by a cow," George said.

Steve looked at him, his mouth open.

"You are serious?!" Steve said. "Is he okay?"

"He is up on orthopaedics, two broken legs and cracked ribs," George said and pointed to the counter. "What do you want?" He said. "My treat."

"No, no, no," Steve shook his head and pulled his wallet out from his side pocket. "It is my turn, you got the last few!" He laughed. "Let me."

"It is fine, really Steve," George said. "I am happy to get these."

"Do as you are told, or I will break a ventilator!" Steve held his finger up in warning.

"They are yours, so it's not really going to be my problem!" George smirked. "I don't mind fixing them."

"I will tell Christina that you broke it," Steve started to smile, a crafty plotting smile.

"Wow," George scoffed. "That is low."

"Never piss off a senior sister," Steve said. "Not many live to tell the tale!"

George laughed.

"Could you let me know where Harold is later?" Steve asked. "I would like to check up on him and check over his file, make sure he is getting looked after."

"I will do when I find out," George said.

The girl behind the counter passed a large paper cup through and a baguette.

"Here you go sir," She said. "Anything else?"

"I am getting those," Steve said. "Put it on my bill and could I get the same please, but a small coffee with an extra expresso."

The girl nodded and walked away.

"Does your wife know about the expresso?" George teased. "Or is it a secret?"

"You do know my wife is a matron?" Steve warned him. "She could make us both disappear in a room full of people!" He sniggered. "Oh, I have a question."

"What's that?" George said, picking up the coffee and putting the baguette under his arm.

"My tablet is not working properly," He pulled the tablet from under his arm. "I dropped it last night, is there anything you can do?"

"Unfortunately, no," George said. "That is one for information technology services."

Steve groaned.

"Not the answer you was hoping for?" He looked at the cracked screen on the tablet. "Tell you what," George said. "How about you pop down later and speak to one of my guys, he used to work in a mobile repair shop, he could have a look for you."

"Oh, that would be great George," Steve said. "I would rather avoid going up to the IT department and telling them I have broken another!" He chuckled.

"How many is that now?" George said, turning to walk away.

"Six!" Steve said.

"Jesus man, what are you like?" George scoffed. "Need to get you one of those rubber cases like they have in children's services."

"One of my patients had one," Steve said. "He was autistic, liked throwing things around."

"Can't you tell IT that it was one of your patients?" George said. "They would never know."

"I think that only works so many times," Steve said. "Anyway, I better let you go, enjoy your lunch and good to see you."

"You too Steve," George said. "Don't forget I still need those forms signed before you get your pumps."

"I will do that later," Steve nodded.

"You said that several times last week," George shook his head. "I want them gone by the end of the day."

"I'll do it when I come round later," Steve said. "Now get lost."

George turned the corner by the technical services workshop, stopping when he noticed a patient leaning against the wall, smoking under a large 'do not smoke sign'.

"Excuse me," George said. "You cannot smoke here."

The woman turned around, skinny, and tall with long greying hair. She is pale and held onto a drip stand with two pumps running, the lines attached to her hand.

"I am a patient," She said. "I am allowed to smoke here!"

"This is a non-smoking site," George said. "No one is allowed to smoke here."

"You cannot stop me," She snapped. "What are you going to do, arrest me?!"

"No, I am not a police officer," George sighed. "I just like to be able to get into my workshop without a face full of smoke, so can you put that out or move on."

"You are not a very nice person," The woman moaned. "I think I will complain."

"That is fine," George said. "So, what will you complain about? Getting caught smoking in a non-smoking area where oxygen bottles are stored?" He pointed to the cage with several bottles in it.

"I will say I was given permission and I was not aware that smoking was not allowed," The woman said smugly. "And I will have you fired, for being rude and threatening to me!" She stared at him.

"Okay," George sighed with frustration. "Firstly, you are standing under a non-smoking sign," he said pointing to it. "Secondly you are on camera," He pointed to the small domed camera on the wall by the door. "Thirdly I don't give a toss, because looking at you, you won't even make it to the end of the week, so please take your disgusting habit somewhere else."

George walked past her, swiping his card on the access panel, and giving the shocked woman a sarcastic smile.

Kirsty is a woman in her early twenties, wearing tight blue jeans and a navy-blue blouse. Her light brown hair tied at the back and she is wearing red-rimmed glasses. She stood up when George walked in, pulling the door towards him.

"Hello," Kirsty said and signed slowly. "My name is Kirsty," She signed again.

"Hi Kirsty," George said. "I don't sign."

"How do you communicate?" She said slowly.

"Like this," George said. "Just speak clearly and normally."

"Sorry if I offended you," She said in embarrassment. "When Marvin said you were deaf, I went on google and learned some signs."

"You learned that today?" George was impressed. "That is good going."

"Let me know if I need to change anything when I talk," Kirsty said clearly.

"You are fine," George said. "No sign language or shouting and we will get on great."

"Is that woman still outside?" Kirsty said. "I have told her to leave a couple of times, but she was ever so rude."

"Yeah," George said. "Drop security a message, they will come and move her on," George put the coffee and baguette on the counter in the small office, looking at the three empty tables behind it and then towards the double doors leading to the workshop. By the entrance is a door leading to Harold's office, his name in the centre in block capitals with, 'Head of Technical Services' below it.

"Yes, I know," She nodded. "Saw your photo on the staff board."

"I need to update that," George sighed. "Everything sorted out today for you?"

"Yes," Kirsty nodded with a smile. "Lennie came down and helped me set up early this morning and Marvin went through the phones and helpdesk with me."

"I gather you are aware of the situation?" George said, picking up the coffee and sipping at it.

"Yes, Barbara called earlier and updated Marvin who told me everything," Kirsty said. "I heard you cancelled your holiday!" She gasped, shaking her head. "That sucks."

"Tell me about it," George said. "I am going to use the office, could you get the guys to join us in here say?" George looked at the clock. "Half twelve?"

"Sure, no problems," Kirsty said smiling. "Will do that for you, also Barbara said you will need help with phone calls, is that correct?" She looked uncomfortable.

"Sure," George said. "Either take messages or act as an in-between," George explained. "Is that okay?"

"We can go through it when someone calls," Kirsty said sitting down.

12:32

Kirsty sat at her desk, playing patience on the desktop. Andy sat behind her at the desk, short and skinny, dressed in black trousers and a white shirt, scruffy and creased, his short black hair was overground and his face full of uneven stubble, he rested his feet on the desk, his focus on a mobile phone. Behind him sat Curtis, a middle-aged man with silver hair, black-rimmed glasses, and a smile on his face. Also wearing a well-pressed white shirt and black trousers, he sat with his arms crossed. George opened the door, holding a notepad and pen he looked at the three sitting and then looked at Curtis.

"Where are the others?" He said.

"Well," Curtis said. "Ahmed is on the wards doing his servicing. Erica and Simon are in the community," He sat thinking. "Kevin is off sick," Curtis explained. "And Harold is signed off sick."

"Yes I know about Harold," George breathed out heavily. "What is Kevin off for this time?"

"He hurt his back," Curtis said. "Lifting weights."

"What here?" George asked.

"No idea," Curtis shrugged his shoulders. "He called in this morning and said he would email you later."

"I thought he told Marvin he had sickness and the runs?" Kirsty said. "Sounds like he got his story mixed up?"

"Not heard a thing," George said writing in the notebook. "Did the others know about the meeting?"

"Who?" Curtis said in confusion.

"Ahmed?" George said. "Did he know?"

"Yes," Curtis nodded. "He said his servicing took priority."

"Plank!" George snapped. "Typical of him really."

Kirsty giggled.

"Marvin?" George said. "I know he is in."

"He popped up to see Harold," Kirsty said. "Sorry I forgot to mention it."

"Where is Evan?" George said. "Forgot about him!"

"How can you forget about him?" Curtis laughed. "If he isn't burping or breaking wind, he is moaning about anything and everything!"

"He called in and said he would be late," Kirsty said. "Apparently, he has a gas leak."

"Another?" George scoffed. "How many is that now?"

"Three," Curtis said holding up three fingers. "Maybe this one is leaking from his backside?" Curtis giggled.

"Oh please," Kirsty said. "That is disgusting!"

"What about the duo?" George asked. "Fatman and slobbing?"

"Oh, you cannot call them that," Curtis laughed nervously. "Not allowed too."

"Well Simon is fat because he always feeds his face," George said. "And Erica is a slob, her desk is disgusting."

"That is true," Curtis agreed. "But still not allowed to say it."

"I don't give a shit," George said. "Things are going to be different."

George looked at Andy who was playing with his mobile.

"Andy?" He said.

Andy did not respond.

"Andy?" He said louder.

Andy slowly looked up.

"Sorry," George scoffed. "Am I keeping you from something?"

"No," Andy shook his head. "Just tired."

"Could you put that down for two seconds?" George said. "You won't die!"

Andy put the phone down on the table.

"And get your feet off the table," George snapped. "You are not at home."

Andy pulled his feet off the table and dropped them to the floor, the weight pulling him off the seat and sending him crashing down.

"Oh, Jesus!" George groaned. "And we let this moron loose on medical equipment."

"Are you okay," Curtis said getting up and reaching down. "Hurt yourself?"

"I'll hurt him in a minute!" George groaned. "Okay if you could minute this for me, Kirsty?"

"How?" Kirsty asked looking at George in confusion. "I am new to this."

"Do you know how to take minutes?" George said. "It's basically, taking notes of what is being said in a meeting?"

Kirsty shook her head.

"Okay," George sighed. "I'll do it and go through it with you later."

Kirsty nodded.

The phone began to ring loudly, causing Kirsty to jump.

"I'll get it," Curtis stood up.

"No stay there," George said. "Could you get it, Kirsty, thanks."

Picket up the phone and pressed the answer button.

"Hello," She said. "What can I help you with?" She listened on the end, nodding, and looking more confused by the second. "It's the baby ward," Kirsty said. "They have a new kettle and want us to test it."

"Not us, we only do medical devices," George said. "Tell them to contact estates."

"Hi, you need to contact estates," Kirsty said. "We don't do them," She listened again and after a minute she stood up. "They said it is medical because it is in the ward."

"Tell them it isn't and they need to contact estates," George said.

"They did and estates told them it is us," Kirsty said. "Sorry."

"Estates are a bunch of lazy twats that think we do everything they don't want to do," George walked up to the counter. "Give me the phone," He held out his hand."

Kirsty handed him the phone and he pressed a couple of buttons and then hung up, handing it back to her.

"What did you do?" Curtis asked with a smile on his face.

"Transferred the call to estates," George said and sat on the edge of the desk. "Okay," He took a deep breath.

"Do you want me to go up to the ward and sort it out for them?" Curtis said. "I want them to see us as being helpful."

"No Curtis," George said bluntly. "We are not doing estates work. Especially not you, you have too much to get done."

"Oh, what is one extra?" Curtis laughed.

"Okay," George looked at Andy. "Andy, how many outstanding jobs do you have?"

"Couldn't say without looking," Andy said. "I can guess?"

"Yes guess," George said.

"About twelve items for repair, twenty services and two acceptance," Andy said looking up as he thought. "Give or take."

"That's fine," George said and looked at Curtis. "How about you Curtis?"

"Okay," Curtis laughed uncomfortably.

"How many?"

"I have twenty repairs, over a hundred servicing jobs," Curtis said. "That's it."

"So, you completed all your acceptance testing?" George said.

"No," Andy grinned. "He still has that I was going to help him today."

George groaned and dropped the notepad on the table.

"Okay," He said. "Repairs and acceptance testing is a priority. I will speak to Ahmed when he comes down and can someone tell me where Simon and Erica are?"

Both Curtis and Andy shook their heads, George looked at Kirsty who nodded.

"Service contract in Sheppey," She said with a smile. "They left a number."

"Okay, could you call them after and tell them I need to speak to them, so could they head back an hour earlier?"

"Sure, can do," Kirsty said. "Is it okay if I go for lunch first?"

"Yes that is fine," George said. "Curtis, could you cover Kirsty while she is at lunch?"

Curtis nodded.

"Andy, have there been any requests for the library?" George asked.

19

"I am on it," Andy said. "I have the sheet and bleep."

"Thanks," George said. "Okay, for those of you that may not know, Harold broke both legs in an accident."

Andy sniggered.

"Why is that funny?" George glared at Andy. "How about I break yours so we can all have a giggle?"

Andy looked down at the floor.

"How did he manage to do that?" Curtis asked. "Did he fall off his bike again?"

"No," George said. "He hasn't ridden his bike in years."

"He said he was fed up with his bikes getting stolen," Andy said. "He had three nicked from the front entrance last year."

"Walks everywhere now," Curtis said. "Or gets his wife to drive him."

"Well she isn't well and cannot drive him anymore," George said. "So, I am going to pop up later and see if there is anything, I can do to help him out."

"Shall I get a card?" Curtis said.

"What kind of card?" Andy turned round to face Curtis.

"Well it isn't a birthday or congratulations card is it?" George muttered. "I would imagine a get well soon card," He said sarcastically. "Have you woken up yet?"

"I don't know," Andy shrugged his shoulders.

"Shall I get a couple?" Curtis said. "And we can decide which to give him?"

"No," George shook his head. "Whatever you choose will be fine, but please don't spend two hours looking."

"Oh yeah!" Andy laughed. "When you picked out a congratulations card for the last admin girl and took you two hours," Andy scoffed.

"It wasn't for two hours!" Curtis said. "It was closer to an hour and three quarters."

"Okay shut up Curtis," George said bluntly. "As you may know, I have been stupid enough to agree to help out while Harold is off," George sighed. "I have been made the interim head of Technical Services."

"Wow," Kirsty said. "You must be happy."

"No, not really," He shook his head. "Like running a mental asylum."

Andy giggled.

"Stop giggling Andy," George looked at him. "You are like a five-year-old."

Andy went quiet, looking at his mobile on the desk, fixated on it like a dog to a treat.

"Who is looking after the dog?" Curtis said.

"There isn't one," George said trying to avoid the subject.

"Yes, there is," Curtis said. "Little Tyson."

"Aww I love dogs," Kirsty said loudly. "What kind is it?"

George sighed.

"It's a Jack Russell," Andy said. "Nasty little fucker!"

"Stop swearing Andy," George said. "First and last warning today."

"Nasty little," Andy paused. "Thing."

"I love Jack Russell dogs," Kirsty said. "They are cute."

"This one wasn't," Andy chuckled. "Nearly took one of Harold's fingers off, do you remember that Curtis?" Andy burst out laughing. "When he came in on a Monday, hand bandaged up!"

"Oh dear," Kirsty said. "What happened?"

"It was Harold being bloody stupid," George snapped. "That is what it was."

"Tell her what happened Curtis," Andy giggled. "It's classic!"

"Well," George smiled. "There was this thing online where people were pouring ice-cold water on their dog's testicles."

"Oh no," Kirsty frowned. "I heard about that."

"Well, he tried it with little Tyson," George scoffed. "Who is faster than a speeding bullet."

"Shot up and clamped his jaw down on Harold's hand," Andy giggled. "Only let go when his wife jammed a treat in his face."

"Why did they call him little Tyson?" Kirsty asked curiously.

"When he was a puppy, he tore half of his mum's ear off," George said.

"Evil little sod," Andy said.

The door clicked and Marvin walked in, tall and slim wearing black trousers and hiking boots, a red raincoat that was so bright, George flinched. He has short grey hair and carried a laptop bag. He has a slight limp and struggles to fully lift his right leg.

"Afternoon Marvin," George said. "How is he?"

"Not so good," Marvin shivered. "In a bit of pain."

"Did he have surgery?" Andy asked.

"Yes," Marvin pulled off his coat. "He had it yesterday, plates in both legs."

"Jesus!" George said. "Where is Margaret?"

"With her sister," Marvin said.

"In Cornwall?" George exclaimed. "That is a long trek!"

"No!" Marvin shook his head and took a deep breath. "The one that lives near them."

"The crazy one?" George said. "Oh god!"

"She isn't crazy!" Marvin said. "I think she is very nice."

"Marvin," George said. "She tried to dry her cat off in the microwave back in the seventies!"

Andy burst into fits of laughter, rocking back and forth in his chair.

"Oh no that is awful," Kirsty said. "Did it survive?"

"No," George said. "The microwave blew up."

"Maybe she is Russian?" Curtis said. "A secret and silent killer."

"Well it wasn't a secret, nor was it silent!" George said. "Okay I have a ton of things to do, so if you could all get back onto your repairs and let me know at the end of the day what you achieve," He turned to Marvin. "Marvin, could you do me a favour and help out Curtis before I box him up and ship him off to Russia?"

Curtis laughed.

"What kind of box?" He asked. "Will you find one that I can fit in?" Curtis said all smug.

"I have a chainsaw for a reason," George said. "Shut up!"

George looked at Marvin.

"Sure, can do," Marvin said. "I just need to do an urgent repair on delivery, I believe they called down earlier?"

"Yes, they said that the room is free," Kirsty handed a note to Marvin. "They have cleaned the bed fully."

"What is that?" George asked curiously. "Have they gone and broken another bed?"

Marvin nodded.

"It's a training issue," George sighed in frustration. "How many is that now?"

"Third this month," Marvin said. "I have had to call the company as we don't have the means to lift the bed."

"Pass it onto them," George said. "Don't waste any more time with this one."

Marvin nodded, putting the note into his pocket.

"Any questions?" George looked around the room, no one said anything. "Okay, my door is always open if anyone needs anything, could someone send Ahmed in when he arrives."

George walked back into the office, closing the door. He looked around the room, the shelving down one side, full of books and computer discs, on the other side a desk, covered in paperwork. Behind the desk a large note board with a map, papers and notes pinned all over it.

"Jesus!" He shivered. "What a mess!"

A knock at the door startled him and he turned around as it opened.

"Quick word?" Marvin popped his head in. "Harold asked me to talk to you."

"Sure," George said, looking at the two chairs covered in paperwork. "Going to have to stand."

"You must be having an aneurysm!" Marvin exclaimed. "I know you like it tidy."

"I'm cleaning it up later," George said. "Going to get Kirsty to go through it."

Marvin nodded, looking around the room at the piles of paperwork.

"So, what did Harold say?" George asked.

"He wants to see you," Marvin said. "Also wondered if you could contact his daughter?"

"Why?" George asked. "Surely his son can do that?"

"They aren't speaking," Marvin said.

"Since when?" George said. "Harold never said anything."

"Well you know that his son owes him money," Marvin said quietly.

"Yes," George said. "Thought he would have paid it by now considering the job he has?"

"Well no," Marvin chuckled. "His son was upset that Harold asked for it back."

"Little shit," George snapped. "Does he have contact details for his daughter?"

Marvin shook his head and laughed.

"What is so funny?" George said.

"He lost her number and isn't sure of her address," Marvin said. "Margaret deals with all that kind of stuff and considering she isn't all there," He shrugged his shoulders.

"Fine," George said reluctantly. "I'll try and contact her on social media."

"You okay?" Marvin asked quietly.

"What?" George said.

"Are you okay?" Marvin said. "You look distracted."

"Well," George sat on the edge of the table. "Supposed to be on my way to Cornwall."

"Yeah," Marvin said. "Whereabouts?"

"Falmouth," George said. "Bit pissed off about it, to be honest," He breathed out heavily. "So, what is new in clinical areas? Still wearing masks?"

"Face shields too," Marvin said. "Did you not get the email?"

"I have been off since Friday and came back to over fifty emails!" George scoffed. "Literally one day away and every arsehole emails me!"

"Harold isn't right," Marvin said quietly.

"Harold what?" George said getting closer.

"Isn't right," Marvin whispered. "He doesn't want anyone to know."

"Not surprised!" George said loudly.

"Keep it down," Marvin Cringed.

"Poor sod broke both of his legs and a cow killed his dog," George pressed his lips together, trying not to laugh. "And his wife is not with it," George took his mobile from his pocket. "What happened to the dog?"

"It got squashed under a cow," Marvin said, pulling a disgusted face.

"No!" George groaned. "Is it still on the field or what?"

He rolled his eyes, typing into his phone.

"No," Marvin said. "Harold had to call an ambulance because his wife picked up the dog and carried it home."

George looked up, his mouth opened in shock.

"You are shitting me?" George said. "She walked all the way home with a squashed dog?"

"Well no," Marvin groaned. "I found out when the local vet called me, Margaret walked into the vets with the dog and asked them to fix it."

George covered his mouth, sniggering.

"When they said there was nothing they could do, she picked up the dog, cradled it like a baby and walked home," Marvin said. "I found her at the house, eating a tin of cold baked beans."

"It is almost like you are trying to make me laugh," George said. "Did you bury the dog?"

"Well I couldn't find it," Marvin said. "So, I called Harold in Accident and emergency and asked him for ideas."

"In the freezer?" George said. "She keeps putting things in the freezer."

Marvin nodded.

"She has lost it," George said. "Poor old Harold is going to need all the help he can get."

"I took him out of the freezer, and said that I would bury him," Marvin said, groaning and shaking his head. "When I came back, I couldn't find him, went upstairs in the spare room, and he was tucked into bed."

George snorted, stifling giggles.

"Stop!" Marvin said. "It isn't funny!"

"Oh, it is," George said. "You need to stop telling me these things otherwise I won't be able to concentrate."

A knock at the door and they both turned around, looking at it.

"Sorry to bother you, George," Kirsty stood by the door. "I have a surgical ward on the line, they have requested a faulty bed to be collected."

"Okay?" George said. "And?"

"Apparently, they have requested it twice," She looked uncomfortable. "But the porters haven't collected it and they are desperate for space."

"I'll go and get it," Marvin said. "Will put it into the bed storage shed."

"No," George interrupted. "I will, you need to rest that knee of yours. I'll do it after I have finished this message," He held up his phone. "I've also got Darren from the Agency in shortly."

"How come?" Marvin asked curiously. "Getting another guy?"

"Well yes," George said. "He wants to talk about Eric and has another engineer for us."

"Let's hope it's not another Eric," Marvin chuckled. "We are still sorting out his crap."

"Who was Eric?" Kirsty asked.

"An idiot with a death wish," George replied. "I asked him to leave last week and when he refused, Harold fired him."

"Why?" Kirsty said. "What did he do?"

"Long story," George said. "I will explain after I have sorted the bed out," George put his phone away. "Did they say what the issue was with it?"

"Got to shoot," Marvin said. "Need to get in touch with a supplier."

Marvin left the room and Kirsty came in closer, holding a notepad.

"They said that it doesn't power on," Kirsty looked at her notes. "And the remote is missing."

"Probably the reason it doesn't power on!" George scoffed. "Amazes me how they lose something like that."

"Do you want me to let them know?" Kirsty said.

"No don't worry," George took a mask from his pocket. "I'll go now, and while you are here, the trust has a policy on jeans," he pointed to her blue jeans. "Not sure if you are aware?"

"This wasn't intentional," Kirsty said with a worried look. "My daughter was sick, and these are the only dry ones I had."

"No problems," George assured her. "Hope she gets better."

"Thanks," She smiled. "Anything else?"

George shook his head and Kirsty left, opening the door fully.

13:45

George stopped in the corridor, nodding at the group of nurses that walked past him. Gripping the headboard of the hospital bed, loaded with rolled up pressure mattresses, he was out of breath and sweating. The long narrow corridor was lined with cages full of cardboard and stock, making it awkward to navigate the bed down. The fact that George was invisible to peoples ignorance did not help, and he had stopped several times to let people through.

25

"And here comes another lemming, pregnant too," George said under his breath. "Her nose stuck in a mobile phone whilst she blindly walks down the corridor," He shook his head. "The whale probably thinks she has a Moses complex, and everyone will move out of the way.

The heavily pregnant woman waddled down the middle of the corridor, wearing black leggings and a small t-shirt, her bump poking out at the middle, the badly designed, faded and stretched dolphins in circles around her belly button made George cringe. She had a mask on, hanging under her chin and was chewing gum.

"Lovely!" He scoffed in sarcasm.

The woman got closer to George and he stopped, moving the bed as close to the wall as he could. She was inches away from him when she suddenly stopped and looked up at him, annoyance on her face.

"Careful!" She snapped. "You could have hit me!"

"I stopped some time ago," George said. "I saw you coming towards me and was waiting for you to look up."

"So, it is my fault!" She scoffed.

"Not at all," George said. "But accidents happen when you have your nose stuck in a mobile phone and walking without looking."

"So rude," She said. "I am pregnant!"

"Really?" George said in surprise. "I just thought you were fat."

"You cannot talk to me like that!" She glared at him. "I am going to make a complaint."

"That is fine," George nodded. "I gave up caring ages ago."

"What is your name," She demanded.

"Ivor," George said.

"Ivor what?" She said.

"Ivor," George looked up and rolled his eyes. "Gotten."

"Ivor gotten?" She laughed. "What a stupid name! She scoffed and stormed off, eyeballing George as she walked past him.

"Rabid beached whale," George said. "The bloody wildlife in this place!"

George pushed the bed down the corridor, avoiding patients and staff, stopping, and starting until he got towards the turning that led him outside. He swiped his badge on the access panel and opened the double doors, lining the bed up with them.

An elderly man approached him from the opposite end of the corridor, waving to get Georges attention.

"Are you okay?" George said, looking at the man as he straightened his mask, struggling to get his breath. He is wearing a smart grey suit, old but well looked after. A cap on his head that matched.

"Yes," He nodded holding onto the bed.

"You may want to sit down," George pointed to the ledge. "I would rather you didn't lean against the bed."

He nodded and moved away, slowly lowering himself onto the ledge and giving George a gentle wave of thanks. George went to pull the bed towards him to give the old man some room and was startled by someone tapping him on the shoulder.

George turned round to find one of the porters standing in front of him, a tall overweight woman that was well known for her loudness and overpowering body odour, she had short blonde greasy hair, the pink highlights faded. She is wearing a purple face mask,

"Do you mind dropping your mask," George said tapping his mask. "I need to lipread."

The porter pulled her mask down.

"Sorry George," She said. "I keep forgetting!" She laughed.

George nodded and stepped back when he got a waft of body odour, the stale stench stinging his eyes.

"No problems," George nodded. "What's up?"

"The sky!" She giggled loudly, her laughing almost hysterical.

"Good one," George said bluntly.

"I know," She said. "I'm quick."

"I was being sarcastic," George said. "What do you want?"

"It is easier if you lift the lever," She said and pushed George back, changing the foot switch "That way you will go straight."

"I am going outside," George said. "And I can manage fine thanks."

"You sure?" She asked.

"Yes," George nodded. "Must get on."

"Good," She smiled. "I like to do my bit for the disabled community."

George stopped and slowly looked up at her.

"You like to what?" He said in surprise.

"Your disability," She said. "You probably need more help."

"I am deaf," George replied. "It doesn't affect me physically."

"I know, I know!" She laughed. "I have worked with special needs children, so I understand the struggles."

"Right," George said and sighed heavily in frustration. "I am not a child and I do not have special needs."

"Well," She said, and George held up his hand, putting the palm in her face to stop her.

"These special needs kids?" George said. "Are they still alive or did you eat them?"

She went to speak.

"Okay shut up," George said bluntly.

The old man laughed, smiling and nodding.

"Why do you talk to people like that," George said. "It isn't normal."

"Well I like to be outspoken and honest," The girl said, offended by Georges outburst.

"Really?" George said. "You prefer people to be outspoken and honest?"

The girl nodded.

"Okay," Paul said, smiling under his mask. "Firstly, I recommend a bath, your body odour is offensive."

"Body odour?" The girl said confused.

"Personal hygiene," George said. "Get what I mean?"

"Personal hygiene," She said still not sure what George was getting at.

"Yes," George said, rolling his eyes. "I think you need to invest in deodorant."

"I don't understand," She looked at him.

George looked at the old man who looked back at him, shaking his head.

"You stink," George said. "It isn't a nice smell and the closer you get to me, the more my nose wants to vacate my face and leave the planet!"

The old man laughed.

"That is rude!" The girl said loudly. "You cannot say that!"

"I just did," George said, nodding sarcastically.

"Wow!" She exclaimed.

"Just saying what everyone is thinking," George said, pressing the foot pedal on the bed. "Have a nice day. He gave me a thumbs up and walked away, leaving the girl looking at him as he pulled the bed outside. George watched as the door slowly closed, her bright red face disappearing as the doors came together.

"Fruitcake!" George muttered. "Absolutely, mental!"

George started to push the bed towards the storage sheds when he heard the door open behind him and someone called out.

"Hey," a nurse came outside. "When you have done that could you move the bed from outside the ward?" She asked.

Wearing navy blue trousers and a light blue tunic, the nurse has short blonde spiky hair and thick red glass, short and slim with an angry look on her face. She leaned against the door, holding it open.

"What?" George said. "Could you repeat that?"

"Oh, you are deaf," The nurse said, tutting as she pulled her mask down. "Got a bed for you to move, as quickly as you can please."

"No, I cannot do that," George said. "you will need to contact the porter team."

"Isn't that what you are?" She asked. "Are you not a porter?"

"No, I am not a porter," George scoffed.

"Oh," She looked George up and down. "Why are you moving that one?"

"I am from technical services," George said. "This needed to be done urgently."

"But you cannot move one bed for me?" She asked. "It's urgent." She grinned.

"No," George said. "You need to report it."

"Thanks for nothing," She said and walked away.

"Friendly," George said loudly and got back to moving the bed to the shed, groaning when he saw the entrance to the ramp.

Two ramps are leading to the shed, one was blocked off due to the damaged concrete, and the other had cages in front of it, waiting to be put into the compactor.

"Doesn't anyone have any sense these days?" George said.

George pushed the bed up to the railings, locking the breaks and moving the cages away from the ramp entrance, lining them up against the compactor.

"This will be fun!" George said remembering that this end of the ramp was higher than the other end and required more brute strength to get it up and moving. Pushing it from the headboard, he growled as he managed to get it up halfway, but it sloped towards the railings, getting stuck.

"Oh, come on!" George said and pulled it down a little, taking a deep breath as he pushed again, building up speed.

Again, the bed lodged against the railings, the slight slope causing it to slide to one side.

"Gonna have to pull," George said, looking around to see if anyone could help.

It began to snow finely.

"Oh lovely," He moaned. "Just what we want."

Getting behind the bed, he gripped the footboard and yanked it. Again, it caught the railings and in a sudden rage, George growled and pulled it as hard as he could towards the shed.

"Bloody thing!" He snapped.

There is a snap and splinter as the footboard broke away from the metal frame, George failed to realise that it was a cheaper footboard, and the only support are the metal posts that slide into the bed, the footboard wasn't designed to take any weight.

Everything went in slow motion as the footboard ripped away from the bed, slamming into George's chest, and lifting him off the ground, throwing him up and over.

Yelping in shock and pain, he sees stars when slamming into the concrete floor, knocking the wind out of himself.

Right next to where he landed is a door leading to a seminar room where a manual handling course was in action. The door and window next to it opened at the same time, half a dozen women popping their heads out to see what had happened.

"Oh my god!" One of them cried out. "Are you okay?"

"Ow!" George groaned, trying to get his breath back.

One of the nurses, short and stocky wearing blue jeans and a green fleece, knelt next to George.

"Thought you were on holiday George?" She said. "You better have a good reason for disturbing my moving and handling seminar."

"I apologise!" George said sarcastically, pushing the footboard onto the floor and grunting as he got to his feet. "Bloody cheap rubbish!" He looked at the ruined footboard and the two metal posts still in the bed. "That will teach me."

"Are you hurt?" The woman said, waving at the other woman to go back inside and close the window. "Did you hit your head?"

"I hit everything on the back," George chuckled. "I'll live."

"Why didn't you knock?" She said. "One of us could have helped you."

"Didn't know anyone was in there," George said.

"Vacation cancelled I gather?" The woman said.

"Yeah," George said brushing the dust off his trousers. "Harold has gone and had an accident."

"Oh my god!" She gasped. "Is he okay?"

George shrugged his shoulders.

"Will find out later," He said. "Need to check up on him after this."

"So, are you covering him?" She asked.

"Yes," George said. "Would rather have not, but they were desperate!"

"You will be good at it," She went to pat him on the arm and backed away. "Are they getting you some help with your disability?"

"I hope not!" George scoffed. "They wouldn't do anything when I complained about the lack of deaf awareness in this place," He shook his head. "Still waiting on the details of the radio blogs."

"That is not good," The woman said. "Did they look into the see-through masks for you?"

"I mentioned it a few times, but seems there is an unnecessary cost to them, considering only two or three deaf people working at this trust," George said. "I gave up trying."

"Did they get a new receptionist?" She asked. "My sister applied for the job."

"Did she?" George nodded. "We had a new girl start and I can lipread her, so winning already," George said. "Fancy helping me with this quickly?" George asked. "I steer and you push?"

"Of course," The woman said, squeezing past the bed and gripping the headboard. "Only if you come up and fix my thermometers!"

"I'll get one of my guys to come up this afternoon," George said, grabbing hold of the footboard mounts and steering the bed towards the open shed doors.

14:20

Harold is propped up in the hospital bed, his legs raised and plastered, wearing a white t-shirt, his hair long and messy and the grey blanket was draped over him. Holding a cup of tea in one hand and a newspaper in the other. The blue curtains either side of him are pulled, on one side of the bed an old armchair, on the other a small bedside cabinet with a bottle of water and various fruit.

"I hear you need something fixed?" George said popping his head behind the curtains. "Okay to chat for a bit, I need to be back at the office for three?"

"Of course," Harold put the paper down. "Just keep your mask on!" He said, nodding knowingly. George sat down in the armchair, shaking his head as he looked at Harold's legs.

"You didn't have to come in," Harold said.

"I thought it would be good to see you," George said. "You ungrateful rude old git!"

"No not me!" Harold chuckled. "You were off for a reason."

"Barbara doesn't know," George said. "Does she?"

"It is between us," Harold said. "I have not told anyone at all, and that is a promise."

"Thank you," George said. "But I had to," He said. "I think."

"Marvin would have managed," Harold said. "And everyone knows what they are doing." George sighed in frustration.

"You are still not right," Harold said. "You practically had a breakdown."

"It's fine," George said. "Maybe this will take my mind off things."

"Oh, bollocks will it!" Harold snapped. "I worry about you,"

"You don't need to," George said.

"That doesn't help," Harold said softly. "It was me that sat with you in the resuscitation after they revived you."

"I know Harold," George put his hand on Harold's hand and patted it. "It was too much drink, too many pills and a very dark place."

31

Harold looked at George, tears welling in his eyes.

"Do I need to pull rank?" He said. "Or will you promise you to speak to me, or anyone if things get too heavy for you?"

"No," George said. "No one needs to know," George sighed. "Please."

"Okay," Harold said. Carry on abusing the staff and winding people up otherwise someone is going to suss you out."

George laughed, nodding in agreement.

"I care about you George," Harold said trying to lean forward.

"So why did you go and do that for?" George said. "Ruined my holiday, you selfish old git!"

"I am ever so sorry George," Harold apologised.

"Oh, shut up," George said. "I am pulling your leg," He paused. "Legs."

Harold scoffed and shook his head.

"How are things down there?" Harold asked.

"Bunch of bloody rejects," George scoffed. "Like watching drunk teenagers in a caravan disco!"

Harold laughed and then winced.

"Careful," George warned him. "Might crack a rib."

Harold smiled, leaning back into the pillows, and rubbing his side.

"Did you manage to get hold of Lucy?" Harold said. "Margaret has misplaced my bloody phone!"

"I did," George said. "Found her on social media."

"You don't use it do you?" Harold said. "Always complaining about it."

"I set up a dummy account just so I could message her," George said. "Got her number and texted her earlier," He gave Harold the thumbs up. "She is coming today and is going to meet me downstairs at five so I can bring her up, security is not letting anyone in unless they have a covering letter."

"Oh George," Harold struggled to speak. "What would I do without you?"

"Well you wouldn't tidy your bloody office, would you?" George shook his head. "Looks like a library massacre!"

"It works for me," Harold said.

"Maybe it does," George said. "But why do you have a service manual for a twenty-year-old vital signs monitor on your desk?" George leaned forward. "And there was a three-month-old beef roll in your drawer!"

"Oh, I forgot about that," Harold chuckled. "You can have it."

"Pass," George gagged. "Bloody disgusting. It was green!"

"I don't think I am going to be back for a while," Harold said. "You may have to cover for longer."

"Got an email from Barbara," George sighed. "She has made me the interim head until further notice."

"Oh, very nice," Harold said. "Always said you would do well at it."

"Well I don't want it," George moaned. "I am happy fixing things, keeping away from idiots and politics as much as possible. I was up to date on everything come Thursday, and now I am back dealing with kids!"

"Calm down," Harold said. "You will only give yourself a stroke!"

"Fatman and Slobbing are trying their luck, Kevin and Evan both off sick again, Ahmed doing his own thing," George took a deep breath. "And Curtis wants to do anything and everything, but doesn't get sod all done, and Jesus, he never shuts up!"

"Finished?" Harold said staring at him. "Like an old woman you are!"

"Yes, you keep saying," George laughed. "I just want to get things running smoothly."

"You have no chance of that!" Harold laughed. "Are you okay?" Harold asked.

"I am fine," George said. "I think."

"What time is Darren due?" Harold said.

"Three, give or take," George looked at the clock on the bedside cabinet. "He is always late."

"Sorry you will have to deal with that," Harold said pulling a worried face. "I was hoping to get all sorted before you came back."

"Wonder if he has cut off that stupid ponytail?" George said. "Looks like an eighties yuppy."

"Oh no," Harold said. "He came in last week, dyed his hair jet black, still has the ponytail!"

"You are kidding," George scoffed. "It looks awful."

"You remember that day when he showed you his phone?" Harold said.

"Yeah," George muttered. "Threw me to the bloody dogs didn't you!"
Harold laughed.

"I thought it was his daughter!" George said. "Looked a right idiot when he said it was his girlfriend."

"Tell me about it," Harold said. "She was nearly twenty-five years younger than him, his face when he showed you the private photo."

"Oh, the photo of the young girl in skimpy underwear?" George said. "Why would you have a photo of your girlfriend in underwear set to wallpaper?" George scoffed. "Fruitcake!"

"Then we had that issue when he told the receptionist about losing one of his balls," Harold said. "She wanted to take things further, funny how she managed to get him to buy pizza for everyone in return for her to forget."

"That was a lot of pizza," George smiled. "He told too many people different stories, fell out the loft and landed on his nuts, someone trod on him playing football and so on, when it turned out he was born with only one." George sighed. "Mental nut!"

"You going to be okay dealing with him," Harold said. "He is coming in to discuss the Eric situation."

"I can deal with the Eric situation," George said. "And hopefully the next guy is better."

"Woman," Harold said. "The agency is sending in a young woman this time."

"About time," George said. "She can kick some sense into the guys."

"Keep Kevin away from her!" Harold held a finger up. "We cannot afford another issue with him and human resources."

"I can see it," George chuckled. "Bloody women, put them up against the wall and bloody shoot them!" George said. "All he does is complains."

"Until he meets one that he likes," Harold said. "He met one on Friday."

"Ah," George suddenly had a thought. "No wonder he has gone sick!"

"Maybe she killed him?" Harold said with a crafty smile.

"Wouldn't be a bad thing would it?" George said. "He always seems to drop a wench in the works when he is around."

"Wrench," Harold said trying not to laugh. "You keep saying wench."

"You know what I mean," George said, waving it off.

"Yeah but after your email last week, Barbara didn't get what you meant and thought you were being rude about women," Harold sighed. "Just say, spanner in the works, everyone knows that."

"I don't give a crap," George said. "Anyway, enough about work, what else do you want me to sort out for you?" George said looking up at the clock.

15:10

George sat down at the desk, having cleared all the papers off and pulling them into storage boxes, The old pine desk, clean of clutter with only a laptop at the centre and a coffee mug on a mat.

"It's a start," George said, looking at the three boxes full of paperwork in the corner of the room, the two chairs now clear. "Just need to get the hoover and mop in here."

He looked at the door when someone gently knocked it and he was not sure if someone did.

"Someone there?" He said.

Kirsty opened the door, popping her head in.

"Hi," She said. "Darren is here and wants to know the policy."

34

"Policy on what?" George said.

"On accessing the department with the pandemic and everything," She said pulling a confused face.

"Tell him we are safe," George said. "We are a green site."

"Okay," Kirst said and walked away.

George got up and moved one of the chairs closer to the desk, checking it before sitting back down. Darren knocked on the door and stood by it, tall and slim wearing a black suit, he has jet black hair and a small ponytail. He is wearing a black face mask and carrying a laptop case.

"Hello," He said. "No Harold?" He asked unsurely.

"Do you mind removing your mask?" George said. "I need to lipread, we have plenty of room but if you are unhappy, I can get a face shield for you?"

"No problem," Darren said sighing in relief as he pulled the mask off, putting it into his pocket. "Hate these bloody things!" He chuckled. "I am Darren, we spoke on the phone."

"I am not Harold," George said. "Long story short, Harold is off sick, and I am covering."

"Oh," Darren said. "You are?"

"Sorry," George said realising he had not introduced himself. "My name is George."

"I think we met before," Darren said. "Must have been a while ago. Probably emailed me a few times too."

"Yes," George said. "Still waiting on a reply from you."

"Ah yes," Darren said uncomfortably. "Sorry about that."

Darren sat down, and Kirsty knocked on the door.

"Anyone want a drink?" She smiled.

"I would love a white coffee," Darren said. "Thank you."

"Could I have a black coffee please," George said. "I put a new jar on top of the microwave," He picked up the white mug from the table, handing it to Kirsty. "Thanks."

"You are welcome," Kirsty said and then stopped at the door. "I finish at three-thirty by the way," She said. "Not sure if you knew?"

"That is fine," George nodded. "Could you give the phone to Curtis?"

Kirsty nodded and closed the door.

"I see that you are deaf," Darren said pointing to Georges implant. "Do you want me to do anything differently?"

"Like what?" George said smiling. "Can you do a handstand and talk?"

Darren laughed nervously.

"I am kidding," George said. "Just carry on as you are, if I have any problems, I will let you know."

"Has Harold updated you?" Darren said. "About why I am here?"

George nodded, closed the laptop, and pushed his chair back.

"Yes," George said. "You are here to speak about why we asked Eric to leave and also talk about a new technician you have."

"Eric," Darren sighed. "Could you explain roughly what happened?"

"Well a couple of things we have concerns with," George said leaning forward. "We had a call from one of the wards, a porter had issues getting a regulator off a cylinder, so he called us. Eric took the call, the porter wanted a wrench and some lubricant."

"Oh dear," Darren said, understanding where George was coming from.

"I was watching the conversation, as his telephone manner isn't great," George said. "I was relieved when he refused and explained he would go up and sort it out for them."

"Okay, that is good, a simple case of releasing the pressure to the regulator?" Darren said.

"Yes, he went up to one of my colleagues, asking to borrow some WD-forty and a monkey wrench so he could go up there and do it for them!" George exclaimed. "I stepped in and told him not too and said it was dangerous, to which he said I was wrong."

"Clearly, he had no idea!" Darren said.

"Lucky for us, he didn't have what he needed!" George said. "So, I asked him not to do it and I would deal with it."

"What did he do?" Darren asked.

"He went up with a monkey wrench and a rubber mallet," George said holding up his arms. "Marvin was working on the ward and took over."

"What was the other thing?" Darren said, removing a small notebook from his inside pocket. "Is it okay for me to write this down?"

"Sure," George said. "I am doing an email for you anyhow, detailing everything due to the incident report."

"Incident?" Darren asked.

"Yes," George nodded. "Classed as a near miss and misconduct because he ignored me and did his own thing."

"Great," He said. "Could I get a copy of that?"

"Can do," George said. "The other thing was that afternoon, he went out for lunch to the local pub, which isn't an issue, but he had two pints with his dinner."

"What an idiot," Darren put his hand over his face, shaking his head.

"I know, and that is why I told him to leave," George said. "Cannot have an idiot like that in the department/"

"I fully agree!" Darren said. "He is making a complaint, but this information helps. Also, we had a complaint from his last location, about his drinking."

"Mad," George said. "We also have two pumps we need to look into, that he has broken."

"Do you want me to foot the bill?" Darren said frustrated.

"I don't know yet," George said. "Curtis is looking at them, so they may be obsolete by the time he bloody does!"

Darren laughed.

The door opened and Kirsty walked in carrying two mugs, she handed one to Darren and the second to George.

"Thanks," Darren said.

"Welcome," Kirsty said. "Need anything else from me?" She asked George.

"No," George said. "You have been great, finish up and go if you want."

"Sure?" Kirsty said. "Thanks."

George nodded, and walked to the door, waving as she closed it.

"New girl?" Darren asked.

"Yeah," George said. "First day today."

"What happened to the other one?" Darren asked. "I forget her name, never smiled, snappy."

"Sandie," George laughed. "Yeah, she was brilliant. She is moving back to her mother in Canada, with the current situation and her father being sick, she wanted to help out."

"Oh," Darren said. "Poor kid."

"We said we can try and help her with redeployment if she wanted to come back," George said. "Kirsty is on a short-term contract."

"Back to Curtis," Darren said. "How is he doing otherwise?"

"Talks too much, but is a very good tech," George said. "Just needs to speed up a little and stop offering to fix everything that isn't anything to do with us."

"Okay," Darren said. "I have a new tech available if you are interested?"

"Can she do infusion pumps?" George asked curiously.

"How do you know it's a woman?" Darren asked.

"Saw the email to Harold," George said. "I am looking after those too."

"Yes," Darren said. "She also does ventilation."

"Oh great," George said. "I need help with acceptance testing and infusion pumps."

"She is available to start as soon as possible," Darren said. "She needs a days' notice."

"Wednesday is great," George said. "We start at eight."

37

"I will send the forms over to you in the morning," Darren said. "And I will let her know, she lives locally."

"Great," George said. "Look forward to meeting her, hopefully, she can kick some sense into the morons I have."

Darren laughed, shaking his head nervously.

"What happened to Harold?" Darren asked. "Not got the virus, has he?" He said worryingly.

"No nothing like that," George said. "He is too messy and even the virus wouldn't touch him!" He scoffed, indicating the mess in the office. "He was mauled."

"Oh, no way!" George said. "By a dog?"

"No, a cow," George said bluntly.

Darren laughed and then stopped when he realised George was being serious.

"Really?!" Darren said loudly, his hand covering his mouth.

George nodded.

"How?" Darren asked. "Well I can imagine how, but what caused it to happen?"

"His dog agitated a cow, Harold went to pull it away and it fell, crushing the dog and landing on Harold."

"Damn!" Darren said, trying not to laugh. "How bad?"

"Two broken legs and cracked ribs," George said opening the laptop. "Dog is a pancake."

Darren sat with his mouth open, shocked.

"Was bound to happen sooner or later," George shrugged his shoulders. "Dog was a maniac."

"What kind?" Darren asked.

"Jack Russell," George said, typing into the laptop. Snappy little shit."

"My aunt has one," Darren said. "Friendly and quiet."

"Harold had two," George said looking up. "The other decided to play tag with a car, didn't turn out well."

"Oh no," Darren said sighing. "Well I better let you get on, is it okay to speak to Curtis for a bit?"

"Go for it," George said. "As soon as I get the paperwork from you, I will get an order raised."

"Thanks," Darren said getting up, the chair scraping against the floor as he pushed it back.

"Just so you are aware, if you need to go around the trust for anything, you need to book in at the desk," George explained. "If you go onto the wards you need a face shield, Kirsty has some behind the counter."

"Could I nick one?" Darren asked. "For home?"

"Sure," George said.

Darren walked to the door and George followed.

"I would shake your hand," Darren said. "Next time."

"It's okay," George looked over at Kirsty behind the desk. "Kirsty, could you hive Darren a couple of shields and masks please?"

Kirsty nodded and smiled.

"I'll see you soon and look forward to getting the information tomorrow," George explained. "Might be a delay in replying as I am running a nuthouse."

Kirsty giggled.

"Take care and speak soon," George said, closing the door slowly and then leaning against it, looking around the room. "Right let's get this cesspit cleaned up."

16:50

George zipped up the fleece, shivering when the cold blast hit him. He stood near the entrance to the hospital, barriers erected to slow people down until security let them in.

"Busy today," He said looking at the line of fifteen plus people, all holding letters and waiting patiently. "Hurry up Lucy, I am freezing my nuts off." He dropped his mask down a little, breathing in the fresh air through his nose.

George turned around when someone tapped him on the shoulder, he smiled and expected to see Lucy.

"Oh hello," He said in disappointment. "Thought you were someone else."

"Can you let me in?" The man said pointing to the locked door near where George stood.

The man is wearing black jeans and a thick woollen jumper, his hands tucked into his pockets and his face pale from the cold. Average height and build, the smell of alcohol was overpowering.

"What?" George said not understanding him.

"Didn't you hear me?" The man asked.

"No," George said. "That is why I said, what."

"Oh," The man pointed to the implant. "You got one of those deaf things!" The man raised his voice. "My grandmother has one, but it doesn't work."

"Oh," George said.

"Are you deaf then?" The man asked.

"Obviously," George said, turning away.

"How do you know?" The man said, leaning against the wall next to George.

"How do I know what?" George said, slightly annoyed.

"That you are deaf," The man said nodding, the drunkenness becoming obvious.

"Because I cannot hear a single thing?" George scoffed.

39

"What," The man said. "Nothing at all?"

"Nothing," George said bluntly.

The man laughed and leaned forward, prompting George to step back.

"Do you mind mate?" His tone is angry. "Social distance huh?"

The man held up his hands, stepping back.

"So, you cannot hear anything?" The man scoffed. "What if I shout really loud in your ear?"

"You will probably get a slap," George said facing him. "So, don't do that."

"Can you let me in?" The man pointed to the door.

"No," George said. "You need to queue up," George pointed to the queue.

"He won't let me in!" The man moaned and sighed, looking at George who shook his head. "Can you hear anything with that on?" He pointed to the implant.

"Yes," George said. "A fair bit."

"What do I sound like?" The man said smiling curiously.

"Bloody annoying!" George snapped.

"That isn't nice!" The man said. "I should complain about you!"

"Go for it," George said.

"I am understanding," The man said slurring his words. "My bothers kid is like you."

"What deaf?" George asked.

"No, he has that Cerebral palsy thing," The man said. "Walks and talks funny!"

"Jesus Christ!" George rolled his eyes. "The only disability that poor kid has is you for an uncle!"

The man laughed and then looked at George, thinking.

"So, are you going to let me in?" The man pointed to the door again. "I need to go to the emergency department, I ain't well." The man breathed out heavily.

George groaned, waving the air, and stepping back.

"Smells like you are dead inside," He coughed. "You don't look sick enough for emergency care."

"I have a headache," The man rubbed his forehead. "My brain is gonna burst."

"Unlikely," George turned away. "You need a brain for that mate," He said under his breath."

A tall slim security guard walked over, wearing a uniform, black bomber jacket and a black beanie hat, he wore a white mask and black gloves.

"Everything alright George?" He said.

George pointed to the mask and the security guard pulled it down.

"Sorry mate," He said. "Everything okay?" He looked at the man.

"Well he keeps asking me to let him in," George said. "Doesn't understand what, no, means and keeps getting in my face," George moved away again. "I think something climbed into him and died judging by his breath."

"I was only saying hello," The man said. "Special needs people need support and encouragement!"

"Special needs?" The security guard burst into fits of laughter. "George doesn't have special needs, he is a grumpy bastard mind you, but nothing special about him!" The security guard crossed his arms. "Told you to go home mate."

"I am sick," The man said defiantly.

"No, you are pissed!" The security guard said. "Leave please or I will call the police."

"You have to treat me!" The man shouted. "I am entitled."

"Weedkiller might do it," George whispered.

The security guard sniggered.

"If I get you a coffee," The security guard said and sighed. "Will you go home?"

The man nodded.

"Promise?" The security guard said. "Going to leave my friend alone?" he pointed to George.

"If I must," The man said patting George on the shoulder.

"The only reason you are alive is that George doesn't fancy going to prison," The security guard grinned. "So, leave him alone okay, he could probably kill you and make you disappear," he nodded. "No one would notice."

The man nodded and walked towards the entrance.

"Sit on the bench," The security guard said loudly, pointing to the bench. "Don't bother anyone else or you will get iced water instead!"

"Thanks, Mark," George said. "Thought he would never leave!"

"You haven't lost a hearing aid, have you?" Mark said looking at both of George's ears.

"Nope," George said. "Why?"

"Someone handed one into reception," Mark rubbed his hands. "I only know one deaf person and that is you."

"Take it to audiology on level two," George said. "They will be able to track it if is loaned."

"Good idea," Mark said. "See you later mate!" He grabbed hold of George's hand, Shaking it. George watched as he walked away.

"So many nut cases in this place," He muttered, taking a small bottle of alcohol gel, and squirting it into his hands, rubbing them together.

"George?" A woman's voice from behind him. "Wow, you haven't changed a bit!"

George turned round to see Lucy, slightly shorter than him wearing light blue jeans, brown boots, and a thick grey coat. Her long brown hair tied up at the back and her face pink from the cold.

"Hey," George said lost for words, stuttering, and trying to speak. "Lucy?"

Lucy stepped forward, getting hold of George and hugging him.

George felt awkward, his arms hanging by the side, he did not know how to react.

"You can hug me back," She said. "I am not going to bite you."

George raised his arms slowly, hugging her back and rubbing her back gently. After a few seconds, be broke away, noticing Mark who stood by the door giving him the thumbs up.

"Have we actually met?" George asked awkwardly. "Sorry if we have already."

"Yes," Lucy said. "Forgotten me already?"

"Sorry," George felt bad. "My memory is terrible, and I am sure you know my people skills suck."

Lucy laughed, nodding gently.

"When did we meet?" George asked.

"About seven years ago," Lucy said. "I looked very different back then, bigger and short hair."

"Christmas day?" George said.

Lucy nodded.

"That was you?" George scoffed. "I never caught your name at the time."

"Really," She laughed. "That is, you all over."

"Oh, bloody hell I picked you up from the station!" George said, his hand went to his mouth.

"No that was my friend," Lucy said. "You are getting us mixed up."

"I do that," George slapped his forehead. "Sorry."

"When did you get that?" She pointed to the implant. "My friends' boy had one, they are brilliant."

"Five years ago," George said. "I was in Vegas and my hearing just went in that ear, thought it was the hearing aid. Turns out it was deeper, so got the ball rolling and had surgery."

"How much did you get back?" Lucy said.

"About eighty percent," George said with a smile. "It has been amazing, to be honest."

Lucy shivered.

"Let's go inside," George said. "I can catch you up over a coffee."

Lucy nodded

"Got a mask?" George asked.

Lucy nodded, pulling the black mask from her pocket.

"Follow me," George said, swiping the access panel on the door behind him and checking before opening it, letting Lucy go through first.

The small canteen had several tables, only two occupied. The long room was on the lower level of the building, with an outdoor seating area. Several food display cabinets and a counter displaying and heating hot food. In the corner a self-service coffee station. The walls bright green and the floor an eggshell green rubber matting. The tables and chairs are plastic and red, the colour coding enough to give anyone a headache. On the wall near the entrance are several framed photos with names under them.

Lucy smiled when George handed her the coffee and sat down opposite her. She removed her coat, to reveal a red top underneath.

"Thanks," She said sipping at the coffee. "What do I owe you?"

"Nothing," George said.

"Sure?" Lucy said squinting. "I don't mind."

"It's fine," George said looking around the room, the elderly couple at the end catching his eye.

"So," She said. "How's dad doing?"

"Surprising okay," George said. "Just bored."

"You probably think I am horrible," Lucy said her head in her hand.

"No," George shook his head. "Why would I think that?"

She shook her head.

"What?" George asked.

"No," Lucy sighed. "Don't worry."

"If you mean the fallout over your mother," George said. "I heard. For what it is worth, your dad regrets it."

"Really?" Lucy leaned forward. "Why didn't he say."

"You know the old sod," George chuckled. "Never does the right thing."

"I tried to call him the other day," Lucy said. "But couldn't get through."

"He tried, but your mother lost your details," George said. "Also lost her phone, we haven't been able to find it."

"Oh, I have it," Lucy said. "Mum mailed it to me, still no idea why."

George laughed.

"Sorry about the email earlier," George said. "I didn't want to freak you out or anything."

She put her hand on his.

"Thank you," She said. "I am glad you got in touch."

She pulled her hand away slowly.

"So, two broken legs and fractured ribs?" Lucy sucked in her breath. "That is going to sting!"

43

"Yeah," George said. "He is more upset about the dog though."

"Little Tyson?" Lucy said. "Why?"

George groaned, covering his mouth.

"I forgot to mention," George said. "I am sorry, but he passed away."

"Oh no," Lucy said. "What did mum do?"

"It wasn't your mum," George said, hesitating. "A cow fell on him," He whispered.

Lucy looked at him, her mouth open and her eyes wide.

"Are you okay?" George said.

Lucy burst into hysterics, loud laughter that echoed around the canteen. After several seconds she quietened down, little giggles escaping her as she struggled to control herself.

"Don't do that in front of your dad huh?" George said looking at the elderly couple that are not impressed, shaking their heads in disgust.

"I always thought it would be a car or die getting into a fight with another dog!" She said. "Or the little shit would actually chew through a mains cable and fry!" She sighed. "Oh, Jesus I would never have thought of a cow!"

"I have been trying so hard not to laugh or comment," George said.

"He was a little shit," Lucy said. "look at this!" She rolled up her sleeve to reveal scars on her forearm. "Three years ago," She said. "He bit me so deeply!"

"Why?" George asked curiously.

"The neighbour's cat got into our garden," She clicked her tongue. "and Little Tyson got hold of his tail and it was screaming," She shivered. "Mum was scared, and dad froze, so I went out and grabbed him, trying to get him to let go but he wouldn't."

"What did you do?" George asked.

"Pressed on his bad leg," Lucy said. "He yelped, let go of the cat and shot round, clamping down on my arm until get got bone."

"Jesus!" George said looking at the scar.

"Dad had to spray him with cold water to get him off," Lucy said. "Didn't work."

"How did you get him off in the end?" George said.

"Bit the little shit," She said smiling. "I just wanted him off, so I bit his leg."

George scoffed, his mouth open in amazement.

"Bloody let go of me then, running away with his tail between his legs," Lucy pulled her sleeve down. "Stayed away from me after that too."

"Marvin buried him," George said. "Eventually!"

"What do you mean?" Lucy leaned forward curiously.

"Well the body went missing, and he eventually found it in the freezer after searching," George smiled, shaking his head. "After Marvin took him out to get ready to bury him, he went missing again and he found him upstairs in the spare room, tucked into bed!"

"Oh, Jesus Christ!" Lucy groaned. "Mum has lost it! She did the same thing with my old dolls." George nodded.

"Apparently," George said, hesitating. "She thought she was putting your brother to bed!"
Lucy sniggered, covering her mouth.

"Heard from him?" George said. "Your brother?"

"No," Lucy frowned. "I contacted him and asked him to help sort things out, but it seems that money is more important to him now."

"Damn, Sorry," George said, drinking from his mug and flinching. "This is horrible," He said, his eyes looking down at the mug. "Don't judge me if yours is the same!"

"It's fine," She sipped at hers. "I have had worse."

"Why did you and your dad fall out?" George asked outright.

"I offered to move back home, to help out with mum," Lucy explained. "But dad didn't want me to get dragged down, seeing as I had a new place and a job."

"Where are you working?" George asked curiously.

"Working from home currently," Lucy said. "Bloody bored."

"Can you fix medical equipment?" He said. "I need someone with a brain."

"Afraid not!" She said. "You managing at the moment?" Lucy picked up her mug, blowing on it. "While dad is off?"

"Yeah," George leaned back in the chair. "Are you moving into the house?"

"Yes, I have a spare key." She said. "Where is dads car?" She asked. "I was going to borrow it while mine is in the garage."

"It is here," George said. "Marvin went and picked it up from the park where the accident happened, it was all over the place that day."

"Oh Marvin," She said. "Not seen him in ages."

"Did your aunt contact you?" George asked. "About your mum?"

"Yeah she did," Lucy said. "Glad she is safe and has someone to care for her."

"Finish your coffee," George said. "I'll take you up to see him."

"They don't mind?" Lucy said. "I was told that visitors are not allowed."

"Harold and I do a lot for people here," George said. "They bend the rules a little, just make sure you do what they ask."

"Will do," Lucy stood up, pulling her coat on. "I know where to go so," She sighed happily. "Thank you!"

"You are welcome," George said. "Hopefully see you again?"

"Definitely," She held out her arms, offering a hug. "Leave me hanging and I will mess up your office!"

George stepped forward, hugging her tightly.

"Text me later," She said.

"I will," George said. "I am going shopping, need anything?"

"I have no idea," She chuckled. "Will find out when I get there, but I will let you know."

George nodded.

"level three blue zone, right?" Lucy asked. "Will I get into the ward?"

"Just give your dads name," George said. "Any issues then text me."

Lucy nodded and walked away, looking back, and waving at George who waved back and sat down, finishing his coffee, and leaning back in the chair, yawning.

19:22

George stood in the queue, waiting for the elderly man in front of him, struggling to pack his bags. Frail and bent forward, he held onto the conveyor, red-faced and stressed.

The woman behind the till, overweight and bored, stared at him. She is wearing Bright pink gloves and a mask, pulled down under her chin,

"Do you need some help?" George moved closer to the elderly man.

The old man looked at him and nodded.

"I am sorry," He apologised. "My hands don't move as well as they used to," He said, peeking over his glasses. "I am very sorry."

"Don't be sorry," George said picking up a carrier bag and carefully placing the items in the bag. "Some stores will actually have what we call customer service," George looked at the woman behind the screen. "And actually, offer to help people struggling."

"I am busy!" The woman behind the till said. "And we are not allowed to help!"

"Here you go," George handed the bag to the elderly man. "All done," He smiled.

"Thank you," He said taking the bag and lopping his arm through it. "You have a nice day now."

George watched as the man walked away, his overcoat catching the floor as he walked, he took a cap from his pocket and put it on his head, pulling it down tightly.

"We are not allowed to help," The woman said.

George nodded.

"It's a choice," He said. "You are wearing gloves so it wouldn't make a difference regardless."

"I don't want the virus!" She snapped and pulled her mask back up, under her nose.

"You are behind a screen, attempting to wear a mask, badly!" George scoffed. "Anyway, could I get two carrier bags, please," He said looking at the several items laid out on the conveyor belt."

"Which type?" The woman asked.

"Sorry I didn't catch that," George said. "Could you repeat?"

"What. Kind?" The woman said louder.

The background noise in the superstore was overpowering and George could not focus on what the woman was saying.

"Sorry, still cannot understand," George got closer to the screen. "Do you mind dropping your mask?"

"Yes, I do mind!" The woman said shaking her head.

"It would really help me," George said. "And you are behind a screen."

"Why?" The woman demanded.

"I am deaf, I cannot understand you," George said.

"You chose to be deaf!" The woman snapped. "Not my problem."

George took two bags from the rail as the woman passed his items down the conveyor, hard and fast. When she finished, she tapped the display showing the total cost.

"Pay that!" She said in annoyance. "Do you understand?"

A man waiting behind George looked at him, shaking his head, wearing a suit, and holding a basket full of several items he placed them on the counter.

"What is wrong?" George asked as he slowly packed, making a point.

The man moved his mask down.

"She was rude!" The man said shaking his head.

The woman looked at the man, like a child that had been caught doing something they should not, her eyes closed as she realised, she had been caught.

"What did she say?" George asked. "Couldn't hear her over the noise.

"She said, 'No, you chose to be deaf!' the man said.

"Really?!" George scoffed.

"I have family members that are deaf," The man explained. "There was no need for her to be like that!"

George looked at the woman and then back at the man.

"Well wow!" He chuckled. "Ignorant."

George moved closer to the screen.

"Really?" George looked at the woman. "You chose to be disgusting," He looked her up and down. "But I didn't say anything did?"

The woman lowered her mask, sighing in frustration, ignorance on her face.

"Well, you had no right to tell me to take off my mask!" The woman said.

"I didn't tell you to do anything," George said. "I asked if you minded, so you could help me to understand you."

"My health is important," The woman said.

"Well," George said grinning. "You chose to be overweight."

"You cannot be rude to me like this!" The woman said. "I will have you banned!"

"Fine by me," George said. "Make sure you tell them that you abused me because of my disability."

"I am disabled myself!" She said loudly.

"Being fat isn't a disability!" George said. "Stop eating!"

George paid and packed his backs, looking at the open-mouthed woman, her face becoming redder by the second.

"You are wrong," He said to the woman. "I didn't choose to be deaf, that is genetics," He clicked his tongue. "But you chose to be rude, fat and pathetic."

The man behind George sniggered, looking at the floor and shaking his head.

"Bye, bye," George said sarcastically, giving the woman a wave.

The man at the checkout is laughing, holding up a thumb and shaking his head.

"Bloody wildlife in this place," George said under his breath. "Even the zoo wouldn't touch them!"

20:19

George groaned when he closed the front door, putting the bag of shopping down on the floor and sniffing in disgust.

"Debbie?" George called out. "You here?"

There were loud footsteps and Debbie appeared at the top of the stairs, wearing only knickers and a small t-shirt.

"Hi!" She said. "Long day for you!" She knelt. "What's up?"

"Got the heating on full blast again!" George complained. "Why don't you put some clothes on instead of ramping it up?"

"Oh, someone is in a mood," She rolled her eyes.

"Did you do the bins?" George said. "Surely you can smell that?"

"I did wonder what it was," She said curiously. "Was going to check it earlier but have been busy."

"Busy doing nothing," George said. "Don't bother!" he scoffed.

George picked up the bag and walked into the kitchen, putting it on the table and looking at the black bin in the corner, rubbish overflowing.

"Bollocks," George said, shaking his head and cringing. "He went over to the sink and reaching underneath he took out some gloves and put them on and took off his jacket, draping it over a chair. He removed the top of the bin and carefully pulled up the sack, moaning when some of the rubbish fell to the floor.

Debbie walked into the kitchen wearing black jogging bottoms, George looked around at her and nodded.

"That is more like it," He said.

"Does it embarrass you?" Debbie asked.

"What?" George looked at her. "The rubbish overflowing?"

"No!" She exclaimed. "Seeing me in underwear?"

"No, it doesn't," George said. "You look great, but it's just inappropriate. What if I walked in with a friend or even a date?"

Debbie laughed.

"What is so funny?" George asked.

"Walking in with a date!" She said.

"And?" George pulled the bag out of the bin, staring at her.

"Would you bring a date back to the house?" She asked, crossing her arms.

"Yes," George said.

"Would you not get permission from me first?" Debbie asked.

"Why would I need permission?" George scoffed. "It's my house!"

"I live here too," Debbie said. "Surely I have a say."

"Okay," George rested the bag on the floor. "When did you last ask me for permission, or even tell me that you were having a drugged-up friend with benefits over?"

"I forgot," She said giggling. "It was no big deal."

"I came home from work to find a random guy with dreadlocks down to his arse, naked in my kitchen drinking out of a carton of milk," George raised his voice. "When I asked who he was, he turned around, making no attempt to cover his junk and asked why I was in the house and he would beat the crap out of me."

Debbie laughed.

"Glad you find it funny," George said. "Don't forget you haven't paid me any rent in three months now."

"I am not working!" Debbie said. "You know that."

"Yes," George sighed. "You said your parents were helping you out."

"I know," She said awkwardly.

"I had to use it to pay off bills," Debbie said. "I just need more time."

"Bills?" George said. "More likely the crap you keep buying online."

"It isn't crap!" She said.

"And you need to stop putting your crap in the spare room," George said. "I need that cleared out."

"I will do it tomorrow," She said.

"You have been saying that for a month," George muttered. "You don't do anything all day," George was getting angry. "You won't pay your bills, won't help out around the house, shit you cannot even empty a bin!"

"Well, why don't we get a cleaner?" Debbie said. "That would help."

"Why would I get a cleaner?" George asked.

"To clean the house," She giggled. "You are the one complaining."

"I keep this place clean," George said. "I clean up after myself every single day, I clean, dust and hoover every Saturday morning."

"I know," She scoffed. "Way too early!"

"Ten in the morning isn't early," George said. "When did you last hoover?"

Debbie thought about it.

"Two weeks ago," She said.

"No," George sighed. "You hoovered your car two weeks ago, in the rain!" He snapped. "You blew up my hoover and tripped the mains!"

"Well I didn't think it would be too bad," She said. "My mate did his when it was raining."

"Yes," George said. "With a battery-powered handheld hoover, not a mains powered operated one!"

"They should make them waterproof," She said shaking her head.

"They should issue people like you with a brain," George said. "Now get lost and let me clean up this cesspit!"

George picked up the bag and twisted it, there was a wet plop and the bag split open, spilling the contents all over the floor. Glass jars, bottles, food, and liquids.

"Jesus!" George growled. "Christ!" He covered his face, gagging and coughing at the overpowering stench of rotting fish.

"Eww!" Debbie said in disgust.

"Why is there glass in the bin?" George said. "You are supposed to put food in the food bin outside!"

"I didn't put it in there," She said.

"Well I don't eat fish," George said pointing to the half-eaten fish. "What is wrong with you?!" Debbie shrugged her shoulders.

"Might have been Gaze," She said. "Sorry."

"Who the fuck is Gaze?" George exclaimed. "Sounds like a knob out of a crappy science fiction film!"

"The guy you met," Debbie said nervously. "With the dreadlocks."

"Oh really," George snapped.

Debbie shrugged her shoulders.

"What is it with you and rejects?" George said. "Why can't you meet someone normal for a change that at least has part of his brain active?"

"He is very intelligent!" Debbie argued.

"Oh really?" George said looking at her. "What does he do?"

"Nothing yet," She said. "He is finding it hard with his criminal record."

"Intelligent!" George scoffed.

"It wasn't his fault," Debbie said. "A friend of his got locked out of his shop and asked Gaze to help him get in."

"Jesus Christ!" George laughed. "That is a true sign of intelligence!" He said sarcastically.

"You think so?" Debbie looked at him curiously.

"No," George replied bluntly. "I was being sarcastic."

"Oh," Debbie said hurt.

"I have had enough," George said. "You haven't paid me in months, you haven't even paid the phone bill and you keep promising."

"But I am not working," She moaned. "I have no money to pay for anything!"

"You are spending hundreds online," George said. "You bought a new phone last week!"

"Well mine was old and needed updating," Debbie sighed.

"It was three months old!" He exclaimed. "Jesus, mine is two years old and still works as it did on the day that I got it!"

"I need more time," Debbie whined.

"You have promised and promised," George said. "You even said you would help out around the house, yet you have done nothing!" George raised his voice.

"I washed up last week," Debbie said.

51

"You washed up one," George held up a finger. "One cup!"

"I'll get the money from my dad," She said. "I promise."

"You said that last time and blew it on online gambling!" George chuckled. "You are taking the piss now."

"I have nowhere to go," She said, tears welling in her eyes.

"All those friends and family members you boast about?" George sighed "You have until Friday and I want you gone," George said. "I cannot do this anymore."

Debbie stormed off, crying as she stomped up the stairs and slammed her door. George let out a long sigh of frustration, looking down at the mess on the floor.

"Lovely," he cringed.

TUESDAY

George stopped at the traffic lights as they turned red, yawning heavily, and muttering to himself.

"Freezing!" he moaned, turning up the heating dial. "Why does this piece of shit take so long to warm up?" He hit the dashboard. "I really need to get this looked at!"

A car pulled up behind him, the lights in the mirror blinding him.

"Bright enough for you?" He said. "Too early for this crap."

The lights turned green and George pulled away, turning onto the dual carriageway, speeding up as fast as he could.

The car followed, matching his speed, and getting close to him, the lights annoying George. They got closer and closer but did not attempt to overtake.

"Go round you moron!" George snapped. "Get your lights out of my mirror!" he moaned.

The car followed for a mile, and George started to get uncomfortable so he slowed down, hoping that the car would get fed up and overtake.

"Overtake me!" George said looking in his mirror. "You don't need to sit on my arse!"

After a couple of minutes, lights on top of the car started flashing and George realised it was a police car.

"Thank god for that," George said as he gently pulled into the hard shoulder.

The car stopped behind him and he pressed the button to wind down the window, hitting the glass when it refused to budge, the thump dislodging it.

"Bloody lights," George said, trying to avoid the flashing blue lights.

George watched the officer get out of the car, slowly walk towards the driver's side. There was a click as he flicked on a torch, blinding George.

"Could you not shine the torch in my face please!" George said looking away. "I am deaf and need to lipread you!"

The officer was tall, towering above Georges car as he leant down, looking into the window.

Athletically built, with a shaved head and a trimmed beard, he is wearing a stab vest and a yellow high visibility vest.

The officer lowered the torch and George blinked several times, trying to get his vision back and get rid of the blobs of light in his eyes.

"Better?" The officer said.

"Yes," George said and rubbed his eyes. "Cannot see quite properly yet."

"Have you had anything to drink recently?" The officer asked.

"No," George replied. "Too early for that!"

"What is wrong with your eyes?" He asked curiously.

"You just shone a torch in them!" George said replied. "Didn't help me much."

"You said you are deaf?" He said.

"Yes." George nodded.

"Where are you coming from?" The officer asked. "You are out early."

"Had to pop to a hospital site I look after," George sighed and took out his hospital identification, showing the officer. "Needed to collect some equipment."

"What kind of equipment?" The officer said shining the torch into the back seat.

"Medical equipment for theatres," George said. "It is in the boot if you need to have a look."

"No that is fine," The officer said. "Are you a driver for the hospital then?"

"No," George said. "Technical services engineer, it was on my badge."

"Oh yes!" The officer chuckled. "Ignore me, I am tired."

"Any reason for pulling me over?" George asked. "I know I wasn't speeding, and my lights work fine."

"No just routine," The officer said. "Not much traffic out at this time of the morning."

"Okay," George said. "Can I go now?"

"Are you allowed to be driving?" He asked. "With your disability?"

"Am I what?" George looked at him, not sure if he heard correctly.

"Do you have a license?" He asked.

"Yes," George replied. "It's in my back pocket, can I get it?"

The officer nodded and George undid his seatbelt, reaching back and pulling out his wallet, handing the license to him. He waved at someone in the vehicle, asking them to come out. The second officer joined him, a short woman that approached the door and looked in, smiling at George.

"Good morning!" She said. "How are you today sir?"

"Tired," George said. "Why have I been pulled over?"

"Just a routine check," She replied.

The officer walked over to the car with the license, leaving the female officer with George.

"Where are you coming from?" She asked.

"Lavender Community hospital," George said.

"And where are you going?" She asked.

"Lavender Park Hospital," George said yawning. "Your colleague doesn't think deaf people should drive," I scoffed.

"Really?" She said in surprise and looked towards the police car.

"Yeah," George shook my head.

"Strange," The woman said. "What did you go to Lavender Community for?" She asked.

"To collect some equipment that is needed at Lavender Park," George replied.

The male officer walked over, looking through the window.

"Is this your license?" He asked.

"Yes," George said.

"Where did you take your test?" He asked.

"Sidcup back in ninety-seven or so," George struggled to remember the correct date.

"I am just concerned because you said you couldn't hear," The officer said.

"So?" George said. "My implant does a pretty good job."

"Well, how do you hear outside the car?" He asked.

George looked at him, surprised.

"Well I don't need to," George replied. "If there is anything wrong, I would feel it, and I have pretty good eyes when I am not being blinded."

"Are you aware of emergency vehicles?" He asked.

"The fact you pulled me over proves that" George exclaimed. "Flashing lights are hard to ignore."

"Okay," He said. "Is the car yours?"

"Yes," George sighed in frustration. "The car is mine, it is taxed, insured for personal and business use and has an MOT."

"Okay," The officer said. "My colleague will just do a quick inspection."

"Jesus!" George snapped.

"Problem?" The officer said.

"No, it's fine," George replied. "You just clearly want to find something wrong after discriminating."

"I have not discriminated against you sir," The officer said. "Not at all."

"You asked if I should be driving because I am deaf," George scoffed. "Would you ask someone the same question if they wore glasses? Or if they had no legs?"

"Of course not," The officer laughed.

"So why are you making my hearing disability an issue?" George asked, waiting for a reply.

"I have never met a deaf driver before," The officer said and handed Georges license back, who took it and dropped it on the passenger seat.

"Well this one is on the house," George said sarcastically. "I also recommend some basic deaf awareness, might prevent someone from taking further action against you."

"I can only apologise if you think I have treated you differently," The officer said, becoming uncomfortable.

The female officer joined him, nodding when he asked if all was okay.

"Have a safe journey," He said. "You may go now."

"Thanks," George replied. "I will keep my windows down in case I need to hear anything important."

George slowly drove away, and they followed him for several miles, before overtaking and leaving at the next junction.

"Something got their scent," George mumbled. "Probably a fucking doughnut shop!"

05:12

George switched on the light and closed the door behind him, yawning heavily as he placed the coffee on the table and turned on the laptop. He removed his glasses, turned, and walked up to the corner of the wall, breathing heavily. He put his head to the wall, groaning softly and started to sob, tears running down his face.

"What is wrong with me?" He said softly. "What is happening to me?" He cried and covered his eyes with his hand, punching the wall several times with the other, moaning in pain and frustration. His mobile phone buzzed loudly, vibrating across the table and he stopped crying, breathing deeply, and wiping the tears from his face, sniffing.

Sitting down in the chair, he took out his mobile phone, checking the messages.

"Blimey," He said. "You are up early!" He said to himself. "Hi Lucy," he said. "Just going online now," He typed out the message. "Give me a minute or two and I will connect with you." He muttered to himself.

Placing the phone next to the laptop, he signed in, watching as it went through the usual, slow motions.

"Slow piece of crap," he said. "I need an upgrade." He rubbed his face and put his glasses back on. George moved the laptop back, watching as the display lit up when the video chat activated.

Lucy is on the other end, her hair tied up at the back, she smiled when she saw George.

"Hey George," She said. "I see you are like me!"

"What?" George said. "Naked?" he chuckled nervously.

"I am not naked!" She laughed and pulled the sides of her top up. "See," She shook her head. "This top is too big."

"I was only kidding," George said. "Wasn't being creepy or anything."

"Oh, it's fine," Lucy dismissed it. "It's an old top from the last time I was here, seems I lost more weight than I thought!"

George nodded, uncomfortably.

"What's up with your eyes," Lucy looked closer. "Something wrong?"

"No," George said biting his lip and thinking. "Air freshener." He replied.

"Air freshener?" Lucy said in confusion. "That makes no sense."

"One of the guys left a curry container in the bin by the kitchen," George said. "Absolutely, stank the place out, so I went to spray some deodoriser and had it round the wrong way because I wasn't wearing my glasses."

Lucy sniggered.

"So, I got a face full of chemicals and now smell heavily of lily of the valley with a combination of Christmas vanilla!" George sighed and shook his head. "I am clumsy!"

"Me too!" Lucy laughed. "I fall over my feet all the time, always burning and cutting myself!"

"I trip up the stairs," George smiled. "Usually with a mug of coffee."

"I can beat that!" Lucy moved the camera down, carefully showing a half circle cut on her abdomen."

"That is a very nice view," George said nervously under his breath.

Lucy looked at him, shaking her head.

"This one is free," She said bluntly. "See that scar?"

"Cannot understand a word you just said," George said smiling and shaking his head.

Lucy moved the camera back up to her face.

"See that scar?" She repeated.

George nodded.

"Got that when I was nineteen," Lucy said. "Came home drunk, got a glass of water and stumbled up the stairs and fell forward."

"Jesus!" George said. "That must have hurt like hell."

"I was too drunk to care, but when mum came out and started screaming," Lucy said. "My dad went into first aid mode after I stood up and the glass fell out."

"And he cut his foot on the glass when he ran down the stairs," George said. "I remember the story now, he had glass in his foot for a couple of days."

"Yeah," Lucy said. "Mum reversed into dads car in a panic and dad just flipped out and drove instead, blood everywhere."

"Damn!" George shivered.

57

"I was lucky," Lucy said. "Very lucky!" She pulled the duvet up to her torso.

"That reminds me of several years ago when I cut my leg," George said. "I was tired and angry over something, cutting cables on the desktop with a box knife, slipped and punched my leg. Did not think I did any damage until I saw blood on my trousers, popped to the loo to have a look and had a cut about an inch on my thigh."

"Bet that dead leg hurt more?" Lucy laughed.

"Damn it did," George chuckled. "I went to your dad and told him, but because I am always winding him up, he didn't believe me. So, I limped to the walk-in centre and got two stitches and updated my tetanus."

"Sore!" Lucy sucked in her breath.

"Next day was worse," George said. "Couldn't walk properly!"

"Lucky," Lucy shook her head. "Could have hit your femoral, and we may not have been talking now."

"Yeah, that is what the consultant said," George said, sighing heavily. "How come you are up so early?"

"I don't sleep too well," She said. "I usually work throughout the night and sleep throughout the day. What about you?"

"I needed to pop to the community hospital to collect some equipment," George said. "I was fuming last night so never really got to sleep."

"Yeah, you said in your text it was a bad one, what happened?" She asked curiously.

"I have a lodger," George said. "Well more of a favour for a friend."

"Oh right," She nodded.

"She is a nightmare," George sighed. "Messy, disgusting and useless."

"Oh dear," Lucy said. "How come?"

"She hasn't paid rent in three months due to not working, but her parents are helping her out," George scoffed. "But she blows it on gambling and online shopping."

"Oh no that isn't good," Lucy said. "So why the argument last night?"

"She didn't bother doing the bins," George cringed. "The house absolutely, stank of fish last night, and when I emptied the bin, it split open everywhere."

"Oh my God," She covered her mouth. "I cannot stand fish!"

"Me neither!" George laughed. "So, I was cleaning the kitchen for nearly an hour, I am nuts like that."

"Is she going?" Lucy asked.

"I told her Friday," George said. "I was in a mood, so left her a note today saying she has a week from today."

"She sounds crazy," Lucy said.

"You don't know half of it," George said. "Not long ago I came home to a guy called Gaze in the kitchen, naked with dreadlocks down to his arse drinking milk out of a carton!"

"What kind of a name is Gaze?" Lucy laughed. "Sounds like something out of a post-apocalyptic film!"

"I know the feeling," George said. "He even challenged who I was, in my own house!"

"So, what happened this morning?" Lucy yawned. "You mentioned the police!" She laughed. "Did you get caught with a body in the boot again!"

"Oh, your dad told you that story!" George exclaimed. "Anything he hasn't told you?"

"Sort of," She said. "Tell me what happened."

"Well I was driving back from an event in Brighton and got pulled over for speeding slightly," George said. "The police did the usual checks, warned me about speeding, but when they asked what I had in the boot, I was honest."

"What was in the boot?" Lucy smiled.

"A body," George said. "The officer froze, looking at me like I was some kind of psychotic maniac, so he asked me again, what do I have in the boot."

"So, what did you reply?" Lucy said.

"Again, a body," George said. "I paused a little and then added, not a real body though, no one is that crazy!"

Lucy burst out laughing, the laptop juddering all over the place.

"So, I showed them the anatomy correct mannequin in the boot with a grin on its face, and put his mind at rest," George explained. "He was more fixated on the penis."

"He what?!" She scoffed.

"It had a rather large, detachable penis for catheter training," George chuckled. "So, I pulled it off to show him and he groaned."

"Did they leave you alone after that?" Lucy said.

"Yeah," George nodded. "They recommended in future I sit it in the back seat with a belt on!"

"Mental! Still at the same place?" Lucy said. "I remember you moved out for a while."

"Yeah," George chuckled. "When the bath went through the ceiling!"

"Lucky you weren't in it!" Lucy said. "Would have been a great moment to catch on film!"

"Absolute nightmare," George said. "It ripped the pipes out of the wall and then landed on my brand-new television cinema system, destroyed my aunts' glass coffee table, and flooded the living room!"

"Insurance cover it all?" Lucy asked.

"No, the company that put installed the bath had to, appeared they had not replaced the rotten wood under the bath," George laughed. "The very issue they were supposed to deal with first."

"Mental," Lucy said. "You okay otherwise?"

George nodded.

"What time do you usually start?" She asked curiously.

"Nine," George said. "Before all this pandemic crap I used to sit in the Café and read but that is on hold."

"Why do you get in so early?" She asked.

"So, I can get a car park space," George said. "Less hassle when there are fewer morons about."

"Still not a people fan then?" Lucy grinned knowingly.

"Oh, people suck!" George said. "I like a select few."

"Am I one of them?" Lucy asked.

"Working on it," George laughed.

"Considering you are disabled," Lucy said with a growing grin. "Can't you get a disabled parking space?"

"Very funny," George said. "That joke has been done to death!"

Lucy burst into hysterics.

"I can get a dog for the deaf," George shook his head. "If I wanted to, but I really don't need one!"

"Dad told me about your dog," Lucy said sadly. "Sorry to hear that."

"It's okay," George said. "He was old and sick."

"He was your aunts, wasn't he?" Lucy said. "You took him in when she got sick."

"Yeah," George nodded. "He only listened to me."

"How was your dad yesterday?" George asked.

"Depressed?" Lucy said.

"I am sorry to hear that," George said. "Did you talk about it with him?"

"It's mum," Lucy said. "It is getting to him, I think he realises he needs more help at home, or she goes into a home."

"Shit," George exclaimed.

"Yeah, the first time I have seen him cry since Liam." Lucy wiped a tear from her eye, chuckling nervously.

"Liam?" George said. "Not heard of that name before."

"Oh, shit he probably never said!" Lucy groaned. "I'll tell you but please don't repeat it."

"Okay," George said. "I won't say anything."

"My brother," Lucy said. "Liam was my brother."

"I had no idea," George said. "Harold never said anything, I am sorry."

"It's fine," She smiled. "Don't be."

"When was this?" George said.

Lucy sighed, thinking, and sitting up in bed, trying to get comfortable.

"I was twelve," Lucy said, her tone sad. "Liam was eight."

"You don't have to talk about it," George said.

"It's okay," She said. "Liam was hit by a car when he was riding back from school on his bike, the driver wasn't paying attention and hit him from behind, crushing him against a parked car."

"Jesus!" George said.

"Yeah," She shook her head and breathed in heavily. "They switched his life support off a couple of days later, there was nothing they could for him."

"I am sorry," George said. "Does he ever talk about him?"

"Not in years," Lucy said. "Last time was when he had that massive argument with my brother."

"Oh yeah," George nodded. "I remember that."

"It was a bloodbath," Lucy said. "Not seen my dad that angry before."

"What is your brothers' name?" George tapped his head. "I forget!"

"Stephen," Lucy said. "After my mums' dad."

"Do you speak to him?" George asked.

"Not in a while," She rubbed her eye, stifling a yawn. "He isn't one for keeping in touch, and I said no to loaning him money, so he had no reason to keep in touch."

"That is sad," George said.

"What about you?" Lucy said. "Do you have any family?"

"None I want to keep in touch with," George said. "Not worth talking about."

"Sorry," Lucy said.

"It's okay," George said. "They had such a negative impact on my life, walking away was the best thing I ever did, and I won't look back."

"Good for you," Lucy said. "So, my dad!" She exclaimed. "Nearly forgot!"

George laughed.

"He was okay otherwise, depressed and fed up and missing mum," Lucy said. "He wasn't feeling too great. I didn't stay long, apparently, they were going to put him on another infusion."

"Should have let me know," George said. "Would have met up with you."

"I didn't want to bother you too much considering what you have done for me," Lucy said. "I am sure you are fed up with me by now?"

"No," George said. "You are the only sane person I know!"

"Sure about that?" She grinned. "I went to drama school, I am an excellent actress." She leaned closed to the camera. "Don't let this innocent set up confuse you!" She burst into giggles. "Plans for the day?"

"Got a boring meeting at eight," George groaned. "Otherwise catching up, need to get to a ventilator in intensive care."

"Oh, that sounds interesting," Lucy said.

"No not really," George said. "Usually user error when they go wrong, there is one particular nurse up there that gets bored and touches things she shouldn't."

"My dad mentioned a fire on one of the wards," Lucy said. "When was that?"

"Well not so much a fire," George said. "It was one of the respiratory patients, a regular. He is a smoker that cannot give up, even though it is slowly killing him."

"Oh dear," Lucy said. "What happened?"

"He decided to go into a storeroom for a cigarette," George scoffed. "However, he forgot to turn off his oxygen while he was in there."

"Enclosed space!" Lucy said. "Did he survive?"

"He did, pretty much blew out the window," George chuckled. "Minor burns and set off the alarms."

"Oh wow, that could have been so much worse!" Lucy said. "Did he get into trouble?"

"That is where it got worse," George explained. "The sister gave him a stern telling off, and the family didn't like that, apparently he is a very important person at his camp."

"Camp?" Lucy interrupted.

"Gypsy," George said. "So anyway, they laid into the sister and she refused to be intimidated, even when they started throwing racial abuse at her," George shook his head in amazement. "Security threw them out, along with the old boy after he started bashing people with his brass handle walking stick."

"Crazy," Lucy said.

"It got worse," George said. "A lot worse!"

"How?" Lucy was curious.

"Someone sent the sister a parcel, quite large and security called the police due to it smelling bad and leaking," George said. "Guess what it was!"

"I dread to think," Lucy sighed. "Horses head?"

"Close," George said. "It was a rotting cows head."

"That is disgusting!" Lucy covered her mouth. "Poor cow!" She exclaimed. "I mean the cow, not the ward sister!"

"They tracked it to the farmers' field where the camp also happened to be," George laughed. "The old man himself still had a table set up behind his caravan, covered in dried blood and cow guts"

"That is just wrong," Lucy said.

"Farmer pressed charges and had them all evicted from the field," George said. "Nothing has happened since, but the sister didn't bat an eyelid."

"Good for her," Lucy said. "Some of these travellers like to intimidate people to get what they want. I remember a story my father told me years ago about a girl from a travellers camp that died in childbirth and the family came in with bats to teach the staff a lesson!"

"Before my time, but I heard about that," George chuckled. "They couldn't get past the security doors."

"Idiots!" Lucy said. "Will you be around later?" She asked softly. "So, I can grab you a coffee?"

"Yeah," George said. "Are you seeing your dad?"

"Briefly, I am just dropping off some things for him," Lucy said. "I still cannot find the tablet that he wanted."

"Marvin has it locked in our safe," George said. "Harold left it on the back seat of the car, I'll get it charged and bring it to you."

"You are a star," Lucy said. "Thanks."

"No problems," George said. "Well, I better shoot."

"Sure," Lucy smiled. "Thanks for the chat."

George waved and ended the call, closing the laptop.

"Time to see if the café is open," George said. "Cannot keep up with the opening and closing times.

05:42

There were several tables in the café, spaced out according to the social distancing, George saw an empty table to the end by the window.

"Good morning," The man said from behind the counter. "What would you like?" He is wearing black trousers and a white shirt, a large coffee stain down the front. Tall and slim, he was higher than the screen, his eyes peeking over the top.

"Sorry what?" George said turning around. "Didn't catch that."

63

"Deaf, are you?" The man chuckled.

"Yes, I am actually," George replied bluntly, shaking his in frustration.

"Oh, I am sorry," The man said. "I am tired."

"Me too," George said. "But I don't say stupid things."

The man looked at George.

"Could I get a plain coffee please," George said. "And a couple of scones."

"Anything else?" That man asked.

George shook his head.

"To have in?" The man asked. "Or take out?"

"In please," George said.

George placed his card on the scanner, watching as it beeped and flashed green.

"Receipt?" The man asked.

George shook his head.

"Take a seat and I will bring it over," The man said. "Will be a few minutes."

George nodded and walked over to the table, sitting down on the chair closest to the window.

"Lovely!" He said quietly and brushed the breadcrumbs and sugar off the table, wiping the arm of his suit jacket.

"Good morning!" The man said loudly from the next table.

"Jesus!" George jumped. "You scared the crap out of me Mr Khan!"

Mr khan leant back in the chair, wearing a dark brown suit, he is average height, overweight and has long hair and a thick beard.

"When are you going to shave that off?" George chuckled, pointing to his beard. "Surely your patients suffer when they come to you?"

"I have not seen you in a while," Mr Khan said. "Where have you been? Have your hearing aids not broken down? What about ear moulds?"

"I am under an audiology in London now," George said, moving his chair slightly.

"Better than us, are they?" Mr Khan said, pretending to be hurt. "Why did you leave?"

"I told you," George sighed. "After all the issues here, you have forgotten?"

"What issues?" Mr Khan said, turning his chair round to face George.

"When I lost my hearing, it took three months to get an urgent appointment," George said and breathed out. "And that audiologist gave me a dirty hearing aid and claims it was battery damage."

"Oh, I remember," Mr Khan said. "Very sorry about that."

"It is done and dusted," George said.

"Yes, Yes," Mr Khan nodded. "Water over the bridge."

George laughed.

"What did I say?" Mr Khan said. "What is funny?"

"The saying is water under a bridge," George said.

"I mean under the bridge," Mr Khan corrected himself. "I always get that one wrong."

"You are in early," George said. "Didn't think audiology opened until ten."

"We have some new equipment coming today," Mr Khan said. "Engineer is setting up for seven sharp."

"Does technical services know?" George said. "I am not aware of any setups."

"Oh I don't know," Mr Khan said, pulling a confused face. "I was not aware that you needed to know."

"It's trust policy that all equipment is added to the asset register, commissioned and safety tested," George shook his head. "It shouldn't be used until it is."

"Oh dear," Mr Khan said. "What do you recommend?"

George looked up and sighed.

"I'll send Andy up," George said. "Just email me all the details and work reports from the engineer."

"Thank you, George," Mr Khan held his hands together. "You are truly a lifesaver!"

"I am not," George said. "I am only doing this to avoid the fallout."

"Have you considered a Cochlear Implant?" Mr Khan asked.

"I already have one," George said. "That much is obvious."

"Did we recommend you?" Mr Khan said thinking.

"No," George said. "They said at the time I had no options, so I got my doctor to refer me to the implant team in London."

"And was it successful?" He asked, looking at the implant.

"About eighty-five percent," George said. "This is my second processor, and it is quite different."

"Very impressive," Mr Khan said giving George the thumbs up. "What do I sound like?" He asked.

"Annoying as always," George said smiling.

Mr Khan burst into loud laughter, echoing around the room, and causing several people to look.

"Sure, you don't need a hearing aid?" George said. "I think Scotland heard you."

"Here you go," The man from behind the counter said. "Coffee and scones, no charge by the way."

"I have already paid," George said.

"I cancelled the transaction, so you won't get charged," The man smiled. "My way of apologising for my stupid comment back there."

"It is fine really," George said. "No hard feelings."

The man nodded and walked away.

"What was that about?" Mr Khan asked.

"His gob went into gear before his brain," George said.

"Gob?" Mr Khan said. "As in mouth?"

George nodded.

"Ah fair enough," Mr Khan stood up, groaning as he held onto the chair to steady himself. "My damn knees!" He chuckled. "I need new ones!"

"Well take care," George said. "I'll speak to you soon."

Mr Khan picked up his coffee, waving as he walked away.

"Fruitcake," George whispered.

George sipped at his coffee, watching videos on his phone. He felt a tap on his shoulder and turned around to find two nurses standing behind him, looking rather annoyed. Both are eastern European, wearing uniforms and carrying face shields.

"Hi," he said. "How can I help?

"Why are you ignoring us?" One of them said.

"I'm not," George explained. "I am deaf."

"But we were right behind you," She said. "Surely you heard that?"

George turned around, starting to get cramp in his neck.

"It is noisy in here," He said. "Makes it harder to focus and track sounds."

"Okay," She said. "So?" She asked.

"So what?" George was confused.

"Oh god!" She moaned. "This is hard work!"

The other nurse whispered something to her, telling her to calm down. She then looked at George with a smile and clearly spoke.

"Is anyone sitting there?" She pointed to the empty chairs on the other side of the table.

"No," George said. "Waiting on a colleague but will be going when he arrives."

"Can we sit there?" She asked.

"Go for it," George smiled. "Plenty of room."

The girl sat down, and her friend joined the long queue that was now near the door.

"Sorry about her," She said.

"No problems," George said. "I get it a lot, people always are rude when they are embarrassed."

"She is having a bad time lately," She said. "Not an excuse I know, but she is usually really nice."

"Okay," George nodded and checked his mobile.

George noticed the girl looking at him curiously.

"What?" George asked, feeling a little uncomfortable.

"Do you work here?" She asked.

"Well not here no," George smiled. "I work in technical services."

"What is that?" She said curiously.

"When you smash a bladder scanner or rip the wires out of a vital signs monitor," George said. "We take it away, repair it and then bill the department."

"Our thermometers are not working," She grinned. "Do you look at those?"

"Have they been reported?" George said.

"No," The girl said. "Not yet."

"Okay, once they are, we will look at them," George said and returned to his phone.

The girl looked closely at the side of his head.

"What is it?" George said in frustration.

"What is that?" She pointed to my implant.

"It's an implant," George said. "Helps me to hear."

"Oh wow," The girl was surprised. "That is amazing!"

"Yeah," George said. "It has been so much help."

"How long have you worn it?" She asked.

"Since about half three this morning," George replied bluntly. "Or so."

She laughed.

"You don't sound or look deaf," She said.

"How does someone look deaf?" George asked. "That is like me saying you don't look Polish."

"How do you know I am Polish?" The girl asked curiously.

"Random guess," George said

The girl stuttered and then sighed, shaking her head embarrassedly.

"Anyone can be deaf, regardless of how they look or sound," George said shaking his head.

"I didn't mean it that way," She said. "I meant you don't come across deaf. Your speech is good, and you can understand me fine."

"I wasn't born deaf," George said. "So, there is a big difference there."

"Can I ask something," She said.

"Sure," George nodded.

"How did you go deaf?" She asked.

George thought about it, a smiling breaking on his face.

"Ah," I said and paused. "I was shot."

Her mouth opened in shock.

"Shot?!" She said. "How!?"

"By a gun," George scoffed.

"No, I mean," she stuttered. "How did it happen?"

George paused for a bit, trying to think of a story.

"I used to work as a bodyguard," George said. "Several years ago."

"Oh my god!" She gasped. "That sounds amazing!"

"It was," George said. "Until I was shot in the head."

"I'm sorry," She said looking away. "It was wrong of me to ask."

"No, it is fine really," George said.

"Was it long ago?" She said.

"About eight years ago or so," George explained. "I was working with a musician that received death threats."

"Oh wow!" She gasped. "Who?"

"I cannot say," George said. "However, on one night someone took a shot at her and I got in the way."

"Oh god!" She sat back in her chair nervously. "That was brave of you!"

"Well it was my job," George sighed and leant back in the chair. "I didn't do it for me."

"Amazing!" She exclaimed.

"So, after the bullet pretty much destroyed my hearing in my left ear," George picked up his coffee, sipping at it. "I left the trade and came home, got the surgery and it gave me my hearing back."

"That is great," She said. "So, what do you do now?"

"Medical engineering," George said. "Bit different, less chance of getting shot."

"Do you miss it?" She asked.

"Getting shot?" George said and pretended to be confused. "Not at all!"

"No!" She laughed. "I mean the job."

"The money was good," George said. "Jumping on stages and saving famous people was fun," George smiled. "But I rather live."

"So, you cannot hear anything?" She asked.

"Without my implant I cannot, I rely on lipreading to communicate and sound," George explained

"What is that?" She looked at me curiously. "What is lipreading?"

"Hard to explain," George said thinking. "But when you speak, rather than hearing, I look at the way your lips move and get the words from that."

"Oh right," She said, looking at George but not quite sure.

Marvin approached the table, carrying a carrier bag and wearing a full-length black overcoat.

"This is my colleague," George said. "I am going to make a move now."

"Well, it was nice meeting you!" The girl said. "Maybe we could swap numbers and talk about your old bodyguard days?"

Marvin looked at George confused.

"Bodyguard days?" He said. "You never told me that."

"Really?" George said, looking at him and trying not to smile.

"He told me he was shot saving someone on the stage," The girl said.

"Sounds like a famous film to me," Marvin said. "He is pulling your leg!"

"Pulling my leg?" She said. "What does that mean?"

"Winding you up," Marvin said.

"Have you been winding me up?" The girl said looking at me.

George nodded.

"That is so mean!" She said. "Why would you do that?"

"I couldn't help it," George sniggered. "Every time I meet someone, they want to know about how I lost my hearing, and the same old story gets boring."

Marvin laughed, slapping George on the back.

"He tried the same with us when he first started," Marvin said. "Kept it going for a good six months!"

"Arsehole!" she said, bursting into laughter.

"Just a bit of fun!" George said. "I think your friend wants you."

The girls' friend stood by the counter, waving for her to go over.

"I better see what she wants," The girl said. "See you later."

George watched as she walked away.

"She works on delivery," Marvin said. "Remember that incident report that was done on us last month?"

"Yeah," George said. "What about it?"

"She did it," Marvin said. "All because Andy forgot to put the batteries back into a doppler."

"I remember," George said. "That was signed off as a training issue their end."

"You coming up with me?" Marvin said. "They are trying to get Harold his own room."

"Sure I can pop up for a few minutes," George said. "How is he?"

"Spoke to the nurse last night," Marvin shook his head. "He isn't too well apparently."

"Let's go see how he is," George yawned. "I need to pop into Intensive Care at half six."

"How come?" Marvin said as they both walked towards the exit.

"Ventilator has gone down on bed one," George scoffed. "Again."

"That nurse likes you," Marvin teased. "That is why she keeps breaking things!"

"Oh please!" George moaned.

06:30

George closed the door behind him, looking down at the light blue scrubs he had on, the top too big for his slim frame. The theatre shoes slapping against the bottom of his feet as he walked towards the nurse sitting by a small table, wearing the same type of scrubs, a mask, and a pink hairnet.

"Morning," George said. "I am George from Tech Services."

"Hello," The small nurse said and stood up. "How are you this morning?"

"Do you mind lowering you mask while we talk?" George asked her. "I am profoundly deaf and need to lipread."

"Of course, of course!" She pulled her mask down. "That is better, are you here to look at the faulty ventilator?"

George nodded.

"Bed twelve," She said. "It is empty currently."

"Full Protective gear? " George asked.

"Unfortunately, yes," The nurse nodded. "Five confirmed patients in that bay."

"Okay," George sighed and walked over to the shelving next to the table, removing a gown, face shield, mask, and hat. "Is my kit in the office?" He asked. "I forgot it last time, it is in a small green box with VT on the front."

"I'll go look," The nurse said and walked away.

George pulled on the gown and tied it up around his waist, covering his head with the hat, he then put on the mask and face shield.

"Here you go," The nurse said frightening George. "Don't forget your gloves!" She took a pair of large gloves from the box and handed them to George, watching as he pulled them on.

"Thank you," He said. "Is Kim on?"

"Yes," The nurse said.

"That's a shame," George said and picked up the box, making his way through the double doors and heading for bed twelve.

The main intensive care was made up of three large bay areas, twelve beds on one bay and in the other two, five in each. The nursing station was at the far end of the bay, with monitors mounted above the desk. Down each side of the bay are six beds, on one side five of the beds are in use, ventilators hissing, monitoring and pumps beeping, the curtains pulled around each bed. On the left side, all six beds are empty, stripped and the curtains open. The ventilators, monitoring and pumps all switched off.

George saw bed twelve, closest to the nursing station and walked towards it, noticing a woman by the desk.

"Oh shit," He mumbled to himself. "Not my day."

The nurse turned around, waving when she saw George. Short and stocky, she was wearing full protective clothing.

"Good morning George," She shouted. "I am so glad to see you!"

George waved back at her in embarrassment.

"I don't feel the same," He mumbled to himself. "Morning Kim," George said.

"I thought you forgot about me!" She shouted walking down to meet up with George, putting her arms around his shoulders.

"Personal space!" George said. "Hope you are clean!"

"You are funny," She laughed. "It is bed twelve."

"What?" George said.

"Twelve!" She shouted and then pointed to the bed, exaggerating.

"Stop shouting," George said. "It doesn't help."

"Okay," She nodded.

"So, what happened?" George asked. "Did you touch something you shouldn't have?"

"No!" Kim exclaimed. "No, I didn't"

"So, what is wrong?" George said, stopping by the ventilator and looking at him who shrugged her shoulders. "Okay," George said and turned the ventilator on, putting the box down on the shelving next to it.

"The day staff said it would not work when they set it up," Kim said. "I had a look earlier, but it wouldn't let me do it."

"Who said?" George asked.

"Day staff," Kim said louder.

George went into a menu using the touchscreen, reading the log that is displayed.

"There," George said. "Someone tried to run an extended test and didn't respond to requests," He scrolled up. "They then turned the machine on, so it went into safety lock mode."

"Oh," Kim said.

"Yes," George shook his head. "At seven yesterday morning." He turned around and looked at her. "Did you try and do an extended test again?"

"No," Kim said.

"Really?" George said knowing she was not telling the truth.

"Can you fix it?" Kim asked nervously.

"Yes," George said. "But you need to bugger off and give me space."

Kim nodded and walked away, George waited until she disappeared behind the nursing station.

"Bloody fruitcake!" He said, turning the ventilator off and then back on again.

Someone tapped George on the shoulder, and he sighed heavily, turning around.

"Morning George," Steve said. "Nice and early today!" Steve was in a disposable bodysuit, wearing a hood, a tube running from the back to a pump on the side of his hip.

"Speak of the devil," George laughed. "What are you doing in so early?"

"Double shift," Steve yawned. "Had a very sick patient in bay two so I stayed on to help out."

"Are they doing okay?" George said.

"No, he died," Steve said. "Crashed his motorbike at ninety miles per hour, injuries were too extensive, but we gave him the best we could."

"Sorry to hear that," George said. "Never a nice thing."

"No," Steve said.

"Why the hood?" George asked. "Thought you were fit tested?"

"I failed the new batch," Steve moaned. "So, I have to wear this bloody thing!"

"Better than nothing," George said.

"What is up with it?" Steve said looking at the ventilator. "Kim buggered it up?"

"Well someone did an extended test," George grumbled.

"Not good then?" Steve said. "You didn't get this from me, but she was showing the new student the setup yesterday."

"Might have to password the service menu again," George said. "Either that or get an office up here."

"Share with me," Steve said smiling.

"I have seen your office," George said. "I'll pass."

"I have the config by the way," Steve said. "Signed the paperwork so will bring it down later for you."

"Great!" George said. "Took you long enough, the pumps are probably out of warranty now."

"Mr sarcastic!" Steve said. "Do you ever stop moaning?"

"When I am asleep yes," George grinned. "Going to bugger off now and let me fix this?"

Steve pat George on the back and walked away, pulling off his hood as he approached the double doors. George watched him, shaking his head.

"looks like something out of a sixties sci-fi film," George said. "Right let's sort this out."

George ran the extended test on the ventilator, looking around the bedsides while it was running in the background. A nurse came over from the nursing station, walking up to George. She was in the same protective equipment that Steve had on, only her overalls are pink.

"Good morning," She said to George. "How are you?"

"Fine thanks and how about you?" George said, smiling under the mask and the realising she could not see. "I smiled under this by the way," He tapped the mask."

"Very well thanks," She looked at the ventilator curiously. "I am new here, by the way, started last week, but last night was my second night on intensive care."

"How did you find it?" George asked.

"Not too bad," She said. "This hood is annoying though, but it is only until I get my mask fitting."

"Fair enough," George nodded.

"Kim said you are deaf?" she said. "Can you understand me okay?

"Obviously!" George laughed. "As long as I can lipread you it's fine."

"Let me know if I do anything wrong," she said. "Not spoken to a deaf person before."

"Just carry on as you are, I am George by the way," George said. "From technical services."

"Maisie," She said smiling. "Student nurse."

"Did you get shown how to do this?" George pointed to the ventilator.

"Yes," she said. "Did I break it?"

"No," George said. "The test was cancelled out, so it locked the ventilator, wouldn't let anything be done until a full test was run again."

"It's my fault," Maisie said in embarrassment. "It all went wrong when I was left to it."

"Who trained you?" George asked. "Kim?"

Maisie nodded.

"No harm was done," George watched as the ventilator finished the testing and then he shut it down.

"What did I do wrong?" Maisie asked.

"The wrong test," George said. "I'll show you how to do it if you want?"

"That would be great," Maisie got closer to the ventilator while George stood back, watching her.

"Go into new patient menu, and then click setup checks," George pointed. "You need to press the flashing button on the panel within five seconds or it times out."

George watched as Maisie navigated the menu and the ventilator beeped, displaying the self-test mode.

"Now connect the circuit and follow the screen prompts," George explained. "If you do it wrong or miss anything, it will remind you to do it again."

Maisie gave George a thumbs up.

"Hey!" Kim said loudly from behind them.

"Jesus!" George snapped. "How can someone be a ninja and an elephant at the same time!?"

Maisie laughed.

"So, have you fixed it?" Kim said. "Maisie here has probably told you she messed it up."

"Well if you had gone through it with her, then she may not have," George said bluntly.

Kim scoffed.

"I was busy," She said. "And I explained to Maisie what to do."

"You shouldn't be cascade training," George said. "Causes too many issues."

"Well it didn't," Kim said.

"Would have done if you needed it in the middle of the night," George said, packing up the test gear laid out on the bed.

"We would have called you out in that case," She said. "They are twenty-four-hour cover," Kim said to Maisie.

"No, we are not," George said. "We never have been."

"But you were here late last year, looking at that monitor for me," She said. "That was nine at night."

"I was here because a friend's father was dying," George said. "And I only fixed it because you wouldn't shut up."

"Wow," She said. "Rude!" She raised her voice.

George shook his head in annoyance and looked at the ventilator that had successfully finished.

"All done," George said to Maisie. "That is all there is to it."

"Thank you," Maisie said. "That was helpful."

"No problems," George said and made his way to the exit.

Just as he got to the double doors, Kim started shouting at him to come back.

"George!" She shouted across the bay. "Wait!"

George stopped at the doors, sighing deeply as he turned around.

"Wait!" Kim shouted, walking quickly towards him.

"What?" George said.

"Bed one monitoring isn't working," She said loudly.

"The what?" George said.

"Monitor!" Kim shouted.

"Don't shout!" George snapped. "Just talk clearly."

"Do. You. Mean. Like. This?" Kim exaggerated each word, sarcasm in her voice.

"Just speak clearly, without the attitude and exaggeration please," George said. "What did you want?"

"Monitor on bed one," She said. "Not working."

"In what way?" George asked and looked towards bed one, realising the curtains were drawn.

"Not sure," She said. "You need to speak to the nurse on that bay," Kim said, walking away.

"Moron," George whispered and made his way over to bed one and gently opening the curtains.

"Hello," Maisie said. "Can I help?"

"Apparently, the monitor isn't working properly?" George said. "Kim asked me to have a look."

Maisie looked at the male nurse that was setting up an infusion, he looked at George and then nodded.

"I won't be long," George said. "Do you know what the issue is?"

"Keeps cutting out," The male nurse said. "Getting annoying now."

"Sorry, could you repeat that?" George said, struggling with the heavy Scottish accent that the nurse had.

"Keeps cutting out," he said again.

"Sorry, could you repeat what he said please?" He looked at Maisie.

"He said it keeps cutting out," Maisie said.

"Is it my accent?" The man said. "Surely I am not that difficult to understand?"

"He is deaf," Maisie said. "The accent probably makes it harder to understand you with a mask on as well."

"What she said," George held up a thumb. "Spot on."

"I am really sorry," the man said. "No offence intended."

"No problems," George said. "Heard a lot worse."

George bent down next to the monitor, following the monitoring cables that ran to the back, watching as the monitor cut out when he moved them.

"Think I know why," George said and made his way behind the bed, accessing the back of the monitoring. "You will lose the display for a few seconds," George said. "Is that okay?"

The man nodded.

"That is fine," Maisie said.

George pulled the cables free, untangling them and then plugging them back in, looking up at the man.

"Working?" George asked.

"Not yet," Maisie said.

"Odd," George said looking at the cables, following them up to the back of the large display. "Hold on a minute," He said and reached in, pushing the cable up until there is a beep.

"Works now," Maisie said. "Thanks for that."

"Anything else?" George asked and looked at the man who nodded.

"Give me a second," He said.

75

George watched as he set up the infusion on one of the pumps, writing on a form as he did so and then start it, watching as it began pumping

"I am desperate for some more pumps," The man said. "Do you have any of ours?"

"Do you mind?" George said to Maisie.

"Of course not," She smiled. "He asked if you have any of our pumps because we are desperate."

"We still have ten downstairs," George said. "Currently being repaired and fully tested."

"Are they the ten that fell off the drip stand?" The man said.

"Yes," George said getting used to the accent. "The one the porter moved from the equipment storage to here, using a condemned stand."

"Are they all repairable?" He asked.

"Could you repeat that?" George said.

"Are they all able to be repaired?" He said.

"Yes," George said. "Not going to be cheap though but we should get the outstanding parts today," George explained. "I am looking at one because it still fails to work considering the main parts have been replaced."

"Can we get any back today if possible?" The man said. "Would appreciate it very much."

"Sorry," George said. "Didn't get any of that," He struggled with the monitor in the next bed alarming.

"He asked if we could get some back?" Maisie said. "If any are available?"

"I can get six to you," George said. "And I will check with Evan to see if he can spare any from the library if he is in that is."

"Thank you," the man said.

"Okay thanks," George said. "Just need to make sure the monitoring cables don't get wrapped around the cable at the back," He said. "Otherwise it could damage the connector."

"I will mention it in our huddle later," The man said. "Thanks."

George left the bedside and walked back to the double doors, sighing in relief when he walked through them.

"Bloody warm," He said to the nurse at the desk, taking off the shield and placing in in a red box.

"All done?" The nurse said, standing up.

George nodded, pulling off the mask and hat and then the gown, folding it up and putting it into the bin next to the table.

"I need a strong coffee now," George laughed and squirted alcohol gel from the bottle, completely covering his hands with it.

"Matron asked if you could pop into her office for a moment?" The nurse said. "If you wouldn't mind?"

George picked up a fresh mask, putting it on.

"Sure," George nodded and walked to the end of the corridor, knocking on the door, and listening.

"Come in!" The woman's voice behind the door.

George opened the door to the small office with a full-length window at the end, on both sides are two desks with computers and various files and papers. By the door are two filing cabinets on one side and on the other a locked metal cabinet. Posters and charts covered the walls.

"Good morning George," The matron said from the desk in the corner.

The matron is short and athletic with short black hair, she is wearing glasses with a red frame, her red tunic visible under her black fleece jacket.

"Good morning Reo," George said. "Thought you were off this week?" He said in surprise. "Or do we have the same boss?" He laughed.

"I could say the same for you," She sighed. "You were going to ignore any requests and go to Cornwall!" She sighed. "What happened?"

"Bloody Harold," George said approaching the table, Reo pointed to a chair for him to sit down. "Went and broke his legs to stop me going didn't he!"

"Oh no!" Reo said. "Are you serious?" She asked curiously. "I can never tell if you are."

"He did," George said. "Trampled by a cow after his dog freaked it."

"That is terrible!" Her hand went to her face. "Is he here?"

"Yes, on the orthopaedic ward," George said. "Won't be out for a while."

"I must go and see him," Reo said. "Drop him in some fruit!" She pointed to the table opposite her, several fruit baskets covering it.

"Blimey!" George said. "Where did that come from?"

"Donations," She said. "We get too much!"

"Well I can take some off your hands," George said. "My team needs to stop snacking on junk!"

"I will get one of our porters to drop some off," Reo said. "Now the reason I wanted to see you."

"If it is about the four vents in storage," George said. "They are all serviced and ready to go."

"No, it's not about any equipment," Reo sighed nervously. "I have had a complaint."

"About me?" George said.

"No not at all," Reo patted George on the leg. "A member of my team overheard another member of my team, degrading you."

"Would that be Kim?" George said. "Yeah, I am aware of that."

"Why didn't you approach me?" She asked.

"You are busy enough without having to deal with idiots," George said.

"They are my idiots, and I won't have it," Reo said. "Apparently Kim stated that you shouldn't be fixing equipment if you are deaf."

"Yeah, that was it," George laughed. "Very original huh?"

"I will take it further if you wish?" Reo said.

"No need," George said. "I got a few choice words in myself and she hasn't said anything since, however, I do wish she would stop shouting at me across the bay."

"I will bring that up," Reo said. "Could I ask what the choice words were?"

"I was in the staffroom last week having a catch-up and lunch with Steve, " George chuckled. "Kim came in and had three fresh cream cakes in a row, so I reminded her she probably shouldn't be eating so much considering she is on a diet."

Reo exclaimed and started to laugh.

"That is mean," Reo giggled. "True but mean."

"She said the same," George said. "So, I reminded her that talking about a deaf person thinking they cannot hear is also mean."

"Did she apologise?" Reo said.

"Sort of," George said smiling. "Not to bothered really, but I would like her to stop shouting."

"I will sort it out," Reo said. "But please if you have any issues, let me know, I won't have people discriminating."

"No problems," George said. "I sorted out bed twelve."

"I saw the handover, what was the problem?" Reo asked.

"User error," George said.

Reo groaned.

"Kim told Maisie how to do a self-check instead of showing her, and she made a mistake," George explained. "Kim turned it off."

"Was it in use at the time?" Reo asked. "The report said it was on a patient?"

"We were told it was not in use," George said. "And the logs show the patient was discharged the day before."

"Are you able to arrange some training?" Reo asked. "From the company?"

"Well with the current virus situation," George said. "The company are struggling, so I am happy to train staff on set up procedures, I have already shown Maisie, she is a natural."

"I have heard good things," Reo said. "She is only here for a short while, however, I am going to offer her a permanent position."

"She will be great," George said. "Lots of common sense."

"So, are you okay?" She said. "Are you sure you don't want to take it further?"

"No, it is fine," George scoffed. "Really it is not worth the hassle."

"Okay," Reo said. "I am sorry either way."

"It's fine," George stood up. "Anything else?" He asked. "Got a ton of things to do this morning."

"No all good," Reo said. "We are getting some buffet in later, you are welcome to come up with the team."

"They are like puppies!" George said. "They will clear the table in seconds!"

Reo laughed.

"I am actually meeting someone, so will let the guys and gal know," George said. "We have a new administrator, by the way, Kirsty, so far so good!" George said, walking to the door and opening it.

"Glad that it got sorted," Reo said. "Take care, George."

George waved and closed the door quietly.

07:20

George took his mask off when he got outside the hospital, holding a paper cup of coffee. It was a clear day, and cold, he breathed in deeply, and breathed out, watching as the mist escaped from him. The middle-aged woman wearing a floral dress and a mauve cardigan, her blonde greying hair tied up at the back, wearing a mask and gloves, she ran up to George.

"Hello," She said. "Come and help me!"

George looked at her and then looked around, wondering if she was talking to him.

"Sorry do you mind dropping your mask so I can lipread?" He asked her.

She shook her head and continued to talk.

"I am sorry, but I cannot help you unless I can lipread you," George explained. "Reception will be able to help you otherwise," he pointed towards the entrance.

She again shook her head, waving her hands and talking so George went to walk away, only for her to step in front and block him from getting past.

"I cannot understand!" George said.

She raised her voice, speaking slowly and exaggerating every word.

"I need you to come and help me," She said.

"I still need to lipread you," George explained. "I cannot make out a word you are saying!"

"No!" She said loudly. "No."

"Then I cannot help.," George said in frustration and sipping from his coffee. "There is plenty of room between us, so there is no need for the mask."

She shook her head again, repeating herself and George made another attempt to walk away. She stepped in front of George again, putting her hand on my chest, he looked down and then backed away.

"Could you not touch me with gloves please," George said. "I doubt they are clean." He sighed heavily. "And that is also harassment."

She pulled her mask down, looking incredibly angry, her thick lipstick slightly smeared at the sides.

"You stepped into me," She said defiantly.

"No," George laughed. "I walked away, and you stopped me," He shook his head in disbelief. "There is a camera up there," He pointed to the camera above the door. "So, avoid the bullshit please."

"I was asking you for help and you refused," She was angry.

"I asked you to move your mask so I could understand you," George said. "I didn't refuse anything."

"So, you could infect me you mean," She snapped. "How do you think I feel?"

"Infect you?" George scoffed. "I am virus free for your information, I have regular swabs."

"I don't know that do I?" She said.

"Then don't accuse me of trying to infect you when you stepped into me," George said sternly.

"The rules are to wear a mask," She said.

"We are over two meters apart," George said. "Well, we were until you stopped me."

"You should listen when being spoken to," She said with a high and mighty attitude.

"I am deaf and do not appreciate that comment," George said. "I could say a thing or two about you," George looked her up and down. "But I cannot be bothered."

"The customer is always right," She said.

"This is a hospital," George scoffed. "Not a bloody Tupperware store, so do you want my help, or shall I walk away?"

She stared at George and then let out a small sigh.

"I apologise," she said, not meaning it from her tone. "My mother is in my car."

"Okay," George said waiting for her to say more. "Why are you telling me this?"

She sighed in frustration.

"You don't understand me, do you?" She said shaking her head. "Why can't he understand me." She laughed looking around her.

"Who are you talking to?" George asked her, looking around. "Do you have an imaginary friend?"

"You," She said. "You don't understand."

"I understand you fine," George replied. "I just don't get why you are telling me, nor why you are making these insulting comments?"

"I want you to do the job you are paid to do," She said and put her mask back on, pointing to the car."

"Which is what?" George asked. "I cannot fix your mother if that is what you are aiming for?" She lowered her mask and moaned.

"Why do they employ people that cannot understand?" She said. "I. Need. You. To. Get. A. Wheel. Chair. For. My. Mother." She said loudly, emphasized, and plain ignorant and annoying. "Do. You. Understand?!"

"Bloody hell," George scoffed. "What year do you come from, the nineteen twenties?" He said. "Did your slaves all die or something?"

"Fetch a wheelchair," She said. "Please!" She snapped her fingers.

"Don't snap your fingers at me," George huffed. They are likely to be broken," George shook his head. "I think you have me confused," George said.

She laughed.

"No," She laughed. "I do not."

"I am not a porter," George replied. "Or, the help, as your ladyship would put it."

She looked at George confused.

"And even if I was a porter," George said. "I wouldn't put up with that ignorant and outdated attitude from the likes of you."

"Not a porter?" She said. "I am not giving you attitude, I am concerned about my mother who may have the virus."

"Sorry to hear that," George said. "Security at the entrance will be able to help and give you the relevant advice," He added and went to walk away.

"Ignorant and rude is what you are," She said.

George stopped, he probably should have ignored her, and walked away but that was not who he is.

"Said the woman who assaulted me, abused me and harassed me," George said. "I tried to leave, and you blocked me, putting your dirty gloved hand on my chest."

She scoffed.

"I can take it further if you wish?" George spoke softly. "I could have a word with security, who will probably tase you, laughing as you fall to the floor and lose control of your bowels and bladder, reducing you to the pathetic toddler that you are."

The woman looked at him, her mouth opened in shock.

"No need to go over the top," She said. "I apologise if you think I have offended you."

"Takes more than that," George said. "And I have heard a lot worse," He said walking away.

"They should have something in place for deaf people like you, so you don't make it harder for others," She said, looking at George defiantly like she got the final insult in.

"They do," George replied. "It is called common sense, but clearly you missed that boat, lucky for you it isn't the dark ages, otherwise you would have been lobbed in the lake and burnt at the stake!" George walked away, ignoring her calls for him to come back.

08:22

A knock at the door caused George to jump in fright and slowly close the laptop.

"Come in," George said loudly, looking at the door.

Kirsty opened the door and looked in.

"Good morning Kirsty," George said. "Has she shown up yet?"

"Yes, she is here," Kirsty said. "Shall I bring her in?"

"Please," George nodded.

Ananya walked in and stood in the doorway. She is wearing black jeans, a white blouse, and a thick black jacket. Her long hair black, thick, and messy. She wore a face shield, mask, purple latex gloves and held a bag in one hand and a coffee in the other.

"Good morning Ananya," George said. "Just so you are aware, we are a clean zone, so you don't need to wear a mask or shield, but entirely up to you," George explained. "Masks have to be worn everywhere else and if you are on the wards near patients, a shield is required."

Ananya took off her face shield and facemask, placing them onto the chair by the door.

"Please sit down," George pointed to the chair in front of the desk. "Would offer you a drink but I see you have one."

Ananya nodded, placing her cup on the table, took off her jacket and dropped it on the floor next to the chair. She then sat down, smiling nervously.

"Did you get in okay?" George said.

Ananya nodded.

"Did you drive?" George asked.

Ananya shook her head.

"Can you speak?" He chuckled.

"Yes," she said. "I was unsure how to go about it, I was expecting Harold."

"Go about what?" George asked.

"Darren informed me that you are deaf," she said. "So, I studied it online last night."

"Okay," George laughed. "I'll put your mind at rest, just carry on as normal, speak as you would with anyone and if I have any trouble understanding, just repeat it," George explained. "I have trouble with new people usually, accents and background noise."

"Can you understand me with my accent?" She said. "I am from India and it used to be quite strong, but ling in London has changed it a little."

"I can understand you fine," George said.

"Do you sign?" She asked.

"No," George said. "Never learned to and never needed to."

"I thought all deaf people learned to sign?" Ananya said. "How do you communicate?" she looked at him curiously.

"What?" George said.

"How do you communicate?" She asked again.

"You mean like we are now?" George said smiling. "I can hear with my implant."

"Wow," She said looking. "I have not seen one of those before!"

"They are pretty good," George said. "I was lucky with mine."

"Is that fitted to your skull?" She said leaning forward.

"No, not the bone-anchored one," George said. "I have a coil inside my head and a processor on the outside, connected with a magnet."

"So cool!" She said excitedly. "Why did you get it?"

"The implant?" George said. "Because I went completely deaf and hearing aids couldn't do much for me," He said. "Anyway, enough about me. "Where did you work before?"

"In London," Ananya said. "For a private firm."

"Was that patient monitoring?" George asked. "Why did you leave?"

"Personal reasons," She said. "Too many freaks."

"Sorry to hear that," George said. "Has Darren updated you about what you will be doing here?"

"Infusion devices," She said with a smile. "I am really, really excited!"

"I will get Marvin to supervise you," George said. "I have a desk set up for you, but if you need anything let me know."

Ananya nodded.

"Marvin will get you a temporary badge sorted out and show you around shortly," George said. "I have a couple of meetings today, sadly!" He groaned. "Otherwise I would work with you."

"Okay," She said. "Would it be possible to work half eight to half four?"

"That will be fine," George said. "Just let Marvin know."

"Thank you," She smiled.

"Also," He stood up. "No Jeans please, trust policy."

"Sorry," She apologised. "I wasn't sure."

"Do you smoke?" George asked.

"Yes," She said. "But my parents don't know that."

"We are a non-smoking site," He said. "So, you will need to go off the grounds."

George walked to the door, opening it.

"I have left an information pack for you to read, could you also sign the paperwork," George said.

"Of course," She said. "Could I ask something?" She said standing up and picking up her jacket.

"Go for it," George said.

"How long is this post for?" She asked curiously.

"It's a temporary assignment," George said. "But we are looking for another technician to join the team soon."

"I am looking for a permanent position," Ananya said. "And would be interested in applying."

"I will let you know when it becomes available," George said. "But these things take forever, you know how it is."

Marvin appeared at the doorway, causing George to jump in fright.

"Got you!" He laughed. "You must be Anya," He said.

"Ananya," She corrected him.

"Sorry," Marvin apologised. "It's my age."

"He uses that excuse for everything," George said. "We have an iron bar in the workshop when he starts talking rubbish, we belt him with it."

Ananya giggled.

"Could you show her around, set her up at the desk and introduce her to everyone," George said. "She will be doing infusion pumps."

"What all five hundred?" Marvin said with his mouth open in amazement.

"Is that all," She replied in disappointment. "Should keep me busy for a day or two."

George chuckled and then turned to Marvin.

"Is Curtis in?" George asked.

Marvin nodded.

"Could you send him in please?" George sighed. "He is giving me grief."

"Oh dear," Marvin sighed. "Can't we just take him outside and shoot him?"

"If only," George said and returned to the desk, sitting down. He watched as Ananya left, followed by Marvin. Marvin opened up the laptop and signed in, looking at his mobile next to it and then picking up the coffee, leaning back.

A knock at the door followed by Curtis walking in and closing the door.

"You needed to see me, boss?" He said.

"What is with the red shirt?" George asked.

Curtis was not in uniform, he wore black trousers and a blood-red shirt.

"My washing machine blew up," Curtis laughed. "So, I had to use this."

"Well make sure you roll the sleeves up," George said. "Didn't you have something that isn't so," George tried to think. "Loud?"

Curtis laughed, shaking his head.

"Deafinitely!" Curtis laughed.

"Is that another one of your attempts at a deaf joke?" George stared at him. "I am really not in the mood today."

"Well jokes to tend to fall on deaf ears," Curtis said with a smile on his face.

"One more and human resources can deal with it," George warned. "I am not joking."

Curtis held up his hands in an apology and nodded.

"Okay," George scoffed. "Sit down," He pointed to the chair."

"So, what is going on?" Curtis said. "I was hoping to speak to you today."

"Yeah?" George said. "Why?"

"I want to book tomorrow off," Curtis said.

"Oh, Curtis!" George complained. "Not much notice is it? What is it for?"

"Not sure," Curtis laughed.

"You need a whole day for that?" George huffed. "Really?"

Curtis nodded.

"You do realise I have Ahmed and Andy off tomorrow?" George said.

Curtis laughed.

"Why are you laughing?"

"Are you serious?" Curtis said. "I cannot tell."

"Why do you need the day off?" George asked. "Do you have a reason?"

"I don't know yet," Curtis said.

"So, you don't know why you want to take the day off?" George scoffed. "Or are you just being complicated for the sake of it?"

"My wife asked me if I could take the day off," Curtis said smiling.

George looked at him, waiting for him to say something more.

"That means nothing to me," Curtis said.

"I think she wants to go for a walk," Curtis said.

"Okay," George huffed. "No, you cannot have the day off, you are aware of the policy."

"I am sure Andy won't mind changing his day off," Curtis said. "I can chat with him about it."

"You want Andy to change his day off so you can go for a walk?" George scoffed. "Can't you do that on Saturday?"

"Well my wife is very particular," Curtis said. "I like to let her do what she wants to do."

"Can't you grow some balls and say no?" George said. "You keep asking for non-emergency days at short notice without any concern for anyone else in the department."

"So is it a no?" Curtis asked.

"It's a no," George snapped. "End of conversation."

"I'll talk to Barbara," Curtis said.

"You do realise that I am the interim manager?" George said. "If you go over my head, I will take it further."

Curtis looked at him, a nervous smile on his face.

"Okay I won't take the day off," Curtis said. "So, what did you want to see me about?"

"Cancer services," George said. "Does that ring a bell?"

Curtis sat back in the chair, looking at the floor as he thought about it.

"No," Curtis said. "Should it?"

"I had an angry email from the sister," George said. "Stating that you took four of their pumps away two weeks ago for servicing?"

Curtis nodded, scratching his chin.

"That correct?" George said.

"Yes," Curtis smiled. "Harold spoke to me last week about those and asked me to get them back as soon as possible."

"And?" George said.

"I still have them," Curtis laughed nervously. "I need to run the battery calibration."

"You can do that anytime," George said. "You could have run those overnight, why haven't you."

"I got side-tracked," Curtis said. "I have been helping out the other guys."

"What other guys?" George said opening a notepad.

"Well Andy asked me for some help on his syringe pump," Curtis said. "So, I have been doing that with him."

"Andy doesn't do infusion pumps," George said.

"I know," Curtis laughed.

"Stop laughing," George sighed. "You are like an annoying school kid!"

Curtis nodded, chuckling silently.

"So why is Andy doing a pump?" George wanted to know. "No one has told me anything about that."

"That would be my fault," Curtis said. "Harold asked Andy to sit with me when I actioned a repair on one."

"And did he?" George asked.

"No," He said nervously. "I got called out to Maternity to check some things for them."

"What things?" George said.

"They asked if we could fix the television in the waiting room," Curtis said.

"Why would you do that?" George groaned. "Entertainment services do that, not us."

"I wanted to help," Curtis said. "They were very persuasive."

"So you broke policy to make yourself look good?" George groaned. "I will deal with that later, back to Andy, why did he do the pump?"

"I told him to dismantle it," Curtis said. "And rebuild it to learn."

"You did what?" George snapped. "You do realise that the pump was new and still under warranty."

"That isn't a problem," Curtis brushed it off. "I know them very well."

"Yes, it is," George said. "He should have been fully supervised and broke the first rule, you always check the details and history before you look at a repair, you know that!" George moaned. "What is wrong with you!"

"I'll sort it out," Curtis said.

"But you are sending too many pumps way," George said. "The last two were under warranty and we had to pay for the repair because you invalidated the warranty."

"Well no one would have known about it if you hadn't said anything," Curtis said. "I had it under control."

"You didn't you plank!" George snapped. "The invoice came to me and when I asked you about it, you told me to ignore it!"

Curtis shrugged his shoulders.

"Two pumps, sixteen hundred pounds!" George said. "When they shouldn't have cost anything."

"Well they were damaged by the end-user," Curtis said.

"No, the issue was related to an alert," George groaned. "Because you ignored a procedure, did your own thing and made things worse."

"I will sort them out," Curtis said.

"Well we still need to pay the invoice," George said. "They have already done the repairs."

"Who authorised it?" Curtis said, shaking his head.

"You did you, bloody idiot!" George moaned. "You completed the paperwork and sent it to them when you should have passed it to Harold."

"I was just helping," Curtis said. "I like to deal with my work."

"You cannot authorise payments," George said. "You authorised two repairs without talking to Harold or me!"

There is a knock at the door and Marvin popped his head in.

"Everything okay lads?" He said. "Kirsty is getting worried about the shouting."

"You can get her to call an ambulance," George said. "Because I am going to murder someone shortly."

"What have you done now Curtis?" Marvin said. "When are you going to learn?"

"I am stuck in my ways!" Curtis laughed. "Cannot teach an old dog new tricks."

"No," George said. "But you can take it down the woods and shoot it in the bloody head!"

Marvin closed the door behind him, leaning against it.

"Okay let's sort this out," Marvin said. "Are you okay with me staying George?"

George nodded.

"Curtis," Marvin said. "Do yourself a favour stop doing things your way, this is a team, and we have things in place for a reason."

"I am trying," Curtis said. "It is new for me."

"They have been in place for five years and you have been here three years," George scoffed. "Do you want an instruction manual or something?"

"He has a point," Marvin looked at Curtis. "You need to stop this one-man show crap, you are causing lots of problems."

"Did Harold talk to him last week?" George asked Marvin.

"No," Marvin said. "He planned to on Friday, but Curtis booked the day off at the end of Thursday."

"This is what I mean," George said. "You don't have a single thought for the rest of the department and just book days off at a moment's notice."

"I asked for tomorrow off," Curtis said. "He refused it."

"What did you want it off for?" Marvin asked.

"To take my wife to the doctors," Curtis said looking at the floor.

"You lying little shit!" George snapped. "You told me you wanted the day off to go for a walk and I said no because I have people off already."

"Really?" Marvin said. "Why?" He looked at Curtis.

"It doesn't matter," Curtis sulked. "I'll book time off next week."

"Jesus!" George scoffed. "I am going to get this over before I lose my rag," George said.

"I think you have already," Curtis said softly, chuckling quietly.

"Oh, trust me," George said. "This is nothing."

"You need to zip it," Marvin said to Curtis. "We are trying to help."

"Consider this a verbal warning," George said. "You are on thin ice, so try not to break it."

"Could I have that in writing?" Curtis started laughing. "Let's make it written?" He giggled.

"I give up!" George said. "Sure Curtis," George nodded. "I'll do that for you."

"Go get those pumps sorted for Cancer services," Marvin said. "If we get reported, you are in trouble."

Curtis nodded and got up from the chair, walking to the door and smiling as he took his phone out of his pocket.

"Can I show you something funny?" Curtis said, bursting into fits of giggles.

"Get out," George said. "Not today!"

Curtis left, closing the door slowly behind him.

"George," Marvin said. "Chill!"

"I am fine," George said. "I just need him to take responsibility."

"I will deal with him," He said. "When is your meeting?"

"Eleven," George said.

"Go grab a coffee," Marvin said. "Go for a walk, anything. Just walk away."

"Good idea," George said. "Do you want anything?"

"No, I am good," Marvin said. "Are you okay?"

"Yes," George said and got up from the table, slowly pushing the chair under it. "Just didn't get much sleep last night."

"How come?" Marvin said.

"Tinnitus," George said. "Driving me up the bloody wall."

"Oh, that is not good," Marvin sighed. "Nothing they can give you to help or soothe it?"

"Not really," George chuckled, leaning against the desk. "A few years back someone in a chemist suggested I listen to whale songs, and a lady in the queue thought I was going to go to the beach, stick my head under and listen."

"Oh my god!" Marvin sniggered.

"Had to explain to her you can download the songs," George shook his head. "Crazy."

"When did it stop?" Marvin said.

"It didn't," He breathed out heavily. "Still blasting away in my head now. The housemate was being all nice, made me a coffee and took an interest in it. Made me laugh."

"How so?" Marvin said.

"Well she is a little thick," George said. "She asked me how I can hear sounds in my head if I am deaf."

"Oh god!" Marvin sniggered. "You are kidding?!"

"No," He said. "She comes out with crazy stuff. Not long ago, she got drunk and asked me if I had a deaf baby, would I abort it."

"What is wrong with that girl!?" Marvin snapped. "Didn't you say once about when she asked if you tried to learn and hear, and you probably wouldn't need an implant?"

"Yes," George said. "That is the one! Also asked if my snoring wakes me up, I told her no I am completely deaf, so, she asked me, what would I hear if she screamed in my ear."
Marvin looked at George in shock.

"I said, probably my knuckles cracking against your nose!" George laughed. "I could write a book on the things that girl says!"

"What is the worst she has said?" Marvin asked curiously.

"Worse?" George said thinking, "I would say when she asked how long I had been mentally disabled," He nodded, and his eyes widened.

"That is pretty bad!" Marvin said.

"Not long ago she got talking about how much I could hear and asked what she sounded like," George paused for a few seconds. "So, I told her she sounded annoying."

"Damn you can be brutal!" Marvin said.

"Oh," George coughed. "That was a warmup!" He scoffed. "Another was, how do I know I am deaf."

"Oh, no way!" Marvin laughed.

"She asked me today if I ever hear strange things," George smiled. "So, I said, only you."

"I remember that time we had the cute rep in," Marvin said thinking. "From the consumables supplier, I forget her name."

"Corina?" George said. "Always came in with tight tops and so on."

"That's the one," Marvin said. "When she met you for the first time and asked you a million or so questions," Marvin scratched his forehead. "She asked you if you had any special abilities or powers, and you replied." He pointed to George.

"I wasn't bitten by a fucking radioactive spider, I was given crap genetics by my parents!" George said and they both burst into laughter.

"Not seen her in ages," Marvin said. "Apparently, she doesn't work there anymore."

"I saw her last year at the bus stop," George said. "Hadn't seen her in a while and Harold mentioned she was pregnant. I got talking to her, and she asked me if I knew her news. I said what? So, she showed me her bump and told me she was expecting," George paused and smiled. "I replied, oh thank god for that, I just thought you were getting fat from all the doughnuts you forget to give us!"

"Oh, you didn't!" Marvin exclaimed. "What did she say?"

"She was laughing so much she couldn't talk," George said. "Or crying, I don't know. Or care."

"Crazy," Marvin looked at his watch. "Go grab a break and I'll sort out everything."

"Thanks," George said. "Appreciate it."

"Do you want a hug?" Marvin asked, holding out his arms.

George looked at him, confused.

"You bang your head or something?" George said. "Do you not know me at all?" He joked.

"I'll put it down to social distancing then," Marvin opened the door. "Piss off."

11:02

George sat at the desk, looking at his watch and then at the laptop. Against the wall is a small whiteboard on a stand, next to it a presentation pad on a similar board.

There is a gentle knock at the door and George smiled when Kirsty stood in the doorway, holding a business card. She is wearing grey trousers and a white shirt.

"Hi," She smiled. "I have a John Laker here for a meeting with you?"

"Yes," George said. "I am expecting him, send him in."

John was a tall and heavily built man and is wearing a black suit and overcoat, he walks in and waves at George before placing his bag on the floor and removing the overcoat, placing it over the chair.

"Do you want a drink?" George asked him. "Tea? Coffee?"

He shook his head.

"Okay, are you ready to start?" George said. "I don't have much time, so I just need the basics."

John looked at George in confusion.

"Shall we start?" George said.

John stood up and pointed to the dry wipe board. In large capitals, he wrote 'HELLO. MY NAME IS JOHN'. Underneath he wrote. 'ARE YOU GEORGE?'

"Yes," George said.

John nodded and then he proceeded to slowly sign, thinking between each sign.

"Okay stop," George said. "Can you speak?"

"Yes," John said.

"Good," George said nodding. "Forget the sign language crap," He said bluntly.

"Okay," John said. "I apologise if I have offended you. My Name is John," He said in embarrassment.

"Good to meet you, John," George said. "How long have you signed?" George asked curiously.

'Two days," He responded in fingerspelling.

"I don't sign," George said.

He looked at me, shocked.

"Okay," He said loudly and emphasised. "How do you communicate?" He said slowly.

"Like we are right now, normally," George said, the annoyance building said. I can lipread and hear you.

"Normally?" He said confused.

"Yes," George nodded. "As you would with anyone else so there is no need to speak loud or overemphasise."

He came over embarrassed as he walked over to the dry wipe board, wiping the message away before sitting down.

"I feel like an idiot now!" He said putting his hand over his face.

"Don't worry about it," George said. "At least you tried, which is more than some people do."

"You have no idea," He laughed.

"What?" George said.

"I tried to hire a sign language interpreter," He laughed. "And spent all day yesterday learning basic sign language."

"That is pretty full-on," George laughed. "You asked me the other day about it, and I said not to worry."

"It really threw me when you talked," he said. "I didn't think you were the same person I talked to via email."

"Deaf people can talk," George said. "Just some never learnt to."

"I didn't mean it like that," He stuttered. "I mean you don't sound deaf."

"A lot of us don't," George said. "We adapt so we can integrate into the human population."

"Oh," He said.

"Makes the invasion smoother," George said sarcastically. "Our goal to wipe out the hearing scum and keep a select few as slaves."

He looked at George with his mouth open.

"That was a joke," George said. "So, can you show me the specs on this pump and then I will pass you over to Marvin."

"I have brought the manual in various print," John said. "Which do you need?"

"What do you mean?" George asked.

"Normal print, large print and also in braille," John said. "Like to be prepared."

"You do know I am deaf," George said. "Not blind?"

John looked at George, confused and embarrassed.

"Okay," George sighed. "Let me go and get Marvin before I lose the plot," George got up and walked to the door, opening, and then closing it.

16:20

George stood at the counter in the small store that also had a post office section. The counter split in two with general shopping on one side and postal on the other side. A large screen had recently been installed, and labelling put onto the floor for social distancing measures. George had looked at the card aisle, trying to find a get well soon card but could not find anything he liked.

The two women sat behind the counter, their masks under their chins as they talked and laughed, completely oblivious to George standing at the counter. One of them, tall and slim with brown hair down to her hips. The other, shorter, and skinny with short grey hair and thick glasses. Both are wearing a shirt showing the logo of the store.

George coughed deliberately, his hand covering his masked mouth.

None of the women noticed him.

The door buzzer sounded when someone walked in and the woman behind the counter with the short grey hair looked up at George.

"Oh hello," She said in surprise. "Didn't see you there," She said and put her mask on.

The other woman put her mask on and moved to the far end of the counter, waiting for the customer browsing the shop.

"I have a parcel to send away," George said. "And need proof of delivery please."

"Is it a valuable item?" The woman asked.

"Sorry, can you repeat that?" George said.

"Is it a valuable item?" The woman said louder.

"Sorry," George said. "Still cannot understand. Do you mind dropping your mask so I can lipread you?" George asked.

"No sorry," She said shaking her head.

93

"I really cannot understand you," George said. "You are behind a screen and I am wearing a mask, do you mind?"

She shook her head again.

"I need to lipread," George said.

The other woman behind the counter came over.

"She said is it valuable?" The woman said.

"Sorry," George said. "Can you write it down?"

The grey-haired woman sighed in frustration.

"Now you know how I feel," George said. "Try dealing with this crap every day!"

A customer came up behind George and tapped him on the shoulder.

George turned around and recognised the woman behind him.

Ethel worked at the same trust as he did, a Speech-Language therapist in the audiology department. George had worked with her a couple of times on equipment repairs and requests. She was a tall and heavily built woman that was a retired powerlifter, having given up after a car crash damaged her back. She is wearing a nurses uniform.

"Hello George," She said. "Need some help?"

"Oh, it's just the complete lack of deaf awareness as always," George said. "Bored with it, to be honest."

"This gentleman is deaf," She said. "Unless he can lipread he cannot understand you." She explained. "You are behind a screen."

The woman with the grey hair lowered her mask, clearly upset with the request.

"I am putting my health on the line," She said. "Not happy about it."

"Well you weren't too bothered when you were chatting to your colleague," George said pointing to the other woman. "Practically touching toes talking about the Turkish guy that runs the Chinese across the street," George said bluntly. "And you were ignoring me until someone else came in."

"I was not ignoring you," She said. I didn't know you were here," She scoffed. "We are only doing what we are advised with the masks," She said.

"You are behind a screen," George huffed. "And to make things worse, you have a sticker stating you are deaf aware, on the flipping screen."

The other woman looked over the till.

"Oh, that came in the post," She said smiling. "One of those free things that most places put them up."

"So, you don't have any deaf awareness training?" George asked.

"No," She said. "But it cannot be hard can it?"

"You think?" George said. "You failed on a few just by talking."

George leaned forward, getting his nail under the sticker, and peeling it off the screen.

"Why did you do that?" The grey-haired asked. "That is criminal damage you know!"

"Would you have a sticker saying you do manicures?" George asked, looking around the room.

"Well no," She scoffed.

"Hy not?" George asked.

"Because we don't," She said bluntly.

"You don't do deaf awareness either." George snapped. "So, what's the point in a sticker stating you do?"

Ethel laughed.

She looked at George for a few seconds before nodding in agreement.

"How can I help?" She asked, changing her attitude.

"Cannot be bothered now," George said in frustration. "I'll go online and do it, not likely to get any bollocks on that."

"I am sorry you feel that way," She said. "These are very pressing times."

"Only when it suits," George turned and faced the counter. "I'll let the Turkish god with the nice arse, as you put it, that the cranky grey-haired discriminative moron across the street likes him," George smiled. "Got a feeling he won't be too keen considering you are probably old enough to be his bloody grandmother!"

George pushed open the door, storming off down the street.

The woman looked at Ethel, her mouth open in shock.

"Well done," Ethel said. "I don't think I will shop here either."

Ethel turned and slowly left the shop, dropping her items on the shelf.

20:30

George sat at the table, eating a slice of charred toast. He is wearing a white t-shirt and grey jogging bottoms. Looking down at his mobile phone, slowly chewing the toast. He picked up a mug of coffee, closing his eyes and sipping it.

"Just text her," He said to himself. "Say something."

"Who you talking to?" Debbie walked in.

"Shit!" George jumped, spilling coffee down the front of his t-shirt and sitting forward as it burnt him. "Shit!"

Debbie is wearing blue jeans and a red jumper, her hair loose.

"I am sorry!" Debbie said. "Didn't mean to frighten you."

"It's fine," George said and put the mug down, rubbing his chest. "It's my own fault."

"Can I have a quick chat?" Debbie asked.

"Sure," He pointed to the chair. "Do you want a drink or anything?"

She shook her head.

"What's up?" George asked, still nibbling at the toast.

"I have transferred everything I owe you," Debbie said. "The rent and the money I borrowed, including the bills."

"How did you manage that?" George asked.

"Doesn't matter," She said. "I wanted to sort this out."

"I appreciate it," George smiled.

"I don't blame you if you say no," She sighed. "But can I stay longer?" She paused. "Please?"

"Of course," George put the toast down and leaned forward. "I am sorry I flipped out, it has been a bad few weeks for me."

"No don't be," She said, tears in her eyes. "I have been a lazy and messy bitch, and I promise it will change. Gaze won't be coming over anymore, I promise."

"You can do better," George said. "You are a stunning looking girl," George smiled. "Don't waste time with sci-fi villains."

Debbie laughed, shaking her head, and wiping her eyes.

"Are you hungry?" She asked.

"I can always eat," George said. "Why?"

"I am going to get Chinese," She said. "Want to join me?"

George nodded.

"I'll open some wine," George said.

Georges phone buzzed and he picked it up, reading a message.

"Okay if someone joins us?" George said nervously. "It's a friend."

"Sure," She said. "More the merrier."

"Where we getting it from?" George asked. "Your favourite one down the street?"

Debbie nodded with an excited smile on her face.

"Good," He said. "I'll find out what my friend likes."

"Have I met him?" She asked.

"It's her," George said.

Debbie looked at George in shock, her mouth open and her eyes wide.

"Oh, very funny!" George said. "I have had ladies over before!"

"Not that kind!" Debbie said. "Who is she?"

"My bosses daughter," George said, pushing the plate away and leaning on the table.

"Oh, naughty!" Debbie teased. "They make videos like that online."

"Behave!" George said. "I have been talking with her over her father's accident, nothing more."

"Do you talk a lot?" She said.

"Quite a bit," George said. "She is really nice."

"Wow," Debbie said winking. "How is your boss?"

"Not great," George said. "Two broken legs and he is quite unwell."

"Got the virus?" Debbie said in concern.

"No nothing like that," George sighed. "I think it is shock more than anything."

"Okay," She paused. "Do you like her?"

"Who?" George asked.

"You know who!" Debbie said. "His daughter, whatever her name is."

"Lucy," George said. "I think she is really nice."

"But?" Debbie said slowly.

George shrugged his shoulders.

"What do you have to lose?" Debbie said. "Ask her out."

"Not appropriate is it?" George said. "And she wouldn't touch me with a barge pole."

"So negative!" Debbie moaned. "Ask her!"

"She won't be interested in me," George said. "Girls never are."

"How many times have you seen her?" Debbie said.

"Yesterday and today," George said. "Coffee and a chat," He said. "Spoken to her more than anyone recently."

"Tell her to come over," Debbie said. "I want to meet her."

"Is that a good idea?" George said. "You meeting her?"

"I'll be on my best behaviour," Debbie teased. "Besides, you can tell her it's just friends meeting for dinner."

"Fine," George said. "Will you shut up if I ask her?"

Debbie nodded.

"Okay find the menu," George got up. "I'll go and get dressed."

WEDNESDAY

George stood at the counter in the café, looking around at the empty tables.

"Hello?" George said. "Anyone here?"

A door opened at the end of the counter and a woman stepped out, holding up her hand as she stifled a yawn. She is tall and athletic, wearing blue jeans and a uniformed top. Her hair is short, black, and spiked heavily with gel.

"Sorry," She apologised. "Didn't hear you, I am going a little deaf."

"Good morning," George said. "Are you new?"

"Yes," She said. "Worked in the town branch but got transferred here."

George nodded.

"What would you like?" She asked.

"Black coffee," George said. "And a couple of plain scones."

"Sure, coming right up," She said. "Go take a seat."

George walked over to the table by the window, sitting down and yawning heavily.

"Any sugar?" She called out.

"What?" George said. "Any what?"

"Sugar or sweeteners?" She said louder.

"No thanks!" George said.

George took out his mobile, checking it before putting it on the table.

The woman walked over, placing the plate in front of him with the scones and carefully putting the coffee down, filled to the top.

"Could I ask you a question?" She said. "It's a little personal."

"Sure," George said.

"My name is Kath by the way," She said down. "If I am annoying just tell me to get lost."

"It's fine," George said. "What is the question."

"How long have you been deaf?" She said looking at him.

"Thirty-three years," George said. "Give or take."

"How did you lose it?" She asked.

"Personal, aren't you?" George said chuckling.

"Sorry," She smiled. "I work with special needs children," She said and quickly added. "Not that it's a special need, there is a little boy that is deaf, so I am trying to understand."

"It's fine," George said. "Genetic degradation."

"Genetic what?" Kath said. "What do you mean?"

"I mean that the hearing genetics my parents gave me," George paused. "Sucked."

"Oh right," She said. "So how did you first know that you were deaf?"

George looked at her.

"What?" She said.

"Really?" George scoffed. "Have a little think about that question?"

Kath looked around the café and then back at George.

"How did I know," George paused. "That I was deaf?"

She nodded.

"The fact I couldn't hear sod all?" George said. "The fact my mother came into my bedroom, yelling at me to wake up and everything was in complete silence and all I could see were her big flapping lips?"

"Oh," She nodded slowly. "Sorry."

"It was pretty instant," George said. "I lost the hearing gradually over a few months, and then both went overnight."

"That sounds scary!" Kath said. "How did your parents handle it?"

"My father cried, and my mother was upset at the prospect of having a disabled child," George said. "I don't waste my time with them anymore."

"Is that when you got the implant?" She said looking at it. "Did it hurt?"

"No, I got that a few years ago," George said. "No, it didn't hurt."

"Wow that is amazing," She said. "Do you sign?"

"Everyone asks that," George sighed. "No, I don't."

"Why not?" She asked.

"I can manage how I am," George said. "Never got round to learning anyhow, parents were against it."

"Why?" Kath said.

"Embarrassed I guess," George shrugged his shoulders, picking up one of the scones and biting into it.

"I have seen some extreme signers," Kath said. "Looks like karate!" She waved her hands around, pretending to do karate chops.

"If you say so," George shook his head.

"Have you got children?" She asked curiously.

"Nope," George said. "Not met anyone yet."

"Are your kids likely to be deaf?" She asked. "Or have issues?"

"There is a fifty percent chance," George said. "Will deal with that if it ever happens."

"What will you do if they are disabled," She said. "I know some people would consider abortion."
George froze, looking at Kath.

"What?" George said.

"Some people do," Kath said. "Abort babies if they have disabilities."

"I know," George sighed. "But deafness isn't noticeable until the baby is born."

"What would you do?" Kath said. "If you had a deaf child?"

"Give her or he the best possible help," George said. "Probably an implant if suitable."

"Right," Kath nodded. "My sister said they couldn't deal with a disabled child."

"Really?" George scoffed. "Then they shouldn't be parents!"

"I know," Kath said nervously.

"I mean no one wants to have a disabled child, but if it happens," George shrugged his shoulders.
"Deal with it, everything happens for a reason."
"How do you wake up?" She said, looking at him curiously.

"What do you mean?" George picked up the coffee, sipping at it. "No different from how you would."

"No," She giggled. "I mean you probably cannot hear an alarm clock," She said. "So, what wakes you up?"

"An alarm clock," George said bluntly.

"But how do you hear it?" She asked. "Just curious."

"It shakes," George said. "I have a pad under the pillow that shakes instead of an audible alarm."

"Oh wow," She smiled. "That sounds interesting.

"Yeah the girls at college thought the same," George said. "I lost three over two years."

"Why?" Kath asked.

"Go figure," George said.

"Oh!" She giggled. "Naughty! Do you snore?" She said.

"No idea," George said. "Cannot hear a thing when I am asleep."

"Sounds great," Kath said. My boyfriend snores so badly."
George nodded.
Steve walked into the café, walking up to the counter and tapping it.

"Morning," He said loudly. "Anyone around?"

"I better go," Kath said and go up, running over to the counter.

Steve looked around.

"Morning George," He said. "Okay to join you?"

George nodded, his mouth full of Scone.

"Want anything?" Steve said. "Or you good?"

"Fine thanks," George mumbled.

George watched as Steve spoke with Kath, his usual flirting making him shake his head in disbelief, after a few minutes, he sat down opposite George.

"God she was a bore," Steve said quietly. "Looks like I saved you!"

"She wanted my life story," George said. "Even tried to get rid of her by talking about alarm clocks from college."

"I remember that story," Steve laughed. "One of the girls offered one back after borrowing it for the evening."

"Yeah," George pulled a face of disgust. "Doubt she even cleaned it!"

"You okay?" Steve said. "Just got in?"

George nodded, wiping his face.

"You?" George said.

"Just finished," Steve sighed, yawning loudly. "Rough night!"

"How bad?" George asked.

"We lost two patients," Steve said. "Both from the road traffic accident."

"Shit," George said. "Sorry."

"Two teens," Steve said. "The driver survived, but he will probably wish he didn't when he wakes up."

"That is sad," George said. "Worse during the lockdown when everyone was taking advantage of empty roads."

Steve nodded.

"You may get a repair request for the ventilator on bed twelve," Steve said sipping at his coffee.

"Oh, you are kidding," George snapped. "I am not going to get a chance today."

"It's okay," Steve said. "Calm down, the sister sorted it. What is up with you?"

"Just not feeling too great," George said. "Head is a mess today."

"Want to talk about it?" Steve said?"

"No," George said and pushed the plate to one side. "I just need a break."

"Fancy meeting me for dinner later today?" Steve said. "I am on shift again."

"I have plans tonight," George said. "Another time."

"Oh, who is she?" Steve said. "You kept that quiet."

"Just someone I have been talking to online for a while," George said and got up from the table, picking up his coffee.

"You off?" Steve said.

George nodded.

"Need to get a few things sorted out before the animals come in," George sniggered. "I am really not in the mood for any crap today."

"Let me know how you get on," Steve said. "I have already paid for your stuff."

George stopped and started shaking his head.

"You have got to stop doing that," George said. "I can pay for you for a change you know."

"You do me favours," Steve said. "I am sure I can return the favour."

"Fine," George muttered. "Speak to you soon."

George walked away, pulling a mask from his pocket, and awkwardly putting it on.

10.15

Kirsty sat down in the chair opposite George, holding a notepad.

"Any luck?" George asked.

"No," Kirsty said. "Ananya isn't answering her calls or voicemail and I have been in touch with the agency who don't to know any more."

"This is crazy!" George said. "What is it with techs from that agency?"

The door opened and Marvin walked in, closing it behind him.

"Curtis just called in," Marvin shook his head. "Car trouble apparently."

"Had it with him," George said. "He wanted today off, and I said no, so he is taking it anyway."

"Not the first time he has done that," Marvin said. "What are you going to do?"

"Going to have to find out what happens," George said. "And then deal with it, I'll have a chat with Harold."

"I can manage things here," Marvin said. "Evan and Simon are on-site, Erica has gone to the community alone."

"Kevin?" George asked. "Is he in?"

"No, he has called in sick again," Marvin said. "Squirting from both ends."

Kirsty groaned.

"Lovely!" George said sarcastically. "I am going to discuss his sickness with HR, this has gone on too long."

"Fifty-two days," Marvin said. "Checked earlier for you."

"What is actually wrong with him?" Kirsty said.

"LBS," George said.

Marvin sniggered.

"What is LBS?" Kirsty asked curiously.

"Lazy bastard syndrome," George scoffed. "He has been with the trust for years, knows all the tricks in the book."

"Not right," Kirsty said.

"I can help out where needed, so don't cancel today," Marvin said. "We will be fine."

"Many repairs today?" George looked at Kirsty.

"Nothing since three yesterday," Kirsty replied. "I have checked the helpdesk and it works fine."

"Great," George said. "Ananya better have a good reason for being late."

"Ananya?" Marvin said. "She was at the front of the hospital just now, smoking and drinking coffee."

"Really?" George said.

Kirsty scoffed.

"She waved at me," Marvin said.

"What is wrong with her!" George looked at his watch. "She is over two hours late."

"What are you going to do?" Marvin said.

"Find out why she is late," He said. "She is taking the piss!"

George looked at Kirsty who had become uncomfortable.

"Sorry," George said. "Didn't mean to swear."

"It's fine," Kirsty laughed. "Three older brothers, nothing I haven't seen or heard!"

"Bet that was fun," Marvin said. "I had two sisters, one passed away last year."

"Sorry to hear that," Kirsty said.

"Ah it's fine," He said. "She had been ill for quite some time, so it was a nice release for her and everyone around her."

"I didn't know that," George said.

"You know me," Marvin smiled. "I rarely talk."

Kirsty shushed Marvin and pointed to the door.

"What?" George said.

The outside door opened and Ananya walked past the door.

"Ananya could I have a word please?" George said.

Ananya came to the door, looking in.

"Can I sort a few things out first?" She asked.

"You can do that after," George said and looked at Kirsty. "Can you stay and document?"
Kirsty nodded.

"If you could get the team on repairs," George said to Marvin. "I'll catch up before I go."
Ananya walked in, sitting in the spare chair next to Kirsty, looking at her coffee. Marvin left, closing the door behind him.
Ananya is wearing blue jeans and a t-shirt, a thick jacket over the top and white trainers.

"You were supposed to be here at eight," George said looking at his watch. "you are well over two hours late."

"Trains were messed up," Ananya said. "Lots of delays."

"You were seen at the front of the hospital, smoking," George said. "Considering you are late, this is also a non-smoking site."

"I needed a coffee, so I took a break," Ananya said. "I am allowed to."

"Yes, normally you are, but you are over two hours late," George sighed. "You ignored all our calls and even the agency cannot get hold of you."

"Why did you call the agency?" She moaned. "You should not have called them."

"Well we had no choice," Kirsty added. "You are over two hours late and you have not called back or anything."

"But you had no right to call the agency," Ananya said in annoyance.

"We pay the agency," George said. "So, we have every right to contact them when someone doesn't show up." George breathed in deeply.

"That makes me look bad," She said. "You could have given me a chance."

"We thought something had happened to you," George said.

"I am fine," Ananya said. "Just a bit hungover.

"Hungover?" George said. "Did you say hungover?" He looked at Kirsty who nodded.

"Only a little," Ananya said. "It is my business what I do outside of work."

"Yes, it is, but if it affects your work here then it becomes our business," George said.

"It isn't affecting my work," Ananya said in annoyance.

"Well, it has for the last two hours!" George scoffed. "You could have called."

"My phone is broken," Ananya said. "I could not call."

"It worked okay when you were having your cigarette break," Marin added.
Ananya shrugged her shoulders.

"Payphone," George said.

"Didn't see one," Ananya said. "Look I don't like all this negativity."

"Well I am sorry, but you walked in without saying a word," George said.

"You did not let me," Ananya said. "You called me in as soon as I walked in and refused to let me settle."

"Also another issue I have," George said. "You left the department yesterday eight times during the day."

"Who has been telling tales on me?" Ananya said. "That is petty."

"Doesn't matter," George said. "Is it true?"

Ananya hesitated.

"I can find out with the swipe system, so no point lying," George said.

"Yes, I did," Ananya said. "I am entitled to regular cigarette breaks."

"Said who?" George asked.

"It is the law," Ananya replied defiantly.

"No," George laughed. "You get half an hour for lunch, we don't cater for your smoking addiction for you to come and leave as you wish."

"It is not an addiction!" Ananya snapped. "It relaxes me."

"Well if you have to disappear every three-quarter of an hour, it's an addiction," George said. "Stop smoking on the site or I will end your contract."

Ananya nodded.

"You didn't hand in any work reports yesterday," George said. "How come?"

"What do you mean?" Ananya asked. "I don't understand."

"You are supposed to fill out the worksheets when you have completed a job," Kirsty said. "I gave you a list."

"I didn't complete any," Ananya said. "I was not aware that I had to."

"How many pumps did you do?" George said.

"Two," Ananya said.

"Only two?" George looked at Marvin. "Okay," George sighed. "You shouldn't be wearing jeans, could you remember that tomorrow."

Ananya nodded.

"Go speak to Marvin please about your workloads," He smiled.

"Okay," Ananya said and got up from the chair, leaving the room.

Kirsty sat back in the chair and exclaimed.

"Wow!" She chuckled. "She has an attitude!"

"She does," George said. "Not convinced she is the right person for here, to be honest."

"I'll check with the stations for you," Kirsty said. "And wanted to mention that I have been offered a permanent position."

"Oh that is great," George said. "Have you accepted?"

"Yes," Kirsty nodded and smiled.

"Sorry you will be leaving us," George said. "Was hoping you would stick around."

"I am," Kirsty sat forward. "The job is here."

"How did that come about?" George said. "It is brilliant news don't get me wrong, but I am not aware of the vacancy."

"Barbara called me late last night and asked me," Kirsty said. "I was due to leave in a couple of weeks to go to a new job, but Barbara offered me a higher banding."

"Well thank god for that!" George sighed in relief. "Brilliant news."

"Thank you," She said. "You are finishing early, aren't you?"

George nodded.

"Gas check at my house and then I am going into town for a date," George said. "Bloody nervous!"

"About the date?" Kirsty asked.

"No, the gas check," George replied with a smile. "Yeah I am, dates rarely work out for me."

"Don't be, they are pretty basic," Kirsty giggled. "Where are you going?"

"Meeting at the Italian place on the high street," George said. "If she doesn't cancel."

"Wow I love that place," Kirsty said. "Hope it goes amazing."

"Thanks," George said looking at his watch. "Going to pop up and see Harold for a few minutes."

"Sure," Kirsty said. "If you need me to do anything let me know."

"Could you get in touch with human resources?" George asked. "I want the years' attendance record for all staff."

"Sure will do that," Kirsty said. "Want a cup of coffee?"

"No thanks," George nodded.

Kirsty left the office followed by George who quickly left the department.

10:42

Harold was seated in the bed, wearing a white t-shirt with a coffee stain down the front. Both his legs in traction, a blue blanket covering his legs and torso. Propped up by pillows, he was snoring lightly. The curtains are pulled around the bed, and an infusion pump attached to him was peeping intermittently, loud and piercing. A multiparameter monitor above his bed, recording his vital signs. George opened the curtain, looking at Harold before walking in and looking at the monitor and pump.

"Let's shut this up shall we," He muted the pump. "Bloody staff probably think everyone is deaf."

George removed his suit jacket, placing it over the chair and rearranging his mask.

Harold groaned, opening his eyes, and looking at George.

"Am I dreaming?" Harold said in confusion.

"Yes," George said bluntly. "Welcome to hell, you old git!"

Harold started laughing.

"Thought that would make you laugh," George said standing at the foot of the bed. "What's with all this?" He pointed to the monitor and pump. "Wasting the trust resources!"

"Nice to see you as well George," Harold said. "How are you?"

"Fine," George said. "You?"

"Not feeling so great," Harold forced a smile. "They put me on a fluid infusion because I was dehydrated."

"Probably that Vodka you had smuggled in," George said and sat down. "Seriously are you okay?"

"I am fine," Harold said shifting in the bed to get comfortable. "What's up?"

George looked up at the false ceiling.

"A false ceiling," He replied bluntly.

"Why are you here?" Harold asked.

"To see you," George said. "Is that okay?"

"What has happened?" Harold said softly. "I can see it in your eyes."

"Curtis and the new agency tech pushing my buttons," George said. "She came in late."

"How late?" Harold said. "You are not being too strict, are you?"

"Just over two hours," George said.

"Damn that is pretty late, " Harold scoffed. "Did she say why?"

"Trains apparently," George said. "Bollocks was it, she is hungover."

"Should have sent her packing," Harold said. "And what has Curtis done now?"

"Phoned in, apparently his car has broken down," George said. "But I refused a day off yesterday for him."

"I did too," Harold sighed. "He is really taking the mickey now. Give him a verbal warning."

"I did that yesterday," George chuckled. "For doing his own thing and taking on work that isn't ours."

"Crazy," Harold said. "If you need more ammo, speak to Barbara."

"She gave Kirsty a full-time position," George said. "Found out earlier."

"She must be good?" Harold said.

"Brilliant," George nodded. "She has the system figured out and has caught up on the reports."

"Fast work," Harold said. "What is this about you having my daughter over for dinner?" Harold said, his tone annoyed.

"My housemate invited her," George said. "Just a friend having dinner with a friend."

"What were your intentions?" Harold said.

"Sweet and sour chicken balls with beef fried rice," George said. "But they messed up and I got pork balls, not so nice."

"Seriously," Harold said. "Thank you for keeping an eye on her."

"She is a nice girl," George said. "How is she?"

"She was okay until she called her brother," Harold shook his head. "The little shit told her not to call him again."

"Wow!" George said. "That sucks."

"He is an idiot," Harold said. "No idea why he turned out that way."

"Sorry to hear that mate," George said. "You okay? Looking paler than usual."

"Really?" Harold said.

"I am smiling under this bloody mask," George chuckled. "You must be bored," George looked around. "Not seen you sit still in one place for so long."

"I really am," Harold said. "Do we still have that spare laptop in the workshop?"

"Yeah," George nodded. "Want me to bring it up?"

"Thanks," Harold said. "That would be good."

"Bring what up?" Lucy said before pulling the curtain open, closing it behind her. "Well?" She looked at George and then at her father.

"Just a bottle of vodka," George said. "He finished the three I left on Monday."

"Really dad," Lucy scoffed. "What have I told you about drinking at this time of the day?" Lucy pulled her mask down and bent down, kissing her dad on the cheek, and then walked round to George, holding her arms open.

"Better hug her before she punches you," Harold said. "She fights dirty."

"I do not dad!" Lucy exclaimed.

"Really," Harold said. "How about the bottle when you were eight?"

Lucy burst out laughing.

"What bottle?" George said. "I need to know that story now!"

"He doesn't know?" Lucy giggled. "Tell him!"

"On Lucy's eighth birthday, my wife got hold of those stunt bottles made of sugar glass," Harold explained. "She smashed one over my head and Lucy here was in hysterics, grabbed a bottle off the table," He paused.

"And it was a real bottle?" George said, stifling giggles.

"It was," Lucy said. "I didn't know did I!?"

"She got me on the forehead because she was so short, opened up a nice gash and sent me crashing to the floor," Harry shook his head. "Imagine the look on the nurses face when I said my eight-year-old bottled me."

"What did the nurse say?" George asked curiously.

"Well I told the nurse I bought her the wrong model kit," Harold smiled. "Crack!"

"I felt so bad," Lucy said. "Mum was laughing so much she wet herself."

"You told me a crazy woman cut your head," George said.

"And?" Harold pointed to Lucy.

The curtains shot open and the ward sister stood looking at all three of them, red in the face and not wearing a mask. Tall and stocky, with short black hair.

"What is this," She snapped. "A bloody party?"

"I have permission to be here," Lucy said, putting her mask on correctly.

"I don't have a choice," Harold pointed to his legs.

"I am here to break him out of this prison," George said and paused, the sisters' eyes piercing him. Lucy giggled.

"No not really," George said. "Someone reported this monitor was faulty," George pointed to the monitor. "See it shows this man has a heart rhythm, so clearly it is buggered beyond economical repair."

"You are from Technical services?" She asked.

"Yes," George said. "Why?"

"Could you have a look at our bladder scanner?" She asked. "It isn't scanning."

"Already have," George said. "Saw it when I walked in."

"Have you been able to work out why it doesn't scan?" She asked. "We need it urgently."

Harold covered his mouth, trying not to laugh.

"It has what we called DBABN," He spelt out the words. "That is the official description."

"Which is what?" The sister asked.

Harold started sniggering.

"Destroyed by a bloody nurse," George snapped. "It has been repaired several times this year because people keep dropping the probe, considering the cost of repairs you would be better off buying a new one, preferably made of flipping titanium!"

"They would still break it," Harold sniggered.

"Be quiet dad," Lucy said, putting her finger to her lips.

"I'll get Maud to give you a bed bath," The sister warned. "Behave."

She then looked at George.

"Has it been reported?" George asked.

"Yes," The sister said. "I have done it myself and put the printout on the shelf."

"I'll take it down with me and ask one of the guys to have a look," George said. "How's that?"

"Thank you," The sister said, drawing the curtains as she left.

Lucy started laughing.

"That is the one that scares your dad," George said. "Right Harold?"

"Too right," Harold shivered. "Reminds me of the mother in law!"

Lucy burst into hysterics.

"She agrees!" He pointed to her. "Scared you didn't she Lucy!?"

Lucy nodded.

"Why?" George asked.

"She sat on Lucy's hand, broke two fingers!" Harold said. "Mental she was."

"She wasn't," Lucy pulled her mask down, "She was amazing, and you will agree dad."

Harold nodded.

"Well I am going to love you and leave you," George said. "I need to get home for a gas check and then I am heading into town."

"Date?" Lucy said. "Debbie mentioned a date."

"Yeah," George said. "Someone I have chatted to for a while, but not expecting much."

"Enjoy the evening regardless," Harold said. "What time is it?"

"Six or so," George said and looked at Lucy. "I better make a move, need to go beat some staff to death."

Lucy laughed and nodded.

"Talk later yeah?" George said nervously. "I'll get Marvin to bring the laptop for you," He looked at Harold. "See you both soon."

George left in a hurry, struggling to find the break in the curtain before leaving, waving as he closed it.

11:20

George leant over the desk, looking through the drawer and muttering to himself. Turning around when he heard Marvin knock on the door frame.

"Just dropped the laptop off to Harold," He said. "What you looking for?"

"Implant battery is about to go," George said. "Forgotten to bring some and I am sure I put a spare somewhere."

"Small little black one?" Marvin asked.

"Yes," George said. "Why?"

Marvin removed the battery from his top pocket.

"Found this on the counter earlier," He held it out. "Kirsty thought it may be for your implant."

"That one is dead," George said, holding out his hand as Marvin threw it. "I have one here somewhere."

Marvin nodded and walked away.

"Bloody hell," George muttered and took his implant off, placing it on the table as he rummaged through the drawer.

"George?" Ananya said, standing in the doorway. "Could I ask for a favour?"

George did not respond.

"Hello?" Ananya said louder. "Can I have a word?"

George continued to look through the drawer.

"Rude?!" Ananya said in annoyance and walked up behind George and flicking his ear.

"What the hell!?" George turned around and snapped. "What is wrong with you?"

He picked up the implant, putting it on.

"What?" Ananya said.

"Did you just flick my ear?" George asked. "Really?!"

Ananya nodded.

"Why?!" George demanded. "Why would you do that?"

"I have been talking to you, but you were ignoring me!" She said. "Why did you ignore me?"

"You know I am deaf," George said. "Why didn't you just walk over and tap me on the shoulder?"

"I had to in the end," She sighed frustratedly.

"No," George corrected her. "You flicked my ear!" George pointed to his ear. "This is my shoulder!" George pointed to his shoulder. "Can you tell the difference, or would you like a picture book?"

"Same difference," She shrugged her shoulders.

"No, it isn't!" George scoffed. "It is an assault."

She laughed.

"What is so funny?" George wanted to know. "I don't remember saying anything funny!"

"It is not assault," She said. "I was only getting your attention, I do it to my brother all the time."

"Well, I am not your brother," George grit his teeth. "What gave you the right to flick me!?"

111

"It is no big deal," She muttered. "You are going so over the top."

"So," George said. "If I could not get hold of your attention, came up behind you and punched you in the head. That would be okay?"

She shook her head and laughed.

"That is just mean," She said. "Why are you being horrible to me?" She moaned.

"I cannot be bothered," I said. "I want you gone."

"What?" Ananya looked at George in confusion. "Gone from the office?"

"No," George said. "Gone from this site, you are fired, I don't want you here anymore."

She scoffed, shaking he head in disbelief.

"You cannot fire me," She complained.

"Funny," George said. "I just did."

"You can't," Ananya said. "You are not a real manager."

"What is that supposed to mean," George leaned against the table with his arms crossed.

"Well," She said. "You don't have a degree and you are deaf."

"Yeah," George nodded. "So what?"

Ananya laughed, shaking her head, and holding up both hands.

"You cannot fire me," She said confidently. "I will take you to a tribunal."

"Fine by me," George said. "Are you refusing to leave?"

She nodded.

George got up and walked to the door and looked at Kirsty who was looking up.

"Did you get all that?" He asked.

"Yes," Kirsty Said. "Would you like me to call security?"

Ananya stepped out from the office.

"Why are you calling security?" She demanded. "Why?!"

Kirsty stood up.

"One," She held up a finger. "You assaulted George, that is an instant dismissal," She held up another finger. "You point-blank discriminated against him."

"He assaulted me!" She said. "When I was in the office."

George sighed and laughed.

"There is a camera in the office," George said. "It was mounted after we had another idiot like yourself working here."

"Like me?" She said. "What do you mean by that?"

"Crying assault because you messed up," George said. "Take it further," He said softly. "And I will have a field day making sure you never work in a hospital or any other medical business again."

112

"Why are you being like this?" Ananya said. "I like it here."

"Calling security now," Kirsty said picking up the phone and dialling the number.

"Please give me a chance," Ananya begged. "The agency will fire me, and my parents will kill me, it will be a very big disrespect to them."

"I don't care," George said. "You were more than happy to throw me to the wolves, so please, get your stuff and leave."

"What do you mean leave?" She said, tears in her eyes.

"I mean get lost," George said.

Ananya started crying, her hand covering her mouth.

"Please!" She cried. "Please give me a chance!"

"Call security if she is still here in five minutes," George said. "I have a meeting online with Barbara."

"Will do," Kirsty said.

Ananya stormed off, her crying becoming louder as she walked into the workshop.

George closed the door, leaning against it and then reaching into his back pocket and pulling out a battery.

"Well," He scoffed. "Typical."

Someone knocked on the door.

"Not interested Ananya," George said. "Walk away."

The door opened and Simon looked in.

"I know you have a meeting shortly," Simon said. "Quick chat?"

"Come in," George said and sat down.

Simon is a short and overweight man in his thirties, shaved head, and a rough beard. Wearing black combat trousers and a blue t-shirt that barely fit him, the bottom of his stomach visible.

"You need a bigger t-shirt," George said. "Can you try and be more presentable?"

"I have shirts," Simon said.

"Work shirts?" George asked.

"Yeah," Simon nodded.

"So why don't you wear them?" George scoffed.

"They don't fit," He laughed. "Gotten a little fat."

"A little?" George said. "If you say so," He shook his head. "Can you try and find something a little bigger, so I don't get complaints."

"Who complained," Simon asked.

"Kim," George said. "Our community contact."

"You mean the whale," Simon laughed.

"Are you fat-shaming someone?" George said. "You are hardly in a position to call a fat person a whale, are you?"

"Well she is a woman," Simon said. "It's different."

"No, it isn't," George scoffed. "You look like a whale's obese mother in law!"

Simon nodded and sat down.

"Just sort it out please," George said. "If I hear you out of breath, you are going to Occupation health again."

"Okay, okay chill out," Simon said. "Do you ever get out the right side of your bed?"

"Do you ever stop raiding the fridge?" George replied. "What did you want?"

"If it is okay with you," Simon said. Erica and I are going to do the offsite service tomorrow instead of Friday, it's a half-day job."

"Do the end-users know?" George asked. "They have a parking space reserved and only have a certain time."

"Yes," Simon nodded. "All sorted out."

"Then yes that is fine," George said. "Have you sorted out the new delivery?"

Simon looked at him confused.

"The syringe pumps?" George said. "For cancer services?"

"Oh shit!" Simon's hand went to his face. "I thought you said the syringe drivers!"

"No, I clearly said the syringe pumps," George scoffed. "And you even wrote it down."

"I've done all eight of the syringe drivers," Simon said. "Will they have those instead?"

"No," George groaned. "They won't."

"I'll sort them out another day," Simon said. "Friday."

"That is no good!" George snapped. "I promised the end-user they would be ready by the end of the day!"

"Sorry," Simon said. "I have been preoccupied with other things."

"What the two full English breakfasts?" George scoffed. "You really should slow down on those."

"Huh?" Simon said.

"Occupational Health stated you are extremely obese," George said. "And that you at risk of heart failure."

"Yeah," Simon Said. "So?"

"Well as a first aider," George sighed. "I'd rather not have to get down on the floor and ruin my trousers just to revive you."

Simon laughed and then looked at George, realising he wasn't joking."

"Get those pumps sorted and ask Marvin to drop them off," George said. "Please."

"I can drop them off," Simon said standing up.

"Rather you didn't," George said. "And make sure you wear a mask if you leave the workshop."

"I do," Simon said.

"You didn't this morning," George corrected him.

"Oh, there was no one about," Simon said. "So, it didn't matter."

"I don't give a crap what you think," George said. "Wear a mask or face disciplinary."

"What has put you in a mood," Simon said.

"The brain-dead morons I have in here," George snapped. "Now go."

14:10

George closed the front door, checking that it was closed and turned around, jumping in fright.

"Damn Edith scared the life out of me!" George chuckled. "Are you okay?"

Edith stood in front of George, resting on a walking stick. Thin, short, and hunched over with silver hair and thick glasses. She is wearing a thick red overcoat and a black scarf.

"Good afternoon!" She said loudly. "Are you not working today?" She looked at her watch, struggling to see the face.

"Afternoon Edith," George said. "No, I have the afternoon off."

"Why?" She demanded.

"Had a gas check," George said. "You must have seen the man leave? After all your face is attached to the window."

"What?" She snapped shaking her head.

"Nothing Edith," George shook his head. "I am popping to the shop to get some stamps," He held up a couple of letters.

"So?" She said. "What do you want a medal?"

"Do you need anything?" George asked.

"No," She said. "I need you to stop letting your cat into my garden!" She said angrily. "It keeps shitting all over my patio and staining it!"

George sniggered at her outburst.

"It what?" George said.

"Shitting!" She snapped. "That fat ginger thing squats on my patio and leaves a whip of shit!"

George laughed.

"I don't have a cat," George said. "Told you before, I have no pets."

"Are you sure?" She asked.

"Positive," George said.

"What about the hussy?" Edith said.

"What?" George asked, not understanding her.

"Hussy!" Edith said loudly. "That girl that lives with you that opens her legs more times than the local corner shop opens its doors!" She growled. "Does she have a cat?"

"No," George said. "The hussy doesn't have a cat."

"How do you know?" She asked.

"Because I live here," George said. "I would know if there was a cat in my house."

"Are you sure?" She asked. "Seems strange," She said. "Sharing a house with a woman you are not married to."

"Times are different," George said. "She just rents a room."

"No cats?" She demanded.

"I am allergic," George said. "So yes, I am sure that there are no cats in the house."

"What a wuss you are!" She laughed. "Allergic to cats, we had nothing like that in our day."

"Good for you," George nodded. "Do you want anything from the shop while I am there Ethel?" George asked.

"No," Ethel said. "I can manage myself thank you very much."

"Glad to hear it," George said.

"What is that in your ear?" She asked. "It looks silly!"

"It's an implant," George sighed. "Told you all about it before."

"What's it for, " Ethel said.

"Picking up annoying sounds," George said.

"Really," Ethel looked at him curiously. "Annoying sounds like what?"

"Like your bloody voice for one," George mumbled. "Do you want anything from the shop or not?"

"Milk," Ethel said. "If it is not too much bother?"

"No bother at all," George said. "Mind the raised paving stone, don't want you falling again," He pointed to the raised paving stone on the drive. "Too busy to have to deal with you breaking a hip on my drive again."

George walked past Ethel and made his way up the hill, minutes passed, and he groaned when he saw the group coming towards him.

The group are of four adults and two children dressed in smart suits, carrying bibles.

"Great," George said looking around. "The Bible-bashing brigade."

George crossed the street to give them more room, smiling and nodding when they noticed him. A young man and woman also crossed, heading towards George.

"Bollocks," George mumbled. "Sod my luck."

They are both tall and slim. The woman with short blonde hair and the man, black hair and clean-shaven.

"Good morning," George said politely as they approached him.

"Good morning to young man," They responded. "Isn't it a lovely day?"

George looked up at the grey skies.

"I guess," George said.

"May we have a minute of your time?" The woman said as they both blocked his path, not giving George anywhere to go.

"I am in a rush," George lied, trying to think of excuses. "I am late to meeting a friend at the bus stop."

"The Lord will watch over them," The man said. "While we watch over you for a moment."

"Okay," George sighed. "I am not religious, nor am I interested." He said politely.

"The Lord loves you, regardless of your following or sins." The woman said.

"My what?" George asked, not sure if he had heard correctly.

"Sins," The man said. "Those who lose faith in the lord are sinners in his eyes."

"Okay," George said. "On that note, I am off."

George started to walk away, and the woman called out to him.

"What are those in your ears?" She asked curiously. "Are they media devices?"

"Hearing aids," George responded. "I am profoundly deaf."

She slowly walked over to George and placed her hand on his shoulder.

"Have faith in the Lord Jesus Christ!" She said loudly. "He will heal you and purge you of your sins if you worship him and accept him into your life!" She moved her hand to his forehead and he backed away.

"Could you not do that please," George said. "Don't touch me like that!"

She ignored him and raised her hand towards my head.

"Excuse me!" George snapped. "Social distancing is a thing you know, and I recommend that you practice it."

"The pandemic is a challenge sent by God," She said. "Only those who are worthy and strong will survive his wrath!"

"Okay," George mumbled. "Best of luck with that, I am off."

"The Lord took your ability to hear for a reason," The woman said. "He is preparing you for his tasks."

"No," George sighed and took a long deep breath. "I lost my hearing due to faulty genetics on both my parents' side."

"It was an act of God," The man said.

"If that is the case, he or she is an arsehole!" George said. "If he or she actually existed!"

"That is disrespectful to the lord," The woman said. "You must respect him."

"He took my hearing without consent," George sniggered. "So, he is a thief."

They both looked at George in shock.

"Thou shall not steal and all that bollocks," George shrugged his should.

"That is blasphemous!" The man said. "You must not speak in that way!"

"Look," George said. "I don't really care, and I am late getting to the bus stop."

"But all we want is your time," The woman said. "Mankind is dying and only the faithful will survive."

"Look!" George snapped. "My mate has a virgin and a goat with him," George said keeping a straight face. "I have plans for the clear night when the moon rises, so, please, let me get on," George smiled. "The goat needs feeding, and the virgin wants a bath."

"You can joke, but you know we are correct in what we say!" The man said, the annoyance on his face.

"Are you really?" George shook his head.

"Yes," The woman said. "God loves his children."

"Didn't seem to give much of a toss when his son was nailed to a cross did, he?" George said. "What kind of a shitty father would stand by and watch that."

"You should be ashamed!" The woman said.

"I don't care what you think," George said. "No matter how many times I tell you and your cult that I am not interested, you keep coming back for more. Please take a hint when someone says they are not interested and stop harassing them!"

"We are not harming you!" The woman said. "We are educating you."

"Try educating your legs and get lost!" George said with a smile.

George walked away, leaving them standing in the middle of the path, watching as he walked away.

George leaned against the wall, looking at his watch. The high street is noisy, various people in masks walking up and down the road, cars roaring past. The noise was overpowering and beginning to annoy him. He is wearing blue jeans and a grey shirt, a thick black coat that came down to his knees.

"Where are you?" He took his mobile out from his inside pocket, checking it.
He looked into the restaurant, someone catching his eye,

"You are kidding me!" He scoffed, watching as the person left their table and walked towards the door, opening it.
A tall slim woman, with long brown hair, in heels and a tight dress walked out, pulling her coat on. Kevin followed, wearing a black suit that was tight over his heavy frame, the shirt buttons getting ready to pop off at any moments. His dark hair is cut short and he has a well-trimmed goatee.

"You look well considering you have been sick for three days," George said. "Knew you were pulling a fast one."
Kevin turned around, embarrassed.

"Oh hey," he said looking around. "I am feeling a lot better now."

"Thought you were too sick to come into work?" George said. "We have been manic."

"I was sick," Kevin said, looking at the woman he is with nervously. "I am fine now."

"Right," George said looking at the woman.

"This is Lindsey," Kevin pointed to her. "This is my colleague, doesn't like me very much," Kevin laughed sarcastically. "He would probably fire me if he was a manager, but that will never happen," Kevin laughed, looked at George and then back at Lindsey. "He is deaf too."

"Head of tech services as well," George said. "So, I probably could get you fired."
Kevin looked at him, confusion on his face.

"What?" Kevin said. "What do you mean?"

"Harold had an accident, so Barbara has made me the interim manager," George smiled. "For a while."

"I am sick," Kevin said. "Honestly."

"Sickness and diarrhoea tend to not go away so suddenly," George said.
Lindsey cringed in disgust, stepping backwards from Kevin.

"I know how my body works," Kevin said. "Let's keep this out of work, it is my personal time and I do what I want."

"Then you have nothing to worry about," George said. "See you tomorrow, we will discuss your sickness."

"Are you spying on me?" Kevin scoffed. "I could complain."

"No," George said. "I am eating out at a restaurant." He pointed to the sign. "I hope you didn't have anything contagious."

"I just needed time away," Kevin said. "It's been stressful for me lately."

George nodded.

"We can talk tomorrow okay?" Kevin said. "Let us not make any bad decisions."

"Fine," George said. "See you tomorrow."

Kevin nodded and walked away.

"Dickhead!" George said under his breath. "You are gone by the end of the week."

George sighed and took his mobile from his pocket and then looked up when a woman approached him.

"Hey Gail," George said, smiling.

Gail was the same height as George, wearing black leggings and a white blouse, holding her jacket in her arm and a bag in the other. She has long blonde hair and glasses with a red frame. Her face is red from the cold and her bare arms pale.

"Aren't you cold?" George asked.

Gail nodded.

"Hi," She said. "How are you?" "So good to finally meet you."

"And you," George said. "You look amazing!"

"Aww thanks," she blushed. "You do too."

"Shall we?" George said pointing to the restaurant. "You need to warm up."

She nodded and they made their way into the restaurant, stopping by the counter, waiting to be seated. The waitress did not even look up from the computer. Short and skinny, she is wearing a uniform, a cap covering her hair.

"Yeah?" She said.

"Hi," George said. "I have a table booked for two."

"Name?" She said bluntly.

"George," George said.

"Which menu did you want?" She mumbled.

"Could you repeat that please?" George said. "I didn't hear what you said."

"What menu," She said chewing gum. "Did you want?"

"Sorry I didn't catch that," George said, slightly embarrassed.

"Why not," She snapped. "What are you having trouble with."

"I am profoundly deaf," George replied. "That is the trouble I am having."

Gail looked at George and then at the girl.

"Normal menus please," she said. "Is that okay?" She looked at him.

"That is fine," George said nervously.

They followed the waitress to a table by the window and sat down, George smiled at Gail and they both looked through the menu. Out of the eight distanced tables, only three are in use. A young couple on one, and on the table behind where George and Gail are sat, is a middle-aged couple.

"What do you fancy?" He asked her.

She looked at her menu and shrugged her shoulders, avoiding eye contact.

"What do you want to drink?" George asked her.

Gail did not respond, she continued to look in the menu, becoming uncomfortable.

"What is it?" George asked. "You have suddenly gone all cold on me."

She sighed.

"Talk to me," George said. "What is it?"

"So," Gail said. "You are deaf?"

"Yes," George nodded. "I am sure that is obvious now?"

"Why didn't you tell me?" She asked, looking at George as if he had done something wrong.

"It never came up," George replied. "Didn't think it would be a problem."

"Well, it would have been nice to know!" She said.

"Would you have changed your mind?" George asked.

She looked at George awkwardly.

"Is that a yes?" George said.

"Well I would have liked to have known you were disabled," She said. "I mean I need to think about the future."

"How do you mean?" George asked.

"Well," She took a deep breath. "I don't want kids with special needs."

George scoffed and laughed.

"It isn't a special need!" George exclaimed. "Jeez!"

"And then I have to take my own health into account," She said. "It is selfish what you did."

"Why?" George asked.

"Well imagine if we ended up having sex," She said. "I could have caught it."

A man on the desk behind her looked around and shook his head. George looked at her with his mouth open, speechless.

"Caught what?" He said.

"The deafness," She whispered.

121

George burst out laughing.

"Don't laugh at me!" She said. "That is hurtful." She looked around nervously.

"I am sorry," George shook his head and noticed people were looking. "You actually think that a hearing disability," I paused. "Is sexually transmitted?!"

She nodded.

"Oh my god," George laughed. "You are kidding?"

The guy on the table looked at me and indicated she was crazy.

"I am going to the toilet," She said and stood up, heading towards the back of the restaurant and George watched as she walked off.

The man on the table waved at George to get his attention. Balding with a trimmed beard, he is wearing black trousers and a white shirt. His wife opposite him in a red dress, texting on her phone.

"I don't think she is all up there mate," He said pointing to his head. "Run away now!" He grinned.

"She seemed okay when we chatted online," George shook his head. "Never thought my special needs would freak her out," He said sarcastically.

"Fucking mental case mate," The man said, flinching when his wife slapped his hand. "Speaking of crazy!" He shook his head and turned around.

George took his mobile from his pocket, playing around with it until the same waitress came over that had brought them to their table.

"Hello," She said nervously. "I am sorry, but I just saw your date leave."

George scoffed.

"Really?" He laughed. "Well, that is no surprise."

"What did you say to her?" She asked. "What scared her off?"

"What makes you think it was me?" George said. "So, what if I offered her a spot under the patio," George stood up. "Not like it was going to be right away was it?"

"Okay," The waitress said, confused.

"I am kidding," George sighed. "She didn't like the fact I am deaf," George shrugged his shoulders.

"Are you going to eat?" She asked.

"Not much point now is there?" George said. "Cheaper just to eat at home."

"I will get your bill," The waitress said and turned.

"Bill?" George said. "What bill, are you charging for the air now?"

"Did you have anything to drink?" The waitress said, looking at the table.

"No," George scoffed. "No one came to the table in the time she freaked out and did a runner."

"Okay," The waitress said. "You may leave."

"Well thank you," George said. "Maybe considering some customer services, if I want an attitude,

I'll go to a doctors surgery and speak to a receptionist."

George left the restaurant, giving the waitress a sarcastic thumbs-up as he walked past the window, groaning when it began to rain.

19:05

George stood in the kitchen, wearing grey jogging bottoms and a white t-shirt.

"Stir fry!" He said to himself, laying six sausages on a wooden chopping board and opening the drawer. "Where is it?"

Debbie came into the kitchen, wearing a dress with a leather coat and a small red bag.

George looked up.

"Damn," He said. "Hot date?"

"No," She smiled. "Meeting with friends, do you have a spare mask?"

"Clean ones by the phone in the hall," George said. "Help yourself," He moved the cutlery around.

"Have you seen my knife?" George asked. "The sharp one in its holder?"

"I broke it accidentally," Debbie said. "I bought you a brand new one, it's in the other drawer."

"Oh, you didn't have to do that," George said. "But thanks."

He opened the drawer, pulling the knife out.

"Have a great time," George said.

Debbie hugged him.

"What?" He said nervously. "What are you doing?"

Debbie stepped back.

"Sorry your date didn't go well," Debbie said. "You should give Lucy a call, cook her dinner."

"She is out," George said. "Visiting family."

"What are you cooking?" She looked at the sausages on the cutting board.

"Fish and chips," George said bluntly.

"Love you too," Debbie said and walked away. "I'll be back late."

George nodded as she walked away, removing the knife from the packaging he ran it under a tap, cleaning it.

"Hungry," George said to himself. "Was looking forward to a Polo Pesto," He muttered. "Selfish bitch!"

His phone beeped from the table and he picked it up, smiling. Positioning it on the worktop so he could look down at it, he opened up the video chat.

Lucy came up on the screen.

"Hey," She said looking. "Did you forget to go on the date?"

"No," George sighed. "She walked."

"She what?" Lucy said. "What is that humming noise?"

"That's the fridge," George said. "I'll move you when I have finished chopping my sausage."
George grinned.

"Filthy sod!" Lucy exclaimed. "What happened?"

"I didn't tell her I was deaf," George said.

"Why not," Lucy said. "Does it embarrass you?"

"No, nothing like that," George said. "If I tell girls, they freak, so better for them to see how I
actually am."

"So, what happened?" Lucy said. "Will you see her again?"

"No," George chuckled. "She took it badly and walked."

"No way?!" Lucy said. "That is mental!"

George nodded, looking down at the sausages and lining them up, slicing them.

"I know," George said.

"Why was she upset?" Lucy asked.

"Said that I had no right and that I could have infected her," George shook his head. "With my
deafness virus!"

"She said what?!" Lucy exclaimed. "You are kidding."

George breathed out heavily and nodded.

"Oh my god," Lucy snapped. "If I had been there, I would have beaten her arse out the door."

"She was a little upset," George hissed and groaned, holding his hand.

"George?" Lucy said. "What happened?"

"Shit!" George yelled out. "Bollocks!" He snapped and groaned.

"You are scaring me, George," Lucy said. "What happened?"

George moved into the display, holding his hand, blood running down his hand.

"Just a little cut," George said and looked at his hand. "Cut my finger," He laughed nervously. "I'll
just find a plaster and call you back shortly okay?"

"How bad is it," Lucy flinched. "Do you want me to come over?"

"No stay at your relatives," George said. "I'll sort it out and call you back later okay?"

George picked up a towel, wrapping it around his hand.

"Are you sure?" She said. "I don't mind."

"It's fine," George said. "But thanks, appreciate it, speak later."

George hung up the phone and put it into his pocket.

"Bollocks," he said looking down at the blood on the floor. "It can wait!"

George opened the drawer, taking out a reel of sticky tape and wrapping it tightly around his hand. Putting his mobile into his pocket, he held his hand up and hurriedly left the kitchen.

20:15

The walk-in centre in accident and emergency was packed, with various people in masks. George got to the booking in counter at the entrance doors, recognising the security guard.

"Hey Mark," George said. "Could I get a mask?"

Mark picked up a mask and handed it to George, who awkwardly put it on.

"You okay?" Mark said looking down at George's hand. "What happened to you?"

"Cut myself shaving," George said. "Bloody sore."

"Damn," Mark said. "I'll speak to triage, let them know you work here."

"No it's fine," George said.

"It's not an issue," Mark said. "I'll work my magic."

"You don't have to," George said. "But thanks."

"That guy from Monday," Mark said. "The drunk giving you grief."

"What about him?" George said.

"He died," Mark said. "That evening."

"Jesus Christ," George exclaimed. "Just how bad is your coffee?"

Mark laughed.

"No, he fell and cracked his head," Mark said. "Leaving the pub round the corner."

"Shit, that is pretty sad," George said. "But he made his choices."

"Yeah," Mark sighed. "Stay there a moment."

George stood by the counter, looking around at the various people, groaning when he saw someone throwing up with their mask still on, the brown liquid coming out at every angle, running down the window he leaned against.

"That is wrong!" George cringed. "Bloody drunk!"

Mark came back a few moments later and pointed to the reception desk.

"Go book in," He said. "They will then sort you."

"Thanks, Mark," George said. "Appreciate it."

George walked to the reception desk, pausing when he felt dizzy.

"Woah," He said to himself. "Pull yourself together."

He got to the counter, leaning against it.

"How can I help you?" The receptionist said, looking up with a smile from behind the plastic screen.

"Hi Sandy," George said. "How are you?"

"I didn't recognise you in regular clothes!" Sandy gasped. "Not seen you without your shirt and tie!" She shook her head. "What happened to you? Better get you booked in."

"Had a silly accident with a knife," George held up his hand, the tea towel soaking up the blood.

"Is everything intact?" She asked.

"Yes," George said. "I can still move it, but it has cut right down to the bone."

"Bet that is sore!" She hissed. "As you can see, there is a bit of a wait."

"No problems," George said. "I have no plans for the evening!" He laughed.

"Take a seat, someone will be out shortly to triage," She said.

"Oh," George added. "Could you make a note that I am profoundly deaf and may not hear them." She nodded.

"Just tell them to look out for the guy in a white t-shirt covered in bloodstains," George laughed. "Almost like I just murdered a bunch of people."

"Okay I will let the nurse know," She said.

George sat down on an empty row of chairs, out of the way and overlooking the waiting room. Opposite was an elderly lady in a nightdress, sat in a wheelchair with a blanket covering her legs.

"Hello!" She said. "Are you my grandson?"

"No," George said. "Sorry."

"Are you positive?" She asked.

"Yes," George said. "Very positive."

"You poor boy," She noticed his hand. "What happened?"

"My daughters' guinea pig," George held up the hand with the bloodied towel wrapped around it. "The little sod got rabies off the neighbour's dog, and it bit my bloody finger off!"

The old lady gasped and covered her mouth, shock on her face.

"Oh my god, she said. "Did the dog bite it?"

"No," George said chuckling. "The dog bit my daughter, and then she bit the guinea pig," George giggled. "Then he bit me, serves my right for taking his chicken leg away."

A nurse walked over, unlocking the brakes to the wheelchair.

"He has rabies!" She said to the nurse who looked at her and then looked at George who shrugged his shoulders.

"Confused," He nodded. "Poor soul."

A half-hour passed and George yawned, looking around just as a nurse came towards him.

"Hi," She signed. "Is your name George?" She said, spelling out his name.

"Yes," George replied. "I don't sign, but lipreading is good."

"Brilliant," She said. "Sorry if I have offended you."

"You haven't," George said and followed her into the side room.

George sat down and started to feel dizzy and nauseous, breathing deeply.

"I just need to take your temperature," She said. "Is that okay?"

"Fine," George said. "Use the left ear."

The nurse took his temperature, looking at the thermometer when it beeped and nodded.

"All good," She said. "No symptoms or anything?"

George shook his head.

"So, what have you done?" She said looking at his hand.

George removed the tape and towel, revealing a deep cut at the bottom of his index finger, swollen and bloody.

"Accident with a new knife," George said and shivered. "Wasn't watching what I was cutting."

"Oh, dear that looks sore," She inspected his hand. "What were you cutting?"

"Sausages," George said. "Mistook a finger for a sausage."

"Okay," She held his hand. "Can you feel this?" She ran her finger up and down his finger.

"Yes," George said. "It is throbbing like hell."

"How do you feel?" She asked.

"Tired and sick," George said. "I don't have an issue with blood or anything," George breathed in deeply. "Just not slept or eaten properly for a few days."

"Okay," She said. "I am going to put some gauze and bandage over this and send you out for a while, sorry but it may be some time,"

"I understand," George said looking at the waiting room. "Manic tonight huh?"

"It is," She sighed. "Most of the idiots out there have scratches or colds."

She bandaged up George's hand and held up the towel. "Do you want this back?" She asked with a grin.

George shook his head.

"Get a cup of tea with some sugar and have something to eat if you can," She said. "We will call you in once the consultant is free."

"Thank you," George said and got up. "Could you make sure they are aware I am deaf?"

"It is on your notes," She smiled. "Someone will come and get you."

"Thanks," George said and returned to the waiting room, stopping at the vending machine for a chocolate bar and bottle of water.

Sitting down in the same spot, someone caught his eye and he chuckled to himself, getting up and walking over to the girl sitting in a wheelchair in the corner.

"Hello Gail," George said. "What happened to you?"

Gail looked up, her make-up smeared and her hair messy, dirt down the front of her top.

"I fell over in the alley behind the restaurant," Gail said. "When I left."

"When you made a quick getaway?" George said. "Oh, dear that isn't good."

"I am waiting for an x-ray," She said, snivelling. "I wish today never happened."

"Me too," George said. "If you weren't so judgemental and thick, you wouldn't be sitting here now."

"What?" She was lost for words.

"You ran away," George raised his voice slightly just so people sitting near her could hear.

"I was embarrassed," She said.

"Well I am sorry that my hearing disability embarrassed you," He said. "And that I could have infected you with my deafness," he said bluntly. "How horrible of me."

George walked away, sitting at the far end of the waiting room, watching as Gail covered her face, embarrassed.

"What happened to you then?" Mark said, sitting on the end of the bench.

"What?" George said, not understanding him.

Mark pulled the mask down under his chin.

"What happened to you?" He looked at Gail across the waiting room. "Do you know her?"

"Accident with a knife," George said. "Cut it down to the bone," He looked at Gail and then at Mark. "That was the girl I met up with today, she ran out of me."

"Really?" Mark laughed.

"Yeah, slipped in the alleyway behind the restaurant," He shook his head. "Thought my deafness was contagious."

"You are kidding?" Mark scoffed. "My other half knows her," Mark waved at her. "She is as thick as anything."

"Yeah," George nodded. "I found out the hard way."

"You are going to be in for a wait," Mark said. "Busy tonight, every twat for miles has come in."

"Yes, the nurse warned me," George yawned. "I am so tired."

"You do look like shit," Mark grinned. "Not your day huh?"

"No," George said. "Never mind."

"Well take care, give me a shout if you need anything," Mark slapped George on the back firmly. "Stay safe."

George laid back in the chair, breathing deeply as his stomach started to rumble.

"Why?" He said to himself. "Why did you go and cut your bloody finger?"

He jumped when his mobile buzzed in his pocket, reaching over awkwardly with his good hand, dropping it to the floor.

"Crap," He leaned down, picking it up and then pausing, looking down at the floor. "Stood up too soon there, you dickhead?" He whispered to himself. "Slow down!"

Closing his eyes and breathing deeply, he then unlocked his phone and read a message.

"Hey Lucy, cannot do a video call," He wrote. "I am at the hospital, the cut is pretty bad, not feeling so great," George sent the message and then sat up slowly, sitting back and crossing his legs, resting his hand against his stomach.

"Better text Debbie and warn her," George said and turned on the screen. "Oh crap!" He groaned, bloody battery!" He sighed in frustration and put the phone into his pocket.

THURSDAY

George looked around the waiting room, feeling tired and sick, leaning forward, and breathing deeply, hot, and uncomfortable. He looked down and noticed his hand had started bleeding again, soaking through the bandage, and dripping to the floor.

"Shit," he mumbled and stood up, holding up his hand.

He looked at the reception desk in which is empty, slowly making his way towards it.

"Excuse me," He said to the receptionist. "This is bleeding quite a bit," He held up the hand.

Less than a couple of feet away, George stopped. The room began to spin, and his eyes rolled back. He reached out as he fell forward, catching his head on the screen, sliding down and headbutting the counter, his glasses flipping off into parts as he hit the floor and passed out.

George moaned when the lights blinded him, his hand when to his eyes, covering them. He briefly glanced around, in a bay with the curtains pulled. Monitor leads attached to his chest and an oxygen mask on his face.

"Hello," The nurse said, trying to put George's implant on the side of his head and he clumsily took it from her, removing the mask and putting the implant on his ear and attaching the headpiece to the side of his head. It is the same nurse from the triage room.

"I feel like crap!" He groaned. "Where are my glasses?"

The nurse handed him the gasses, broken in the middle, but secured with tape.

"They broke," She said. "Mark fixed them the best he could."

George took them off her and put them on, bending them slightly so they would fit.

"What happened?" The nurse asked. "We had to cut your t-shirt off."

"I stood up because my hand was bleeding," George said looking at his hand in which another nurse was cleaning. "I came over sick and dizzy and the room went into spin mode."

"Are you George Shades?" She asked holding a sheet of paper.

George nodded, breathing out slowly, his face, neck and chest soaked with sweat.

"We called you a couple of hours ago but had no response," She said. "Thought you left."

"I didn't hear anyone call for me," George said. "Someone was going to get me."

"A consultant came out and called you from the corridor," She explained. "Twice."

"I am deaf," George said in frustration. "That is why I asked for someone to come and get me."

"Oh dear," the nurse said. "Looks like you got lost in the system." She put on a face shield.

"Forgotten about you mean," George said. "Nice to see you look after you own."

"You work here?" She asked.

George nodded.

"Are you a porter?" She asked. "Mark seemed to know you."

"No," George sighed. "I am not a porter!" He snapped. "Why do people automatically think I am a porter? Deaf people can do anything they wish."

"I didn't mean it that way," The nurse said. "I just thought it was because you knew Mark."

"I am the head of Technical Services," George said.

"Is that the department that does the lights and stuff?" She asked curiously.

"No, we look after medical equipment," George sighed. "You break a fair bit on a weekly basis."

"Any pain anywhere else?" She asked. "You have a minor cut on your eyebrow, she said looking. "Probably from where you hit the counter."

"I made it to the counter then?" George chuckled.

"Well your face did anyhow," The nurse said smiling. "Will be sore tomorrow."

A consultant walked in and nodded at George, wearing brown trousers and a white shirt with a brown tie, he had short hair and a thick beard.

"How did you do this Mr Shades?" He asked.

"Sorry I didn't understand," George said. "Could you repeat?" George struggled to lipread the consultant, his lips hardly moving when he spoke.

"How did you do this?" He pointed to the cut.

They all looked at George, waiting for him to respond.

"Sorry," George said again "I cannot understand you."

"I said," The consultant raised his voice, causing George to flinch. "How did you do this!?"

"Shouting doesn't help," George raised his voice. "Could someone translate for me?"

The nurse looked at me in confusion.

"What language?" The nurse said.

"English," George said.

"That is what he is speaking," She said, laughing.

"I know!" George groaned. "I cannot lipread him and wondered if someone could basically say what he is saying."

"Ah, I didn't realise you are hard of hearing," The consultant noticed the hearing aid. "I apologise very much," He turned to the nurse. "Could you repeat my words for this man please?"

The nurse nodded.

131

"He apologises," She said. "He didn't realise."

"Thanks," George said.

"Is it my accent?" The consultant said. "I am from Pakistan."

"He asked if it is the accent?" The nurse said.

"It's the beard mainly," George said. "But it's fine.

"Can you move your finger?" The consultant said, holding up his hand and moving the finger. George copied him, opening, and closing the finger and moving it around.

"It looks like there is no serious damage," The consultant looked at the cut. "Four stitches should be fine." He gave George a thumbs up and walked away, the other nurse following.

"What was that?" George said.

"He said you have been lucky, no damage to any nerves or anything," She explained. "I am going to put some stitches in."

"Great," George said.

"Any allergies?" She asked.

"No," George said.

"Okay," She put on a pair of gloves and picked up a syringe.

"What is that?" George asked.

"A local," She said. "Problems with needles?" She paused.

"I don't want a local," George said. "They make me nauseous."

"It will hurt," She warned. "I advise you to have it."

"I don't care," I said. "I'd rather that than a local. I'll take some pain killers if I need to, but I will be fine."

"Okay if you are sure," she said.

I nodded and laid back, feeling tired and sick.

"Okay I will just go and check on something and will be back shortly," She said. "Will bring you some water too."

"Thanks," George said.

George laid back, his arm across his face as he breathed heavily, trying to ward off the sickness.

"Are you okay?" The nurse rubbed his chest. "You nodded off for a moment there."

"It's so hot," George said. "Crazy."

"Going to start now," She said. "Ready?"

George nodded, looking up at the ceiling and sucked in a deep breath when he felt the first prick, and then a cold numbing sensation. He looked down at his hand and the nurse held a syringe.

"What is that?" I asked.

"The local," She said. "I wasn't sure if you fully understood what I was saying, so I decided to give it to you to be on the safe side."

"I understood everything fine," George said, annoyed and upset. "I think it is you that didn't understand a simple request." I felt the local kicking in. "Locals make me feel sick and I would rather feel the stitches than feel sick!"

The curtain is pushed to one side and a sister walks in, looking at both George and the nurse curiously. She is wearing a visor, mask, and scrubs. Short and stocky.

"Everything okay?" She asked.

"Not really," George said in frustration.

"Hello George," She looked at his hand. "Been in the wars?"

"Something like that," George sighed. "I just wish I wasn't being taken for an idiot."

"What is wrong?" She asked, walking over, and placing a damp cloth on his head.

"I clearly asked for no local, and as soon as I close my eyes, she forces it on me!" George was fuming.

"I didn't force it on him," The nurse scoffed.

"He said that he didn't want a local," The sister said. "Why were his wishes ignored?"

The nurse looked and me and shook her head.

"I don't think he fully understood me due to his communication disability," She said. "So, I made the decision."

"I don't want her stitching me," George said. "Could I have someone that doesn't treat me like an idiot please?"

The nurse looked at me in offence.

"I was doing the right thing," The nurse said. "No need to be rude!"

"So, if someone who could hear, said they didn't want a local," George said taking a deep breath when his stomach lurched. "Would you have gone against his wishes?"

"Well no," The nurse said. "He would have understood."

"Discriminative too," George shook his head. "Could I have a non-ignorant nurse please that understands the words 'no local'?"

She took her gloves off and stormed out, leaving the sister with George. She shook her head and took out some clean gloves, looking at my hand.

"I am sorry about that," She said. "I will give you details after if you wish to complain."

"No," George said. "I just want to get outside in the cool."

George began to feel sick as the heat rushed over him and he started to shiver.

"What reactions do you have from a local?" She asked.

"It leaves me feeling sick, and hot," George took a deep breath. "I will be okay once I get some air."

"I will get you some anti-sickness pills," She said. "I may as well stitch this up and get it out of the way."

George nodded.

"What are these?" The sister pointed to several thin scars on George's chest, on the left lower pectoral. "They look deliberate."

"They are history," George said.

"Are you sure?" The sister asked.

"Positive," George nodded. "Just a silly mistake in a bad time."

"If you want me to stop or if you feel sick," The sister said. "Just say okay?"

The curtain opened and Mark popped his head in.

"What is going on?" He said. "What's this about you upsetting people?"

"She treated me like an idiot!" George snapped.

"Chill out," Mark held up his hands. "Only winding you up, she has upset more people today than I have had fag breaks!"

"I am about to do his hand," The sister said. "Do you mind waiting a bit?"

"Sure," Mark nodded. "Sorry, do you want anything George?"

"Could you get me a bottle of water and a top?" George said. "Scrubs will be fine."

"Sure, will do mate," Mark said giving George a thumbs up. "Will pop back in a bit."

Mark left and the sister looked over George.

"Ready?" She said.

George nodded, covering his eyes with his arm.

01:44

George yawned, stepping out into the cold walkway, and looking up at the clear skies, the moonlight so bright.

"Wow," He said. "Looks amazing."

George pulled his mobile from his pocket and groaned.

"Bloody battery," He said.

"You going to be okay?" Mark said as he walked through the automatic doors.

"What?" George looked around.

Mark dropped his mask down.

"I said are you going to be okay?" Mark said. "You are looking a little off."

"I'll be okay thanks," George said. "I need my bed."

"Want a lift?" Mark said. "I can take some time out."

"My car is in the car park," George said. "Thanks for the offer though."

"She looks angry," Mark said. "You may have to run."

"What?" George exclaimed.

"Scared the crap out of me you arsehole!" Lucy snapped. "Why didn't you reply?"

George turned around to find Lucy looking at him, a worried look on her face. Wearing black jeans, boots, and a black overcoat down to her ankles, and a small beanie cap.

"Hey," George smiled. "Sorry my phone died a couple of hours ago," George said.

"I'll leave you two alone," Mark said. "Don't hurt him, he has only just left."

Lucy smirked and then looked at George.

"The last text I got was that were at the walk-in centre," Lucy shook her head. "When you didn't reply I got worried."

"Oh," George said. "Sorry."

"I got to your house earlier to find a very upset Debbie that came home to find blood all over the floor and a bloodied knife on the side," Lucy scoffed. "She even called the police because she thought you had been attacked or something, so I had to put that right."

George sniggered.

"It isn't funny!" Lucy smiled. "You said it was only a little cut you sod!"

"It is," George said. "Four stitches," George said holding up his bandaged hand. "Right down to the bone."

"I even called my dad," She said softly. "And he went into panic mode, why is that?" She asked.

"Panic mode?" George said. "No idea."

"He said he couldn't handle you hurting yourself again," Lucy said. "Anything you want to talk about?"

George looked at her, the smile disappearing from his face.

"It's fine," Lucy said. "Tell me when you are ready to."

George nodded, his heart pounding in his chest.

"You are cold too and you look like shit," Lucy said.

"Thanks, love you too," George said sarcastically. "You look pretty amazing," He said. "Nice time out?"

"Went to visit a friend," Lucy said. "How's the hand?"

George held up his bandaged hand.

"Throbbing like hell," George said covering his mouth and yawning.

"Are you cold?" Lucy said. "What happened to your t-shirt?"

"They cut it off when I passed out," George scoffed.

"You passed out?" Lucy said sniggering. "You got a problem with blood?"

"No I have a problem with not eating and sleeping," George said as Lucy got closer to him, putting her arms around him, hugging him tightly.

"That hurts," He moaned. "But nice."

"Sorry, you wuss," Lucy broke away. "You cut your eye too," She said. "You are going to have a hell of a black eye in the morning."

"I'm a mess," George said. "I am gonna head home, do you want a lift?"

"Sure," Lucy said. "My car is at yours."

"How come?" George asked as he walked towards the car park.

"Well, the parking here sucks," Lucy said. "And it costs a bomb, so I decided to get a cab here, Debbie was going to come but I told her to stay in case you showed up."

"Sorry," George said.

"It's okay," Lucy said. "Are you working tomorrow?"

George nodded.

"You mean today," George looked at his watch. "Shit it's late."

"Early you mean," Lucy smiled. "Come on."

"You are going to be tired," Lucy said.

"Already bloody tired," George yawned. "Stay for a coffee?"

"Too bloody right I am!" Lucy said, punching him in the arm softly and then taking it, holding onto it as they walked towards the car park.

02:08

George closed the door gently, looking at Lucy, indicating her to go into the kitchen.

"Trying not to wake up Debbie," He said softly.

Lucy shook her head and pointed to the kitchen.

"Too late, I am still up, you arsehole!" She snapped. "Get in here!"

"Yes mum," George said sarcastically.

George picked up a black fleece banging up on the coat rack and put it on, moaning when he caught his finger. He awkwardly zipped it up, kicking his trainers off.

Lucy sat at one end of the table, holding a mug of coffee. Debbie sat at the other end, wearing a red onesie, her hair tied up at the back. She pointed to a mug of black coffee.

"There you go," She said.

"Thanks," George said. "How did you know we were heading back?"

"I told her," Lucy said. "I promised to."

Debbie sighed loudly.

"I came home and found blood," She hesitated. "All over the kitchen and I nearly threw up!"

"Debbie has a thing about blood," George smiled and then looked on the floor. "Thanks for cleaning it up."

"I had to," She shook her head. "Looked like a crime scene."

"No, it didn't!" George scoffed.

"It really did," Lucy giggled. "She went white as a sheet."

"It was my fault wasn't it?" Debbie said, worry on her face.

"No," George rubbed her arm. "I was distracted."

"So it was my fault," Lucy said.

George groaned.

"Will you two stop fighting over the blame," George said. "I wasn't concentrating with a knife, so it was my own fault."

"So how bad?" Debbie asked, looking down at Georges bandaged hand. "Did it need stitches?"

"Four," George said. "It is starting to throb even more now."

Lucy pulled off her jacket, putting it on the back of the chair.

"I'll let dad know in the morning that you are okay," Lucy said. "Put him out of his misery."

"You have been gone hours," Debbie said. "Was it busy?"

"Take a wild guess," George said. "It was mental, so many idiots!" He laughed. "Oh, that reminds me!"

"What?" Debbie said.

"Well my date, when she realised, I was deaf, freaked out and did a runner," George explained. "When I was in the walk-in, she was there!" He burst out laughing. "She tripped in the alleyway and did her ankle in!"

"Karma," Lucy said. "Serves her right for being a shallow bitch."

"She looked so pitiful," George said. "Pathetic really."

"You look rough," Lucy said. "You okay?"

"They gave me a local," George said. "After I said not to."

"It makes him sick," Debbie said. "I drove him there the year before last when he cut his head and after the local, he threw up, all over my lap!"

"Oh dear," Lucy covered her mouth.

"To make matters worse," George chuckled. "I ate a jar of beetroot and they thought something was seriously wrong with me."

"There was," Debbie scoffed. "You ate a whole jar of baby beetroot, threw up all over me and then what did I do?"

"She passed out," George burst into fits of laugher. "Fell right off the chair and bashed her head on the floor!"

"So, you both had minor head injuries?" Lucy shook her head. "You two!"

"It was her fault in the first place!" George said. "She put a vase on the top shelf in the living room and I didn't realise."

"A few movies fell over and caused a chain reaction," Debbie giggled.

"You laugh now, but you cried like a baby!" George said. "God this is sore."

"Want anything?" Debbie said. "Vodka?"

"It's too late for vodka," George said. "Got work at eight."

"You are going to work?" Debbie looked at Lucy and then back at George. "Really? Surely you deserve the day off you masochist?"

"I need to go in," George sighed. "Too much to deal with, I have a ton of emails to sort out."

"Still a masochist!" Debbie said.

"Got a charger down here?" George said taking his phone from his pocket. "I need to put this on charge."

"By the television," Debbie said. "Want me to go plug it in?"

"No, it's okay," George said. "I'll be back in a minute."

George got up and left walked out and Lucy moved closer to Debbie.

"Is he okay?" Lucy said. "He doesn't seem right."

"Tired," Debbie said. "He doesn't sleep much."

"My dad said something on the phone earlier," Lucy said. "Saying that he was worried that George hurt himself again."

Debbie looked away, biting her lip.

"Do you know why?" Lucy whispered.

"Yes," Debbie nodded. "But I cannot say."

"It's fine," Lucy said. "Don't worry."

"Does he know?" Debbie smiled.

"Know what?" Lucy said.

"That you like him?" Debbie said softly. "I know you do."

"How do you know that?" Lucy said nervously.

"Well last night was a dead giveaway," Debbie exclaimed. "You both have something going on there."

"Not sure if he likes me," Lucy said. "I have dropped some hints but?"

"He is hard work," Debbie said. "Has had his heart broken too many times, so he puts up walls, never lets anyone get close to him, but" She paused. "He is different with you, more relaxed."
Lucy smiled and nodded.

"Taking his time," Debbie said. "You okay George?"
No answer.

"George?" She said louder.

"Hasn't passed out as he?" Lucy got up, followed by Debbie who hurried into the living room.
The living room is small, wooden flooring and light grey walls. Against the far wall was a shelving unit surrounding a large flatscreen television. Against the wall next to the door is a two-seater leather couch, in the middle, a large rug with a glass coffee table at the centre. In the corner of the room by the large window, covered with slatted wooden blinds, is a leather armchair where George was sat, snoring lightly.

"Wow," Debbie said. "That is a first."
Lucy looked at Debbie with a confused look on her face.

"He never sleeps or even nods off on the couches," Debbie said. "Doesn't like people seeing him sleep,"

"Leave him," Lucy said. "He needs it."
Debbie reached behind the couch, pulling out a fleece blanket and carefully draping it over George.
They both walked into the hall, quietly closing the door behind them.

"Do you want to stay?" Debbie said. "Plenty of room?"
Lucy hesitated.

"I have a pull out in my room," Debbie added. "Up to you?"

"No, it's fine," Lucy said. "Thanks for the offer though."

"You sure?" Debbie said.

"Thanks, Debbie," Lucy said. "I need to get back."
Debbie nodded.

"Thanks for tonight," Debbie said. "I got really worried."
Lucy leaned forward and hugged Debbie tightly.

"I'll call you later," Lucy stepped back. "What does he have for lunch?"

"He usually gets a wrap from the café at the front of the hospital," Debbie said. "Chicken and bacon, I think, why?"

"I am visiting dad, so will get him some food and check up on him," Lucy said, walking to the front door. "Text if you need anything," She opened the door. "It's cold tonight," She shivered.

"Drive safe," Debbie said, watching as Lucy walked to her car. She closed the door and yawned, turning off the kitchen light, hall light and then quietly walking up the stairs.

09:12

The room was in darkness, the light from the laptop illuminating only George and the wall behind him. George leaned forward on the desk, scrolling through emails.

He is wearing black trousers, a white shirt and grey tie and a fleece jacket done up.

Marvin opened the door, turning on the light and yelped out in fright,

"Jesus George," His hand went to his chest. "Scared the crap out of me!"

Marvin then noticed Georges hand and face.

"Jesus!" he snapped. "What the hell happened to you?"

"Nothing, why?" George said.

"You have a black eye, and your hand is all bandaged," Marvin walked in followed by Keven, who is wearing jeans and a shirt.

"Do I?" George scoffed. "Didn't notice."

Marvin shook his head.

"What happened to you?" Kevin said. "Have you seen someone about that?" He pointed to the cut above his eye.

"Just a bad night," George said. "Nothing to worry about."

"I was just about to do Kevin's back to work interview," Marvin said. "Didn't realise you were in here, sorry."

"No problems," George said. "I'll sit in, I have a few things to add."

Kevin sat down, folding his arms across his chest. "Marvin closed the door and pulled the spare chair out, distancing himself and sitting down.

"Who is the fit bird?" Kevin said. "On the counter?"

"Kirsty," George said. "Stay away from her."

"She can stick up for herself," Marvin said.

"Fair enough," Kevin said. "She looks tasty!" He smiled.

"One more comment like that and I will complain," George said. "I am not kidding."

"Fine," Kevin said.

"Let's keep this professional huh?" Marvin said. "Lot's to do today."

"Before we start," Kevin said. "I think I need to speak out about something."

Marvin looked at him in confusion.

"I wasn't off sick," Kevin added. "I lied because I needed a few days off."

"Oh," Marvin said dropping his notebook on the floor beside him. "I had my suspicions."

"Well I thought it would be an idea to own up," Kevin said. "Considering George would say something."

Marvin looked at George curiously.

"I saw him at the restaurant last night," George said. "Looked pretty well for a sick man."

"Oh, why Kevin?" Marvin said. "You know how desperate we have been?"

"Sorry," Kevin said. "I will take the days as unpaid."

"Not as straightforward as that," George added. "I will need to raise this with human resources."

"Why?" Kevin said. "I have apologised."

"Well in this time, with a pandemic in play, jobs are not easy to come by," George said. "And I cannot have someone that picks and chooses when he comes into work."

"Can he do this?" Kevin looked at Marvin.

"George is the head of this department," Marvin said. "So yes, he can."

"Harold arranged for you to get counselling for stress," George sighed. "You didn't turn up, claiming that you didn't need to."

"It wouldn't have solved anything," Kevin muttered.

"Asides from letting down the department and adding to everyone's stress," George said, closing the laptop. "You are also defrauding the trust."

"It isn't fraud!" Kevin scoffed.

"You are claiming sickness," Marvin said. "When you are not sick, so yes, it is fraud."

"I have apologised, offered to take it unpaid," Kevin moaned. "What more do you want?"

"I want you to follow the same rules everyone else does," George said. "Why should you be treated any different?"

"Okay," Kevin said. "If that is how you want to play the game."

"It isn't a game," George said. "We are a team here and your little sickness holidays are putting more stress on the department."

"I am with him on this," Marvin said to Kevin. "You already have two warnings on your file."

"They were not my fault," Kevin scoffed. "People keep winding me up."

141

"Then get help," George said. "You clearly have issues with your temper."

"When is Harold back?" Kevin asked.

"Not for a while," Marvin said. "He was soft with you because you intimidated him."

"No, I didn't!" Kevin said.

"Okay I have things to do," George said. "I suggest you write a statement."

"Okay to go for a cigarette?" Kevin asked.

"In your break yes," George said. "Not in our time."

"Go catch up with the guys," Marvin said. "They will hand over what you missed.

George and Marvin watched as Kevin pushed the chair to the end of the room slowly, scraping across the floor loudly.

"Really?" George said. "What are you, five?"

Kevin laughed, left the room, and closed the door heavily behind him.

"What happened to you?" Marvin pulled his chair closer to the table. "Harold called me yesterday."

"I got clumsy with a new knife," George said. "Cut my finger down to the bone."

"How did you manage that?" Marvin said. "How many stitches?"

"I was talking to Lucy via a video call, cutting sausages and slipped," George held up his hand. "Bloody hurt!"

"So, what is with the face?" Marvin pointed to his eye. "How did you do that?"

"Sitting in the walk-in for four hours," George chuckled. "Walked over to the counter because it started bleeding and I passed out, face-first into the screen."

"Jesus Christ!" Marvin covered his mouth. "What time did you get home?"

"Two in the morning," George said leaning back in the chair. "Something like that anyhow fell asleep in the armchair and left two ladies in the kitchen."

"Two?" Marvin asked. "Who?"

"Lucy and Debbie," Marvin shook his head. "I texted Lucy just before my phone died, and she got worried. Debbie came home to the house, blood all over the kitchen!"

"Sure, you should be here?" Marvin said. "I can take over for the day."

"I am fine," George nodded. "Got lots to sort out today."

"Well at least let me fix your glasses," George said. "I have a new solder gun I want to try out."

"Sure," George took them off and handed them to Marvin. "Thanks, mate."

"Spoke to Harold?" Marvin asked.

"No," George yawned, covering his mouth. "I'll pop up later."

A knock at the door and Marvin turned around, looking up as Kirsty gently opened the door and looked in.

"Sorry," She said. "Someone here needs to speak to a manager, she asked or Harold," Kirsty shrugged her shoulders. "Kim Jones."

"Our community contact," Marvin said.

"Send her in," George smiled. "Could I have them back for a while," He held his hand out when Marvin handed him the glasses.

"I'll catch up with you later," Marvin said. "Give me a shout if you need me."

Marvin left and Kirsty walked in, with Kim following.

"Hello Kim," George said. "We met before, probably a few years back, George stood up.

Kim is a large built woman with thick black hair, wearing grey trousers and a white blouse, a tanned overcoat down to her heels.

"Do I have to wear this?" She pointed to her mask.

"No, you can remove it in here," George said. "We social distance. Please sit down," George pointed to the chair.

"Can I get anyone a drink?" Kirsty asked.

"No thank you," Kim said removing her jacket and mask, she draped the jacket over the chair and put the mask in her pocket. "I won't be staying long."

"I'd love a black coffee," George said. "Two sugars."

Kirsty nodded and closed the door.

"Oh dear," she said. "What happened to you?"

"Oh, the neighbour's cat," George said. "Frisky little sod, so how can I help you?"

"I was hoping to see Harold," Kim said. "We do keep in touch."

"Harold is off for quite some time," George said. "He had a bad accident."

"Oh no," Kim shook her head. "What happened?"

"A cow fell on him," George said.

"An actual cow?" She scoffed. "Really?"

"Well, I don't know if it were his other half!" George laughed. "No seriously, it was a cow, long story, but his dog attacked a cow, he went to stop it and the how fell over on him."

Kim burst out laughing.

"When it got up, it trampled him," George said. "Poor sod had to call an ambulance because his wife walked home with the dead dog."

Kim was speechless, her mouth wide open.

"He had to have surgery on both legs," George sat back. "But he will be back to normal soon if he was ever normal in the first place," George smiled.

"So, who is the senior person?" Kim said.

"That would be me," George said. "Interim head of the department, for my sins."

"Oh really," She said. "How do you manage with the hearing issue?"

"Well it doesn't give me any problems," George smiled. "And I don't give it any problems."
Kim laughed awkwardly.

"I didn't see anything on Harold's calendar about you coming in," George said. "Or have I missed something?"

"I was going to email," Kim said. "But I thought it would be better to come and speak to Harold," she paused. "Well yourself instead."

"Okay?" George said.

"I am unhappy with the contractors working for us," Kim said. "I have had complaints and I am not receiving reports for completed works."

"They have been on site this week," George said. "And they are finishing up today instead of tomorrow."

"They only came on Monday and Tuesday," Kim said. "The work has piled up and the nurses are fuming."

"Okay I will look into that and arrange for it to be done," George opened the laptop. "What complaints have you had?"

"Well the man," She sighed. "I don't know his name."

"Simon," George said.

"His t-shirt never seems to fit properly, and the brings in food that stinks out the department when he heats it," She said. "In the microwave."

"Ok," George typed up notes. "Anything else?"

"Yes," Kim laughed nervously. "Erica, she is very loud and swears a lot."

"To people?" George asked. "No, on the phone, she is always on the phone."

"Okay I will deal with that," George sighed. "There will be no charge, for any work done this week. Let me call in Marvin," George got up.
George opened the door, looking towards the counter.

"Kirsty," George said. "Could you be kind enough to send Marvin in for me?"

"Of course," Erica said.
George closed the door and sat down.

"Would you know roughly how much has been completed?" George said. "Since Monday?"

"Thirteen items of equipment," Kim said.

"Thirteen?!" George exclaimed. "You are kidding me!?"

"No," Kim shook her head.

"Would you know how many are outstanding?" George asked.

"Over forty," Kim said. "That was up until yesterday. My colleague was going to call me when they arrived on-site, but they haven't so far."

George looked at his watch.

"This is not acceptable, and I promise it will be put right," George said.

The door opened and Marvin walked in.

"Good morning Kim, long time no see," Marvin smiled. "You wanted me?" He looked at George.

"Simon and Erica were not onsite yesterday," George said. "And have not shown up today, they have completed only thirteen items in two days."

"You are joking!" Marvin said. "They handed me site reports for Monday and Tuesday, still waiting on Erica's from yesterday."

"There have also been complaints, about conduct," George said. "I am logging onto the satellite navigation program, it has a journey tracker."

A mobile phone started to ring loudly, and Kim answered it, apologising silently.

"Hello?" She said. "Yeah, I am in a meeting with the head of the department, have they shown up?" Kim said, then looking at George and shaking her head. "Okay, thanks for calling!" She put the phone away.

"Not shown up?" George asked.

"No," Kim said.

"We will deal with this very seriously," Marvin said.

"I don't want anyone sacked," Kim said. "Just that the work is completed on time."

"Okay, this is going to make you laugh" George scoffed. "They are currently parked up in Herne Bay."

"What?!" Marvin snapped. "Herne Bay?!"

"Yesterday," George clicked on a page. "The van never left the car park."

"So where did Erica disappear off to?" Marvin asked.

"No idea," George said. "But certainly, wasn't work."

"Will we look into this Kim," Marvin said. "And I assure you that everything is sorted out by end of tomorrow."

"Thank you," Kim said. "I appreciate it."

"Are you sure you don't want a coffee or anything?" George said.

"No," Kim smiled and stood up. "I have a meeting with your finance department."

"Okay," George stood up. "Do you know where you are going?"

Kim nodded.

"Good," George opened the door. "Thank you for coming."

George watched as Kim left the department, sighing heavily.

"Kirsty," George said. "Could you call Simon and Erica and ask them to come back urgently."

"Sure," Kirsty said looking up from the counter.

"If they come up with any excuses, then say it comes from the top, failure to come back will result in disciplinary."

"Will do," Kirsty said, picking up the phone.

George closed the door, looking at Marvin.

"Had enough," George said. "They are taking the absolute piss now."

"I am surprised and very disappointed," Marvin said. "What are you going to do."

"Put them up against the wall and shoot them," George said with gritted teeth.

"Got a gun?" Marvin grinned.

"Good point," George said. "I'll use a hammer instead, bash their bloody skulls in."

"Going to make a mess," Marvin said. "Want me to talk to them?"

"No," George said. "I will once they are in."

"Do you want me to look at the glasses now?" Marvin asked.

"I have a video call in about twenty minutes," George said.

A knock at the door followed by Kirsty opening it.

"Sorry," She said. "George, you have a visitor."

"Not expecting anyone," George said. "Who is it?"

"Hugh," She said. "Occupational health."

"Wonder why?" George said.

Marvin shrugged his shoulders.

"Sure send him in," George said to Kirsty who walked away. "Can you find out how many items that Simon and Erica are contracted to do at this site?"

"Sure," Marvin said. "Will print off a report."

"Thanks," George nodded as Marvin left and sat down as Hugh walked in. Tall and slim, wearing black trousers and a dark blue tunic, he is wearing a mask and carrying a file.

"Good morning George," He said. "Can I?" He pointed to his mask."

"Go for it," George said. "I would shake your hand, but social distancing and all that."

"That is fine," Hugh said and sat down. "How are you keeping?"

"Good," George nodded.

"I only found out today you were back," Hugh said. "I was under the impression that you had annual leave for one month?"

"Yeah me too," George said. "However Barbara guilt-tripped me into coming back." George laughed.

"That isn't good," Hugh opened the file. "Can I ask why so I can investigate?" He removed a pen from his top pocket.

"Harold had an accident," George said. "Barbara needed me to come in and run the nuthouse."

"She should not have done that," Hugh said. "Your leave was a requirement."

"I know," George chuckled. "If it hadn't been for the pandemic, I would have sent her packing."

"Okay," Hugh sighed. "I am here because a concern has been raised."

"A concern about?" George asked, waiting for an answer. "Someone on the team?"

"You," Hugh smiled. "Are you managing?"

"I am fine," George said. "Honestly."

"Could you tell me what happened?" He indicated to his hand and face.

"Has someone said something?" George asked.

"Yes," Hugh said. "But I cannot state who. With what has happened in the past, I have to act, you must understand that?"

"I do," George sighed. "I just wished that person spoke to me first. Was it Harold?"

"It wasn't," Hugh said. "I cannot tell you who it was."

"I just wish people would keep their nose out of my business," George growled. "Too many people with too much time on their hands."

"Calm down," Hugh said.

"I am fine," George sighed loudly.

"What happened?" Hugh asked again.

"I was distracted at home, cutting sausages," George said. "I was on a video call to a friend, you are more than happy to speak to her if you don't believe me."

"I believe you," Hugh said. "Do you need it checked or dressed?"

"No it's fine thanks," George said.

"And the face?" Hugh asked.

"You are more than welcome to investigate that," George laughed. "I was waiting over four hours due to them 'forgetting' about me," George said. "They forgot I was deaf and thought I had left. I passed out and smashed my face into the screen."

"I am more than happy to take that further if you wish?" Hugh said.

George thought about it for a few seconds and then shook his head.

"No," He said. "No point."

"How are you managing?" Hugh said. "Are you getting support from the team?"

"Marvin and Kirsty have been great," George said. "The others not so much, but I am fine."

"I have to check these things," Hugh said. "You do understand that."

"Yes," George said. "So who knows?"

"Knows what?" Hugh said.

"About my," George hesitated. "My episode?"

"Only Harold," Hugh said.

"So who told you if it wasn't Harold?" George asked. "Surely someone said something?"

"You know I cannot tell you that," Hugh said. "But it was someone who genuinely cares about you."

"Really?" George scoffed. "I am sure."

"Someone that was on the team," Hugh said. "When you were brought into accident and emergency."

George sighed, sitting back in the chair.

"Oh," George nodded. "I think I have an idea."

"Don't confront it," Hugh said. "Just let it go."

"I am not going to confront it," George said. "Just having a ridiculous week."

"Want to talk about it?" Hugh asked.

"No," George said. "I am fine really."

"Okay," Hugh said. "I won't keep you, but will you pop down next week, Monday?"

"What for?" George asked.

"A chat," Hugh said.

George groaned.

"Or I can come here?" Hugh said.

"No!" George said. "I will come to you."

"Okay," Hugh stood up. "Do you need the hand checked or anything?"

"No," George said. "I'm good."

George got up and opened the door, showing Hugh out.

"Okay speak to you soon," Hugh said and put his mask on. "Keep an eye on the hand."

George nodded, watching as he walked out the door and slowly walked up to the counter.

"Everything okay?" Kirsty asked.

"Yeah," George said. "Any luck with the two idiots?

Kirsty laughed.

"They are heading back," She said. "When they finish."

"Fatman and Slobbing," George said. "That is what I call them."

"I get that," Kirsty said. "Erica argued and said that they have a lot to do," Kirsty explained. "But I mentioned Barbara coming in and she changed her tune."

"Good," George said, looking as Curtis approached him. "What do you want?" He said bluntly.

"Marvin said you wanted to see me," Curtis laughed. "Now?"

"No," George said. "Later, less chance of me murdering you."

"Guess what?" Curtis said.

"What," George said uninterested.

"Got my isopropyl alcohol non-spill pot," Curtis said excitedly.

"What!" George scoffed.

"I said," Curtis raised his voice. "That I…" He was cut short by George.

"No," George huffed. "Don't shout."

Curtis held up a red pot with a silver cap.

"Wow," George said bluntly. "What do you want, a bloody medal?"

Kirsty sniggered, ducking under the counter.

"Well we have issues when they are knocked over," Curtis said. "And they leak, so with these you can turn them upside down and they don't!"

Curtis tipped the pot upside down over George's injured hand, and the cap popped off. The clear liquid poured out all over George's hand and within seconds, it started to burn.

"Jesus Christ!" George howled. "What is wrong with you?!" George groaned loudly, shaking his hand. Kirst ran round with a bottle of water, unscrewing it.

"Hold your hand out," She said. "Quickly!"

George hissed through the pain and held out his hand as Kirsty poured the water over it slowly, Marvin came running into the reception area, followed by Andy.

"What is going on?" Marvin said looking at Kirsty. "What happened?"

"This fucking idiot here just poured isopropyl alcohol over my hand!" George snapped breathing heavily. "I am going to murder him in a minute!"

Andy laughed, covering his mouth.

"Get back to work!" Marvin said to him. "You too Curtis, you idiot!"

"It was an accident," Curtis laughed nervously. "I was showing him what I got for everyone."

"I don't get why you had to prove it over George's band hand," Kirsty said. "I know it wasn't deliberate, but still."

"Wait in the office please Curtis," Marvin pointed to the office. "Are you okay?" He looked at George who had gone pale.

"Fine," George said. "I need to get this redressed."

"I am a first aider," Kirsty said. "I can sort that out for you, save you going to the walk-in?"

"Do you mind?" Marvin asked.

"Of course not," Kirsty smiled.

"Thank you," George said.

Marvin walked into the office and a few moments later came out with a green first aid box, he handed it to Kirsty before walking back in and closing the door. George sat down at the desk next to her, removing the bandage on his hand.

"Has it stopped burning?" Kirsty asked.

"Yes," George said. "That was really fast thinking."

"My dad was a fire officer," Kirsty said. "Taught me and my brothers how to react in a crisis."

"That is great," George said. "Did you not want to follow suit?"

"I wanted to," Kirsty smiled and sighed. "But after my father passed away, I couldn't do that to my mum, considering two of my brothers joined the army and the third joined the fire service."

"Sorry to hear about your father," George said. "Did he die on the job?"

"No," Kirsty laughed. "He fell off a ladder, cracked his head on the patio."

"Shit," George said. "Sorry."

"No," Kirsty said. "We still laugh about it!"

George looked at Kirsty, surprised.

"Well he climbed ladders all his life, fought fires and never got hurt," Kirsty opened the first aid box. "And falls off a little ladder, trying to get the neighbours ball down."

"That is tough," George said, pulling the bandage off his fingers, wincing, and looking at his finger.

"Let's have a look," Kirsty said, putting on a pair of sterile gloves and looking at the cut.

"Looks better than it did," George said. "Just swollen."

"Lucky you didn't take it off," Kirsty said. "My eldest brother did this with a carpet knife once, bled like hell."

"At least it doesn't need cleaning," George chuckled.

"I'll wipe it over anyway," She said. "This will hurt."

George breathed in deeply, holding his breath when Kirsty gently wiped over the area with an antiseptic wipe and then put a gauze over it.

"Hold that," She said to George.

George held the Gauze down.

"You are pale, have you eaten today?" Kirsty said.

"No," George replied. "Wasn't hungry."

"Here," Kirsty reached into the bag, taking out a small protein bar. "Eat that."

"I am fine really," George said.

"Don't argue," Kirst warned him. "I have three brothers and an excellent argument winner."

She placed the protein bar on the table and proceeded to bandage up Georges hand, giving him more freedom and movement, after a few minutes she finished.

"Wow," George said. "Did a good job of that, thank you."

"Welcome," She smiled. "Don't get up until you have eaten that!" She pointed to the bar.

George opened the bar, eating it slowly.

"This is actually quite nice," George said. "Never really tried one before."

"Always have a bunch," Kirsty said. "Especially when my brothers are around!"

The office door opened, and Marvin stepped out.

"You available?" He said to George. "Curtis has a couple of things to say."

George stepped into the office and Marvin closed the door. Curtis stood up from the chair, took a deep breath and tried not to smile.

"Firstly," He said. "I am very sorry about the alcohol incident," He chuckled. "It was stupid of me to mess around, I didn't realise you had a bad hand."

"Cut down to the bone," George said. "Four stitches and it is still raw, so you can guess how that felt."

"I am sorry," Curtis said. "Really."

"Fine," George sighed. "Say no more."

"Secondly," Curtis laughed nervously. "I did break down yesterday."

"Did you?" George asked. "Because you asked Harold for the day off and he said no, then you asked me and I said no," George said. "Then you are off."

"I know it looks bad, but I did break down," Curtis said. "I promise."

"Did your breakdown service collect you and the car?" Marvin asked.

"Yes," Curtis hesitated.

"You can download call out reports within twenty-four hours," Marvin smiled. "Would be good to see that."

"I am not sure my breakdown does that," Curtis said.

"They will if you ask," George said. "Unless you have anything to hide?"

"No," Curtis shook his head.

"Still got your walk didn't you?" Marvin said.

"Walk?" Curtis said nervously.

"Yeah," Marvin nodded, "You were showing Andy the photos this morning, I overhead and Andy nearly passed out from boredom."

"Well if we don't get a report," George said. "It will be a disciplinary."

"How can I make this go away?" Curtis asked.

"Breakdown service report," Marvin said. "Dated for yesterday."

Curtis chuckled, looking at the floor and nodding.

"Okay go back to work," Marvin said. "Let me know what you have done at the end of the day."

Curtis smiled and laughed softly, walking to the door, and opening it.

"He is lying," Marvin said. "And he knows we know it."

"Prick," George said.

"Hand okay?" Marvin said. "He said it was an accident."

"It was," George said. "Just don't get why he would do that."

"Not your week is it?" Marvin said. "Video call?"

"Forgot about it," George said. "It will have to wait, meeting Lucy."

"Oh yeah," Marvin said. "How come?"

"Security won't let her in," George said. "Unless she comes in with someone."

"Fair enough," Marvin said. "Give her my best, are you seeing Harold."

"Maybe later this afternoon," George said. "I need to check on bed one in Intensive Care."

"Why?" Marvin said. "I am going up in a bit, want me to have a look?"

"It isn't faulty," George rubbed his hand. "Steve sorted it, but I just wanted to check."

Marvin nodded.

"I'll have a chat with the team," Marvin said. "Take it easy."

"Thanks," George said and left the office, walking to the entrance. "Kirsty, I am just popping out, the village idiots should be here shortly, could you ask them to wait in the office?"

"Will do," Kirsty smiled. "Hand okay?"

"It's fine," George gave her the thumbs up. "Thank you."

"George," Ahmed said. "Just a quick word."

George turned around.

Ahmed is the same height as George, athletic with a thick beard and jet black hair.

"What is it?" George said.

"I have helped Andy with the syringe pump," Ahmed said.

"Okay," George said. "And?"

"Just letting you know," Ahmed said. "I put my work to one side to help."

"That is teamwork," George said and turned.

"Also one other thing," He said. "My mother is coming to stay with me."

"Good for you," George nodded. "Why are you telling me?"

"She is flying over from Sudan," Ahmed smiled.

"Okay?" George said. "I really need to go unless you need something?"

"May I finish one hour earlier?" He asked. "I would appreciate it."

"You need to speak to Marvin," George said. "He is your line manager."

"I have," Ahmed said. "I am just informing you."

"Oh wonderful," George said. "Gold star!" He said sarcastically.

George pressed the exit button and was met by a cloud of smoke that blinded his eyes, he coughed, waving the smoke only to find the same woman from the encounter on Monday.

Wearing a long red dressing gown and white trainers, her hair tied back. She held onto a drip stand with two pumps on it, one flashing and alarming.

"You again!" George said coughing. "Still alive?" He said under his breath. "Thought I told you not to smoke here?"

"You cannot stop me," She said. "One of the porters told me they cannot."

"This is a department entrance," George said. "Could you please move somewhere else or I will have to call security."

"Like you did the other day, you two face little bastard," The woman snapped.

"Wow," George laughed. "That is nice."

"I wish this pump would shut up!" The lady complained.

"I wish you would shut up," George said softly.

"What?!" She snapped. "What are you blabbing on about?"

"Nothing," George said. "Just leave please."

"You should wear a mask!" She said. "Breathing your germs all over me."

"Said the moron that smokes," George scoffed. "Also wasting two pumps that a real sick person could benefit from."

"I am sick," She growled. "I am really sick!"

"Being an arsehole isn't a sickness, it's a choice," George said. "Now," he sighed. "Please get lost!"

"What is your name!" She demanded.

"Really?" George said.

"Yes really," She snapped. "Give me your name."

"Ivor," George said.

"Ivor what?!" She glared at him.

"Ivor Gotten," George said, giving her a little wave as he walked away, leaving her standing and staring, holding a cigarette.

10:44

George stood by the entrance of the hospital, a cup holder in his hands with two paper cups of coffee. A teenage girl, wearing her school uniform came up to him, smiling.

"What do you want?" George said bluntly.

"Could you go to the shop and get me some fags?" She asked.

"No," George said.

"Oh please," She begged. "I let you have a couple."

"No," George replied.

"Why not?" She demanded.

George sighed heavily in frustration.

"Well for one, you are clearly underage," George said. "Secondly, this is a hospital," George emphasized. "Why would they be selling cigarettes?"

She shrugged her shoulders.

"Go back to school you idiot!" George said.

"Arsehole," She blurted out and stormed off, nearly walking into Lucy who moved out of her way.

"What was that about?" Lucy said.

"The little shit wanted me to buy her cigarettes," George scoffed.

"In a hospital?" Lucy said in surprised. "Shouldn't she be in school?"

"Just what I said," George nodded.

Lucy put her arms around him, hugging him tightly and then giving him a gentle kiss on the cheek.

"How are you?" She asked and looked down at his hand. "Hand okay?"

"It was fine until one of the department dickheads poured alcohol over it," George held up his hand and scoffed. "Stings."

"What?" Lucy said. "Who did what and why have you got alcohol at work?"

"Isopropyl alcohol," George said. "We use it for cleaning things." George handed her a coffee. "For you."

"Oh thank you," Lucy took the coffee from George. "Why did he pour it on your hand?"

"One of those non-spill containers wasn't sealed properly," George laughed. "It wasn't deliberate, but he is a bloody idiot."

"Oh my god!" Lucy said.

"Kirsty cleaned it up and re-dressed it for me," George said. "So all good."

"Is that the new girl?" Lucy said. "Sounds like she is doing well."

"Yeah," George said nodding. "Sorry about last night."

"What do you mean?" Lucy said, sipping at the coffee.

"Falling asleep," George said. "I was embarrassed when I woke up."

"Oh don't worry," Lucy laughed. "Debbie and I enjoyed watching you sleep."

"What?!" George exclaimed. "You didn't?"

"No we didn't," She giggled. "You were gone a few minutes and when we found you, Debbie put a blanket over you and I left."

"I put my phone on charge," George said. Came over a little tired and the rest was history!"

"It's fine," Lucy punched him softly in the arm. "Seen dad today?"

"No," George said. "Was going to later when things calm down, got a shitstorm to deal with."

"Bet you wish you stayed in bed," Lucy said.

George nodded.

"Walk me in," Lucy said. "Then maybe we can meet up later? If you are free?"

"That would be good," George said, walking towards the entrance with Lucy.

11:20

George sat at the desk, looking at both Erica and Simon sat behind it. Simon sat with his arms crossed, his shirt too tight on him. Erica, a large woman with short blonde hair, is wearing combat trousers and a dark green t-shirt. She is playing with her mobile phone, a smile on her face.

"Could you put that away," George said crossing his arms.

"In a moment," She said. "Just sending a message."

"Now," George said. "Do that in your own time."

"Wow," Erica scoffed, putting the phone in her pocket. "Someone is in a mood."

Marvin opened the door and closed it, leaning against the wall next to George.

"Right you two," George sighed. "We have had a complaint," George said. "From Kim."

"Oh, what now?" Simon groaned. "She is always complaining about nothing."

"She came in this morning," George said. "Asking why you were not on-site all week as agreed."

"We have been," Simon said. "Right?" He nudged Erica.

"Yeah," Erica said.

"Why were you in Herne Bay today?" Marvin said. "We get reports from the satellite navigation, so no point in lying."

They both looked up.

"You went to the site on Monday and Tuesday," George said. "We have also had complaints about your professional conduct on-site."

"We only stopped off for half an hour for breakfast on the way," Erica said. "Then we went there."

"Did you leave the van in Herne Bay and walk? George scoffed.

"Where were you on Wednesday Erica?" Marvin asked.

"On a site," Erica said. "Catching up from last week."

"Thought you finished?" Marvin said. "Or was that a lie?"

"How did you get there?" George said.

"Drove the van," Erica snapped. "Bit of a stupid question."

"Van never left the car park," Marvin said. "Neither did your car."

Erica and Simon looked at each other.

"It's clear you are not doing the job you are paid to do," George said. "So I am suspending you both."

"What?" Erica exclaimed. "You cannot do that!"

"I can," George said. "And I am."

"We still need to finish," Simon said. "If you suspend us then the site will complain."

"I have that sorted," George said. "I don't want you two going to sites and offending people with your disgusting food," He looked at Simon. "And the fact you cannot dress, pathetic!"

Simon looked down at the floor.

"And you," He looked at Erica. "On your phone, all day, swearing and laughing in the middle of a nursing office, what is wrong with you?!"

"I was on a break," Erica said. "I am entitled."

"How many jobs have you both completely this week?" Marvin asked.

"Tons!" Erica said.

"Define tons," Marvin said.

Erica and Simon looked at each other.

"Thirteen," George said. "In three days, and there is still a lot to be done."

"Where were you Wednesday?" Marvin asked.

She shrugged her shoulders.

"You are both suspended until further notice," George said. "Human resources will be in touch, however, I suggest you go away and think about it."

"You cannot do this," Erica said. "You are not a manager."

Marvin held up his hand in warning.

"He is," Marvin said. "Barbara made him head of the department."

"I wasn't told," Erica complained.

"It was in the minutes," Marvin said. "You are supposed to check those daily."

Simon started to cry, his hand covering his mouth.

"What is wrong with you?" George asked.

"I cannot lose this job!" He cried. "I need this job!"

"You weren't too bothered about it before you came into the office," George said. "Or did you think you would get away with cheating the system as you have been?"

"Pathetic," Erica mumbled.

"What was that?" George asked.

"Nothing," She said with a grin on her face.

"You said something," George said. "Don't do that crap with me."

"What crap?" Erica said.

"When you say something to a deaf person, and then say nothing when they ask you to repeat it," George said. "It is bullying and discrimination, you are already in enough trouble without adding that to it."

"Please don't sack me," Simon cried.

"I am not sacking you," George scoffed. "I wish I bloody could, I am suspending you, so I suggest you get out and buy a dictionary so you can look it up."

"I am going to complain," Erica stood up. "This is discrimination."

"How is it discrimination?" George said. "You have lied about working and doing your own thing when you should be working."

"You can complain all you like, I have a statement so long, you could wallpaper the bloody hospital with it, now leave," George pointed to the door. "Now."

"Come on," Marvin said. "Collect your items and go."

"Keys and fuel card please," George said. "On the table."

Erica pulled the keys from her pocket and threw them on the table, they slid across and fell on the floor.

"Pick them up," George said.

"No," Erica said. "I have a bad back."

"Consider losing some weight then," George said and bent down, picking the keys up. "I will make sure the statement reflects you threw the keys at me."

"You what?" She snapped. "What did you say?"

"Nothing," George said.

Marvin smiled.

"Fuel card?" George asked. "Now."

Simon took the card from his pocket and handed it to George.

"Gave you both an opportunity to help yourself," George said. "But you have done nothing but lie and take advantage. I will be checking all offsite visits, van journeys and also the fuel card."

Erica shrugged her shoulders.

"If anything is out of place, which includes helping yourself to fuel, the police will be informed," George said. "I suggest a statement from you both."

Erica stormed out, pulling open the door and slamming it against the wall.

"You can go too," Marvin said. "Get your things and leave."

Simon sobbed as he left the office, closing the door behind him.

"Have you sorted out the visit?" George asked.

"Andy and Ahmed are going," Marvin said. "Ahmed wasn't too happy about it, but when is he ever?"

"I cannot be dealing with this shit," George groaned. "How did we end up with all the village idiots?"

"Are you feeling okay?" Marvin said.

"I am going to go for a walk," George said. "Will pop up and see Harold."

"I'll make sure they both go," Marvin said. "Hopefully gone by the time you get back."

"I think Barbara is popping down," George said. "To sign off some orders."

"Okay," Marvin said.

"And Ananya emailed a complaint on grounds of discrimination," George scoffed.

"How do you know?" Marvin asked.

"She clearly doesn't realise that I am looking after Harold's emails," George said. "Besides, the agency fired her for misconduct."

"Not going to get far then is it?" Marvin laughed.

"No," George said. "See you later."

12.23

George washed his hands, drying them and then put a fresh mask on looking down the curtained bay.

"Hey!" A nurse called out, walking fast towards George. "Can you help?"

The nurse is in full personal protective equipment, Short and slim, the bottom of her apron was dragging across the floor.

"Talking to me?" George said. "Cannot lipread." He pointed to her mask that she wore under a shield.

"Are you Kevin?" She asked pulling the mask down.

"No," George said. "I am half his weight and a manager."

"Do you know this?" She held up a thermometer.

"Yes," George nodded. "That is a thermometer," he said sarcastically. "It is for taking temperatures."

The nurse laughed.

"Can you understand me?" She said. "Do you know about this?"

"Yes I can understand you," George said. "What is the problem?"

"It is displaying Fahrenheit," She said. "Don't want that."

"So you want it in Celsius?" George said.

She nodded.

"Okay give it here," George said. "Hold down the menu button," He showed her. "And then press this until you get what you want." He handed it back to her.

George looked up when he heard a defibrillator alarming, the automatic instructions echoing.

"Someone not having a bad day then?" George said.

"No," She shook her head. "The old man in bay five, very sick."

George went numb, his heart pounding in his chest as he made his way towards bay five, pausing by the curtain the then opening it.

A nurse stood over the bed, performing chest compressions on Harold, pale and covered in perspiration, his eyes open and looking up. A consultant stood at the base of the bed, his shirt arms rolled up, a mask on his face and a shield covering his face.

Lucy stood in the corner, shock on her face.

"You need to wait outside," The nurse said.

Lucy reached out for George, unable to speak.

"I close to him," George said. "He would want me here."

The consultant nodded and George moved closer to Lucy, she grabbed hold of his arm, shaking, and breathing heavily.

"It's okay," George did not know what to say. "It's okay."

"Okay stop compressions," The consult said. "Anything?"

The nurse checked for a pulse, shaking her head.

"Okay let's shock," He bent down, pressing a button on the defibrillator.

"Analysing the heart rhythm!" The defibrillator blasted. "Do not touch the patient!"

159

The nurse stood back.

"Shock advised," The defibrillator whined. "Stand clear!"

An alarm started to blare.

"Press the flashing button!" The defibrillator boomed and an intermittent alarm sounded, growing higher in pitch.

The consultant pressed the button and Harold jolted, Lucy groaned and turned away, crying into George's shoulder.

"Shock delivered," The defibrillator sounded.

The consultant looked up at the nurse and shook his head.

"I am sorry," The nurse said. "There is nothing more we can do, we have been trying for quite some time."

Lucy sobbed louder, gripping hold of George's arm.

"Okay," George said. "Could we have some privacy?"

"Of course," The nurse said. "I will be back shortly."

The consultant unplugged the leads from the defibrillator and turned it off. The nurse pulled his blanket up to his neck and closed his eyes.

"I am very sorry for your loss," She said looking at her nursing watch. "I will be back shortly to answer any questions you have."

George nodded, rubbing Lucy's shoulder with his bad hand, winching in pain.

"Sorry," She said through sobs. "Sorry."

"Hey," George said. "You are going to have to look at me," He chuckled softly. "Need to see your face."

"I am an ugly crier," Lucy looked up, her face wet and red. "Damn you for needing to lipread," she joked.

"What happened?" George said. "Well I know what happened but," He stuttered. "Unexpected."

Lucy walked around, sitting down in the chair next to her father, her hand going to his cheek.

"His heart failed," Lucy said. "Stress and other things," She breathed in deeply. "Apparently he had a stroke last night, the nurse realised this morning when he struggled to eat and drink," She sobbed, wiping tears from her face. "He called mum earlier, spent over an hour on the phone and he was so happy."

"I am so sorry Lucy," George said. "I am sorry I wasn't here earlier."

"No don't," She said. "I appreciate everything you have done for me and my dad."

George walked around, putting his hand on her shoulder.

"Dad thought a lot of you," Lucy smiled.

"Do you like?"

"So why did the sod give me so much work then?" George laughed. "Now the arse has gone left me with more."

Lucy shook her head.

"He told me," Lucy said. "About what happened."

She looked up at George.

"For what it is worth," She said. "I am glad you are still here."

The curtain opened and Marvin looked at Harold and then at Lucy and George.

"I just heard," Marvin said. "One of the nurses called down for George, but I said he was already on his way up."

Lucy stood up, walking over to Marvin, and hugging him.

"I am so sorry kid," Marvin said. "If there is anything I can do."

"Oh there is plenty you two can do," She exclaimed.

"Are you okay?" George said. "Not putting on a brave face for this old sod are you?" He pointed to Marvin.

"I have been expecting it," She said. "You both know dad had a bad heart."

George nodded.

"How about we give you some privacy?" Marvin said looking at George. "And then we go and grab a coffee?"

"You don't drink coffee," George said.

"No," Marvin chuckled. "But I'll drink one for Harold."

"You two go," Lucy said. "I need to do this alone," She said looking down at Harold. "Can I come to yours later?" She said to George.

"Of course," George said. "Want me to come and get you?"

"No," Lucy said. "I'll get a cab," She forced a smile.

George got hold of her, hugging her tightly and rubbing her back.

"Come on George," Marvin said. "Let's get you an expresso, or two."

13:02

George leaned up against the glass, looking out into the car park. His heart pounding and he felt sick, his hands clenched and shaking.

"Here," Marvin said handing the double expresso to George, noticing his hand. "Your hand is bleeding."

"Yeah," George said. "I'll deal with it later."

Do you like?

"Just called the ward," Marvin said. "Lucy is in with the consultant."

George nodded.

"Why don't you stay out here a while," Marvin said. "Get some air, do you want me to tell the team?"

"No," George said. "It has to come from me."

"Okay mate," Marvin said. "I'll leave you alone for a bit."

"Marvin," George said. "Thank you," He held out his hand.

Marvin walked up to him and hugged him.

"Social distancing?" George chuckled.

"Fuck it," Marvin said. "The situation outweighs it."

Marvin patted him on the arm and walked away, George walked towards a seating area in the middle of the car park. He sat down on the bench, putting the small cardboard cup next to him and his hand went to his mouth, stifling sobs. Tears rand down his face as he looked dead ahead, the sobs racking his body.

13:20

George opened the door and walked into the office, pausing when he looked around the room at everyone waiting. Barbara stood by the office door in a tight grey suit, next to her stood Marvin. Ahmed, Andy, Curtis, and Kevin sat around the tables, distanced. Against the wall next to Kirsty were Simon and Erica.

"Hello," Barbara said. "I am here because I feel I need to step in."

George went to speak.

"Let me finish," Barbara said.

"Actually I think George needs to speak first," Marvin said.

"He can after I have said what I need to," Barbara said firmly. "Please don't interrupt."

George nodded to Marvin, acknowledging him.

"You seem to be on a spree, of getting rid of staff," Barbara said. "And certain members of your team have complained about your unprofessional and self-destructive conduct."

"Really," George said looking at Simon and Erica.

"Yes," Barbara said. "I know recently you had a breakdown and made an attempt on your life, but this behaviour has to stop."

"Excuse me?" George snapped. "Who the hell do you think you are bringing that up, it is confidential!" George growled. "Now you have shared it with everyone!"

Everyone looked at George, silent.

"I apologise," Barbara said. "I thought everyone knew?"

"No," George said. "But they fucking do now don't they?"

"Please watch your language," Barbara said holding up her hand.

"No, you can shove it," George snapped. "Idiots like you have more money than sense!"

"George," Marvin said warning him.

"No I cannot keep quiet any more," George said. "I came here to deliver some bad news, and you know what, I don't give a fuck any more."

"You," He pointed to Erica and Simon. "Fatman and Slobbing that are ripping off the trust by claiming to work offsite when you don't, you are both disgusting, lose some weight, you pathetic morons!"

Kirsty sniggered.

"And you Ahmed," George said. "Selfish prick that only cares about his work, lets people fail and then reaps the glory when asked to help out. Everyone knows that you steal food from the canteen, and when you go down to the chapel every week to pray, bullshit do you!" He snapped. "You go down the canteen for an hour with your friends, probably plotting who's life to destroy next!"

"George!" Barbara said.

"Let me speak Barbara," George said. "I'll get to you soon."

Marvin smiled, covering his face with his hand.

"You have Andy, a man child that sleeps on the job comes in late and eats the contents of his nose," He pointed to him. "Then you have Kevin, who steals toilet paper and sleeps with other men's wives, and only this morning was taking photos of Kirsty's arse," He turned to Kirsty. "Sorry, I was going to tell you."

She nodded and smiled.

"Curtis," He pointed. "A walking, talking disaster of a man, who has no balls because your wife keeps them in her handbag!" George bellowed. "You think everyone gives a shit about your new toys and your photos?" He laughed. "No one gives a toss!"

"No, come on George!" Curtis said laughing.

"Curtis," George said.

"What?" Curtis smiled.

"Shut the hell up!" George growled.

He turned around, looking amongst everyone.

"We have Evan," He scoffed. "Our porter that is never here, always off sick!" George said. "He has so many missing teeth, that he confuses the barcode readers everywhere he fucking goes!"

He turned to Kirsty.

"You are great," He said. "A beautiful person with an amazing outlook in life, keep going!" He gave her the thumbs up.

"Thank you," She whispered, slightly embarrassed.

"Marvin," George walked up to him. "A man who probably bails out all the village idiots," He laughed. "Just to keep the peace and keep this department running smoothly."

"George!" Barbara said.

"Okay Barbara I am getting to you now," George said. "And we have Barbara," He scoffed. "Absolutely no use or helps, gets paid to let other people solve her problems, but when it all goes wrong, she washes her hands of it," George said. "You constantly promise to visit and solve issues, but no, you are just setting the department up to fail, so you can get your husband in as a contractor to fix it!"

"That isn't true!" She said nervously. "You are overstepping the mark."

"Not finished," George held up a finger. "As well as finding out about my breakdown, and reporting it to occupational health, you also shared my confidential details with the whole team, because you are an idiot!" George looked her up and down. "In fact," He said. "You look like the cow that broke Harold's legs!"

"Rude!" She exclaimed.

"And I know it was Ahmed that came to you," George looked at Ahmed. "Because he also went to occupational health where his so-called lady friend works!"

Ahmed looked at George, his eyes wide and his mouth open as he tried to speak.

"It's okay buddy," George said sarcastically. "I have told her that you are married, and funnily enough, she knows your wife!" He laughed. "Small world!"

Ahmed got up and left in a hurry.

"By the way," George faced everyone. "Harold just passed away, but why would any of you care huh?"

"Harold?" Barbara said. "Died?"

"Yes," George said. "And it has opened my eyes!" George pulled off his identification badge. "Seeing as I am such a liability with my breakdown and suicidal tendencies," He handed her the badge. "Stick the job, it isn't worth it anymore."

"You cannot do this," Barbara said. "You have a contract."

"I could sue you instead?" George said. "For disclosing private information?"

She stuttered, shaking her head,

"Thought so," George walked to the door. "Sorry Marvin, catch up with you later/"

"It's fine George," Marvin said.

"Take care," Kirsty said.

"I'll send you an email Barbara, don't worry I will also attach your boss too, with some very interesting information about yourself and the idiots in here!"

George tried to open the door, but it kept sticking, in a rage he punched it several times with his band hand, leaving a bloodied fist mark.

He stood by the door, breathing heavily through the pain.

"That is better," He hissed. "Have a nice day."

He pressed the button and kicked open the door, slamming it against the wall before storming off.

FRIDAY

01:23

George lay in bed, sitting up against the headboard, snoring gently. The bedside lamp is on, dimly illuminating the room.

A knock at the door.

"George?" Debbie said, pushing the door open. "You awake?"

No response.

Debbie stepped in, wearing a black bra and white hotpants.

"George," She said louder.

George continued to snore.

Debbie walked over to the bed, checking the floor as she approached it. She gently nudged George's arm.

"Hey," She pushed him. "wake up."

George opened his eyes and then closed them.

"What?" He opened them again, widely when he realised.

"Wake up," Debbie said.

"I am awake," George said. "Jesus, I thought you were naked!"

"You wish," She grinned. "Lucy just called me, she asked if you were awake?"

"Well I am now," George said. "Is she okay?"

"Yeah," Debbie said. "She said could you drop her a video chat, she wants to give you a striptease."

"She what?" George stuttered.

"Only kidding," Debbie giggled. "She just wants a chat."

Debbie left the room, George watched as she walked out, shaking his head.

"Nothing to the imagination," He whispered.

He sat is sat up in bed, wearing a grey t-shirt, the duvet pulled up to his waist. He opened the laptop, logging into video chat. After a few moments, there is a loud ping, and the screen lights up.

"Hey," He said. "Glad to get your message, still at your aunts'?"

"Hi," Lucy said smiling. "Yeah, sorry I blew you out."

"Hey it's fine," George said. "Family is important."

"How did it go?" George said.

"It was," Lucy paused. "Surreal," She laughed nervously. "I told mum, that dad passed away and she didn't really react, she told me to check on the fish fingers, so they didn't get burnt."

George's mouth opened, shocked.

"It's her illness," Lucy said, rubbing her eyes. "My aunt explained it to her later, and she said he is in a better place, I suppose it is better for her that way."

"Must be horrible for you?" George said. "How are you?"

"Drunk," Lucy giggled. "Half a bottle of vodka," She pulled a worried face. "I don't usually drink so much so don't think bad of me. How are you?"

"Also drunk," George said. "And also, Vodka," He smiled and stifled a yawn.

"Marvin told me about today," Lucy said. "I am sorry if it was my fault."

"No," George said. "It has been boiling for a while, and the dickheads pushed me too far."

"Promise me something," Lucy said.

"Anything," George said.

"Promise me you won't hurt yourself again," Lucy said. "Getting to know you, has been the best thing for me in a long time," She paused. "Don't take that away."

"I am not going to hurt myself," George said. "I am out of that pit."

"I cannot believe that your boss brought that up," Lucy exclaimed. "In front of everyone."

"I know," George said. "I got an email from Human Resources, saying I am in breach of my contract, so I told them everything."

"Oh wow," Lucy chuckled. "Should keep them busy for a while."

George nodded.

"Marvin contact you yet?" Lucy said.

"No why?" George said. "I feel bad for him."

"He resigned," Lucy said. "He is moving to Cornwall."

"Good for him," George said.

"So," She said. "What are you going to do?"

"Well I am not in any rush to find a job," George said. "I have savings and a couple of properties, so I can manage," He sighed. "I might travel."

"Where to?" Lucy said.

"I went to Yosemite National Park several years ago," George said. "I would love to do that again, San Francisco, Grand Canyon and then Las Vegas."

"Sounds interesting," Lucy said. "I'll join you," She smiled. "If you don't mind?"

"That would be cool," George said. "Going to have to wait for this pandemic to be over and done with."

"Tell me about it," She sighed. "It is the people that are getting to me, the people denying the virus is real."

"Oh yeah," George said. "Stick them in our intensive care unit for the day, they will then change their mind."

"Yup," Lucy said. "Don't give them a mask or anything."

"I agree," George said.

"Will you miss it?" Lucy said. "You have been working closely with intensive care, haven't you?"

"Yes," George said. "Only because I was the only one that would go into the bays where we had viral patients."

"Did it bother you?" Lucy asked.

"No," George shook his head. "Not really, a couple of weeks ago my mask came off, just as I leaned over a patient."

"Bet that was a scare?" Lucy said. "Got checked, didn't you?"

George nodded.

"Hand okay?" Lucy asked.

"Yeah," George said. "Had it cleaned and got some new stitches."

"You need to look after yourself," Lucy said. "What are you doing later today?"

"No plans," George said. "Long bath and chill I guess."

"Meet up with me," Lucy said. "We can grab lunch and go for a walk."

"I am up for that," George said. "Where?"

"Do you know Holland Park?" Lucy said. "It was dads favourite place."

"Yeah I know it," George smiled. "He introduced the place to me a few years back, along with the little terror."

"Okay then," Lucy said. "Meet me at South Kensington Station."

"Will do," George said. "Look forward to it."

"Great, it's a date," Lucy said smiling and then ended the call, the screen going black.

"A date?" George whispered. "Shit."

A gentle knock at the door.

"You can knock louder," George said.

The door opened and Debbie put her head in.

"Hey," She said. "Can I come in?"

George nodded.

Debbie walked in, wearing jogging bottoms and a grey t-shirt.

"Just wanted to say," She paused. "Thanks for putting up with me."

"It's okay really," George said.

Debbie said on the edge of the bed.

"I got a job," She said. "At the hospital."

"The admin job?" George said. "On the children's ward?"

"yeah," Debbie said. "How do you know?"

"I might have put a word in," George said. "I know the sister there quite well."

"Oh, George!" Debbie exclaimed, covering her mouth and bursting into tears.

"What?" George said. "Why are you crying?"

"You are so good to me," She sobbed. "And I have been an arsehole to you!"

"Stop crying you daft cow," George said. "If anything, I have been an arsehole, just make sure you empty the bins," George grinned.

"Are you okay," She sobbed.

"I am fine," George said.

"Are you really?" She wiped tears from her face.

"Seriously," George said. "I am fine."

Debbie leaned over, throwing her arms around George, and hugging him.

"What is it with everyone hugging me?" George scoffed.

"She likes you," Debbie blurted out.

"Who?" George said, he knew the answer but wanted to hear it from Debbie.

"Lucy," Debbie said. "She really likes you."

"I am seeing her tomorrow," George said.

"Are you not working?" She asked.

"No, I quit," George said. "Not going back."

"Oh yeah," She said. "Ignore me," She smiled. "I am drunk."

"Go to bed," George said. "Let me get some bloody sleep."

Debbie nodded and got up, walking slowly to do the door.

"Make sure you kiss her," Debbie said to George who threw a pillow at her, hitting the shelving unit and knocking several books over.

"Missed," Debbie poked her tongue out and closed the door.

"George laid back in the bed, pulling off his implant and glasses, smiling.

George sat back in the seat, looking out the window as everything shot by. There are only a few people in the train carriage, and opposite George is a young mother and her son. The mother is wearing a dress, with a grey jacket over the top. The little boy has a superhero t-shirt and bottoms on, red gloves and a blue jacket.

"Is it your first time?" The little boy says.

"Sorry?" George said, trying to understand the boy over the noise of the train.

The boy looked at him, confused. The mother leaned down.

"That man is deaf," She said. "You have to repeat what you said," She looked at George and smiled.

"Is it your first time!" The boy yelled at the top of his voice and George cringed.

"I am sorry," The mother said to George. "You don't have to shout," She said. "Just speak clearer."

"Granddad is deaf!" The boy said.

"Quiet," She whispered. "Don't shout."

The boy looked at George and then sighed, shaking his head.

"Is it your first time?" He said again.

"On a train?" George said. "No."

"It's my first time on a train," The boy smiled.

The mother shook her head.

"What is that?" The boy pointed.

"Don't point," The mother said. "What have I told you."

"What is that in your ear," The boy said.

"It's an implant," George said.

"Why?" The boy said.

"I am sorry," The mother said embarrassed. "He is always asking questions."

"Do you really want to know why?" George said. "It's a secret."

"I can keep a secret," The boy said. "Please!" He whined.

"Shall I?" George looked at the mother who nodded.

George leaned forward.

"I am a cyborg," George said.

The boy looked at George, his eyes full of amazement, his mouth opened wide in shock.

"Really!?" He asked.

The mother laughed, shaking her head.

"Is he?" The boy looked up at his mother.

"Yes," She said. "Are you from the future?" She asked George.

George nodded.

"He is from the future," The mother said. "He punishes children that misbehave on trains."

The boy looked at George and then at his mother.

"I don't like cyborgs," He started to cry.

"Oh, don't be silly," She said. "We are only playing."

"I am not really a cyborg," George said to the boy. "But I am from the future."

The boy wiped his eyes.

"Really?" He said. "Why?"

"Why what?" George said.

"Why are you from the future?" He asked. "Why did you come here?"

"I fancied a burger," George said. "They are very difficult to get in the future."

"Why?!" The boy moaned. "I like burgers!"

"Aww," The mother said. "Why are they hard to get?"

"Well," George said. "Someone tried to make a beef, chicken burger!"

The boy exclaimed in disgust.

"So now we have cows that fly!" George shook his head. "Very difficult to catch!"

"Wow," The boy said. "Do people fly them?"

George leaned forward.

"I do," He whispered.

"Looks like we are here," The woman said. "Thanks for the entertainment," She laughed.

George watched as they got up, leaning against the window as the train came to a stop, he yawned and put his mask on.

George got to the ticket barrier, and the machine failed to read his card.

"Bloody thing," George said, trying again.

The man behind him was getting impatient, wearing a three-piece suit and an overcoat, he kept nudging George.

"Do you mind?" George said. "Stop touching me please."

"Then hurry up!" The middle-aged overweight man said. "I am in a hurry."

"My ticket isn't working," George said holding it up. "Nudging me in the ribs won't help."

The man mumbled and tried to push past George, who stood his ground.

"What was that?" George asked.

"I said buy a ticket!" The man snapped. "Are you deaf or something?!" He stared at George.

171

"Yes," George nodded. "Profoundly deaf in both ears."

"Not my problem," The man said bluntly.

"Never said it was," George replied. "I'd rather be deaf than you!" He stared back at him. "Now move out of the way you moron."

George made his way to the coffee counter, looking at the pastries before deciding just to get a black coffee. The server handed it to him, and George added some sugar, stirring it slowly.

Someone tapped him on the shoulder, and he turned round to see a colleague from an old job, he just about recognised her.

"Hey!" George said. "Sorry, but I have forgotten your name."

"It's Emily, "She smiled. "I thought it was you!" She said. "Not seen you in years!"

"Must be nearly fifteen years now!" George said. "How are you keeping? Still at the mortgage shithole?"

"No!" She laughed. "I left just after you did."

"Don't tell me," George laughed. "The bitch?"

"The bitch!" She laughed knowingly. "Do you know several people left due to her?"

"Really?" George said. "I had to leave before I ended up punching her in the face."

"She got fired a year later," She said. "Turns out she discriminated against the daughter of one of the directors."

"Doesn't surprise me," George said. "She was constantly dropping comments about my deafness." He shook his head. "Was this the girl in the wheelchair?"

"Yes," She said. "Bitch didn't know who she was, no one did in fact."

"I met her briefly," George said. "Nice girl."

"Well the bitch was slagging her off," She explained. "She asked for some changes to be made to make the department more accessible and went to her boss with it and slagged her off, stating it would be easier to get rid of her and employ someone without wheels!"

"But her boss was the girl's father!" George said laughing out loud.

"Yeah!" She said. "It was amazing, he fired her in front of the whole department after several people wrote complaints against her."

"That explains why I got a letter asking for a statement," George said. "I even hand-delivered it myself!"

"She tried to get you to come back, temporarily didn't she?" She asked.

"Yeah, offered me double pay but I said I would rather play in a volcano," George shook his head. "She was vile!"

"Well she has gone and apparently some of the people that left went back," She said.

"What do you do?" George asked.

"I worked for a small firm doing their accounts," She held up her hand to show me her wedding band. "Got married and had a couple of children!"

"Wow, that is amazing!" George said.

"What about you?" She asked.

"I got into medical engineering," George said. "Was made a manager on Monday, walked out yesterday."

"No way!" She exclaimed. "Why?"

"A close friend died, and everyone is either pathetic or selfish," George sighed. "I snapped, it just wasn't worth it."

"I am sorry," Email said. "What are you doing here?" She asked. "I am upstairs for a work do."

"Meeting a friend for lunch," George said. "Or a date, apparently."

"Any idea on why there are so many police?" She said quietly.

"Not noticed," George looked around. "Probably know I am here."

"What happened?" She pointed to George's hand/ "You were always hurting yourself before."

"Oh," George shrugged it off. "Cooking accident."

"Mad," She said. "Anyway, I better go back, will hit you up later online if that is okay?"

"Sure," George said and hugged her and then watched her walk back upstairs.

George made his way to the underground, sipping at his coffee and checking the train times on the board before walking way.

A uniformed police officer stepped in front of him, holding up his hand.

"Hello?" George said. "Can I help you?

"You are wanted," He said to me bluntly. "Please comply with the request," he pointed behind George.

George turned around and the two-armed officers waved him over, shaking their heads in annoyance. George walked over to them, one of them held up his hand to indicate George to stop, their hands trained on their automatic weapons.

"Want to explain why you ignored me?" The first officer asked.

"I didn't hear you," George said.

"Take your Bluetooth device off," The second officer said pointing to his ear. "And you will probably be able to."

"It is actually a hearing device," George said, emphasizing on the hearing.

"A what?" The first officer said, looking at George unimpressed.

"An implant," George said. "A hearing aid."

The officers spoke to each other quietly, turning so George could not lipread.

"Okay," The first officer said waving his hand at George. "You can go."

"Well, why did you need to speak to me?" George said. "Surely you didn't pull me over to complain about my hearing aid?"

"It doesn't matter," The first officer said. "You can go."

"Fine," George said walking away.

The police officer that stopped George came over to him.

"Everything okay?" He said.

"You tell me," George replied and looked back at the officers. "I think they are both on a power trip."

"Why," The officer said. "They wanted to do a brief identification check."

"Well they thought my hearing aid was a Bluetooth," George explained. "And when I corrected them, they told me to go."

The officer looked at the armed police, shrugging his shoulders in confusion. They called George over again.

"What is the problem?" The first armed officer said.

"You wanted to run an identification check on this guy," The police officer said. "Curious why you didn't."

George took his driving license from his pocket, holding it out for the police officer.

"No thanks," The armed officer said. "We don't need to."

"Why not?" George asked.

"Well you are disabled," The armed officer said. "Unlikely you will pose an issue and we haven't got time to mess around."

"Wow!" George replied. "Ignorant too."

"Only doing our jobs," The second armed officer replied.

"Not really though," George said. "You called me over, you were rude and then didn't check my identification because I am disabled?"

"Nothing to do with your disability," The first armed officer said. "I just changed my mind."

"Okay," George said. "Your choice."

George walked away with the Police officer.

"Sorry about that," He said. "Strange one."

"Bloody ignorant is the word," George said. "At least they didn't shoot me," George laughed.

"Well I can only apologise," The officer said.

"What is going on anyway?" George asked. "Why so many police out today, did an old lady get her bag stolen?"

The officer laughed.

"No," He said. "Something a lot worse, you have a nice day now."

George nodded, making his way for the escalators down to the underground.

14:30

George leaned against the lamppost, watching as the traffic went by, the various people going about their daily lives.

Someone covered his eyes from behind and he smiled.

"Guess who?" Lucy said.

"A stunning lady that keeps stalking me?" George said.

"Wrong!" Lucy giggled. "Just me!"

George turned around and Lucy hugged him tightly.

"Thank you," She said.

"For what?" George asked.

"This," She smiled. "I really needed it."

"Me too," George said, looking into her eyes.

"You didn't mind me texting Debbie, did you?" She said. "To wake you up?"

"No," George said. "I just wished she had put some clothes on first!" He laughed.

"She was naked?" Lucy covered her mouth laughing.

"No, she had a tiny bra on and these little hotpants things," George said nervously. "Didn't leave much to the imagination."

"Oh," Lucy said. "Lucky little sod, you got a free show!"

"Oh behave," George said.

"She is attractive," Lucy said. "Just a bit thick!" She burst out laughing.

"Tell me about it," George said, breathing in deeply. "How are you?"

"Tired," She said. "Bit of a headache," She looked at George, he is wearing brown hiking boots, blue jeans, thick grey top, and a brown jacket.

"We had the same idea," She pointed to her blue jeans and brown boots. "Nearly."

"You look good," George said nervously.

"You too," Lucy punched him in the arm. "How was the visit to the walk-in yesterday?"

"Awkward," George said. "Walked out of my job, and then went to the walk-in after ripping my stitches."

"Bet that hurt?" Lucy hissed.

"Yeah it did," George said. "Serves my right."

"Going to grab some coffees," Lucy pointed to a small café. "Won't be a minute!"

George smiled as Lucy ran to the store, he looked up at the grey clouds.

"Wow," He exclaimed as it started to snow lightly.

A few minutes passed and someone tapped George on the shoulder, and he turned around to find a middle-aged man standing in front of him, average build and stocky, wearing black boots, blue jeans, a shirt and a tanned leather coat. He is balding and is wearing thick glasses.

"Hi," He signed. "Deaf?" He signed.

"I cannot sign," George said. "But can understand a little."

"Hearing?" The man nodded in disappointment and walked off.

Lucy came walking over holding two cups of coffee.

"Friend of yours?" She asked.

"No," George said. "No idea who he was."

"What did he want?" She said.

"He asked if I was deaf," George said. "I told him I didn't sign, and he said 'hearing' and walked away."

"Why?" Lucy said. "That is weird."

"It's a community thing," George said. "It pisses me off, but basically this is how it is. You have the deaf community and the hearing community, I don't really mix with deaf people, and because I had the implant and I don't sign, I am classed as an outsider."

"That is crazy," Lucy exclaimed.

"I know," George said. "I lost some deaf friends when I got the implant, some said I went against my culture, some said I was made this way, blah blah blah!"

"Do you still meet up with deaf friends?" Lucy said.

"No," George said looking down at the coffee.

"Do you want one?" She teased.

"Not fussed," George said.

She handed one to George.

"Let's walk," Lucy said, pulling him gently by the jacket.

After several minutes of walking, they crossed the road.

"Can you lipread me okay?" She asked.

"Perfectly," George nodded.

"Let me know if I do anything wrong," She said. "It must be hard with all these people and noise."

"I will do," George laughed. "You are doing okay."

Lucy reacted and grabbed George's arm just as he was about to walk into a lamppost, spilling his coffee slightly and hitting his lip.

"Ow!" George moaned, tasting the blood in his mouth.

"Are you okay?" Lucy said. "I thought you would have seen it."

"Yes," George said. "Blind as well as deaf. Lipreading and walking is dangerous."

"Walk on my side," Lucy said and gently pushed him next to her.

"What if you walk into one," George asked.

"Then we have something else in common," She scoffed. "Come on let's get to the park."

They both arrived at the park and it was practically empty, other than dog walkers and the odd runner.

"It's a nice day," Lucy said. "Grey but nice."

"It is," George said. "Snowed briefly earlier."

"Did you get things sorted yesterday?" George asked. "With your dad?"

"Sort of," Lucy said. "I contacted the undertakers and will be seeing them Monday," Lucy breathed out heavily. "Dreading it."

"Who are you going with?" George asked.

"My brother would have been ideal," Lucy said. "But we know how that will turn out."

"Does he know?" George said. "About his dad?"

Lucy nodded.

"Okay," George said. "I am happy to help," George paused. "Happy to help out with anything."

"I appreciate that," Lucy said. "Thank you."

"Moneywise too," George said. "It is my way of thanking Harold, for everything."

"Aww," Lucy exclaimed. "You are a beautiful soul, thank you, but money is good."

George nodded.

"My parents put away a whole ton of money," Lucy laughed. "They got the house from my grandmother, as a wedding gift."

"Wow," George said. "Was that the landlady that had several properties."

"That is the one," Lucy said. "She was amazing."

"Not to be rude," George said. "What is happening with your mum?"

"My aunt and I have made the decision, to put her into a specialist home," Lucy said. "It will be safer for her and everyone else."

"That is true," George said. "Sad, but true."

"Well, my aunt decided she would take her on," Lucy chuckled. "That was before mum blew up the microwave."

"How?" George asked.

"Tin of baked beans for breakfast," Lucy said, looking at George with a growing smile.

"Oh no," George said. "She didn't put the whole thing in the microwave?"

"Blew the door clean off," Lucy giggled. "She was sat in the living room, had a go at my aunt for blowing it up."

"Oh dear," George said and hissed when he walked into a bollard, jolting, and giving himself a dead thigh.

"Shit!" George groaned, placing the coffee on the wall. "Jesus!"

"Are you okay?" She said in concern. "Did you not see it?"

"I was too busy lipreading," George laughed. "I am okay."

"Is it my fault," She asked.

"No," George shook his head. "One of those things."

"Bad things happen in threes," She laughed.

"Oh, please no!" George joked. "No more!"

George stopped, his hand went to his mouth.

"What is it?" Lucy said. "What is wrong?"

George sobbed, tears welling in his eyes and he turned away, hiding.

"Oh George," Lucy said walking over to him. "It's okay." She put her arms around him from behind, resting her head on his back.

"I am sorry," George cried. "Things have really gotten to me and this week has been a fucking nightmare." He said. "I just feel like I am going to cry all the time!"

"Over walking into a bollard," She scoffed. "Really?"

George laughed.

"Dad told me everything okay," Lucy said softly. "Let me help you?"

George breathed in heavily.

"I am sorry," George said, sniffing and wiping his eyes. "I am sorry."

"Stop it," Lucy said. "Never be sorry for how you feel," Lucy said. "Things are going to be fine," She smiled. "I promise."

George stepped back, wiping his eyes.

"Pathetic huh," He said. "A grown man crying.

"There is nothing wrong with crying," Lucy said. "It's a good thing and I bet you feel a little bit better now?"

George nodded.

"I understand how you feel," Lucy said. "I have been there, what you see now is a whole new me."

George smiled.

"Dad also told me that you had a thing for me," Lucy said.

George looked at her, embarrassed.

"Don't," She warned him. "I have a thing for you too."

"I don't know what to say," George said.

"Right," She said. "I am going to take you to my dad's favourite place, no talking!"

"Why?" George asked. "Is talking not allowed?"

"No!" Lucy scoffed. "Cannot have you walking into shit and blaming it on the deafness, now can we?"

"Okay," George said, rubbing his knee and picking up the coffee, he followed Lucy.

There were only a few people at the Japanese gardens, George and Lucy slowly walked around a couple of times. Admiring the fish, plants, and ornaments.

"Been here before?" Lucy said.

"Yes," George said. "Your dad got into trouble for letting the little monster off his lead."

"Is that when he chased a peacock?" Lucy said. "I remember that," She said. "Peacocks scare the shit out of me!"

"Really?" George said. "Why?"

"I don't know," Lucy shivered. "It's the whole evil stair and massive display."

"Fair enough," George said. "Wuss."

Lucy punched him in the arm.

"Could you get some photos of me on the bridge?" Lucy asked. "And then we should get some food?"

"Okay," George said.

Lucy handed him her mobile phone and stood on the bridge, posing, and smiling. George took several shoots, stopping when a couple walked into the shot.

"Thank you, " He said to them sarcastically with a smile.

He walked up to Lucy, handing her the mobile phone, she looked through them.

"Thank you," She said, leaning forward and kissing George gently on the cheek.

"Want any more?" George said.

"You just want another kiss," Lucy looked up smiling. "Don't you?"

George stuttered, trying to find his words.

"I am kidding," Lucy said. "Don't pass out!" She shook her head. "I like this one!" She said and showed George the photo.

"That is nice," George said. "Brings out your eyes."

Lucy put her phone into her pocket and turned to come off the bridge, a peacock on the grass opened up in a display, shaking its feathers. Lucy yelped out in Fright and jumped back, accidentally shoving George.

George stepped back, realising he had nowhere to go and slipped off the bridge, feet first into the water. It only came up to his waist, and he yelled out as the freezing water soaked his boots and jeans.

"Jesus," George's voice wavered. "Christ!"

The couple looked over with concern on their faces.

"Oh my god!" Lucy said, her hand went to her mouth. "Are you okay?" She asked.

"Wet," George said in embarrassment. "Didn't you say things happen in threes?"

"I am so sorry," Lucy said, laughing behind her hand. "I didn't mean it."

"Really?" George said, panting. "This is all your fault."

"There was a peacock," Lucy said looking behind her to realise it had gone. "Well, there was!" She looked at George standing in the water, disgust on his face.

"This water stinks!" George groaned.

Lucy burst out laughing and bent down, holding out her hand.

"I'll talk to the bank," George said. "Don't want to pull you in accidentally."

George walked to the bank, the thick mud clinging to his boots as he strained, slowly getting closer. Lucy slowly walked around, heading for the grassy bank to meet him.

As George climbed up the bank, his feet gave way under the slippery grass and he fell face-first into the wet grass.

Lucy let out a howl of laugher, stopping at the top of the bank, her hands on her thighs as she laughed hysterically.

George looked up, shaking his head at her amusement.

"What would your father say if he were here?" George asked in a firm voice.

"Nothing," Lucy climbed down the bank. "He would laugh and take some photos," She paused. "And laugh some more."

Lucy slipped on the grass and her feet went from under her, she landed flat on her backside, squealing with laughter, and moaning when the wetness got to her. George got up, shaking his head, and holding out his hand.

"Serves you right," George said. "Wet arse?" He asked.

"Oh my god it's cold," She said.

"You think?" George pulled her up, holding onto her when he slipped slightly.

"You okay?" Lucy said.

"I stink," George said. "God knows what is in that water."

"Peacock and fish shit," Lucy said with a serious look on her face. "Probably all the crap the local druggies leave behind, beer bottles, condoms and so on."

George looked behind him, checking the back of his legs and backside.

"What you looking for?" Lucy said.

"Just making sure that there are no syringes or bottles sticking out of my arse," George said.

Lucy burst into hysterics, trying to talk.

"Things happen in threes," I said and chuckled. "Not a bad date huh?"

"So, it is a date?" Lucy said.

"Do you want it to be a date?" George asked.

Lucy leaned forward, kissing George on the lips. She broke away and looked at him, a little smile on her face. George pulled her closer, kissing her passionately, after a few seconds, they held each other tightly.

"You have no idea," Lucy said. "How long I have been waiting for you to do that."

"Happy now?" George said bluntly. "So needy!" He smiled.

"I think we need to head back," Lucy said. "Finish this date at yours, with a takeaway? Movie?"

"Debbie is at home," George said.

"No, she isn't," Lucy smiled. "She is staying with her friends for a couple of days."

"Really?" George said. "Since when?"

"Since this," Lucy said smiling deviously as she kissed George on the lips.

George's feet slipped and they both fell down onto the bank, side by side, yelping out in fright and laughing hysterically.

"People are going to think we are nuts!" George said.

"Let them," Lucy said, pulling George closer and kissing him passionately, moaning when he kissed her back.

He broke away, holding her hand.

"Let's head back," He said. "I have lost the feeling in my feet!" He said. "And that peacock behind you isn't too impressed.

Lucy yelled out and jumped to her feet, slipping as she struggled up the bank and ran from the Japanese garden. Seconds later, George followed, water dripping from his jeans and his boots sloshing.

Printed in Great Britain
by Amazon

50874588R00108